# THE OWL AND THE RAVEN
## A Sheriff Lansing Mystery

**Books by Micah S. Hackler**

**Sheriff Lansing Mysteries**
Legend of the Dead
Coyote Returns
The Shadow Catcher
The Dark Canyon
The Mutes
The Owl and the Raven


**Coming Soon!**
**A Sheriff Lansing Mystery**
The Weeping Woman

# THE OWL AND THE RAVEN
## A Sheriff Lansing Mystery

## Micah S. Hackler

SPEAKING VOLUMES, LLC
NAPLES, FLORIDA
2019

THE OWL AND THE RAVEN

ISBN 978-1-64540-032-5

For my sisters
Jean Iverson and Jeri Huggins

# Acknowledgments

Writing, for me, is not a vocation . . . or an avocation . . . or a hobby. In my later years it has become a compulsion . . . which is not a bad thing. But a compulsion is only possible if you have an enabler. My wonderful wife, Olivia, is my enabler. She has coffee waiting for me in the morning, my meals prepared for when I'm hungry, a clean bed ready for my naps and evening slumber. I am blessed, and I can never thank her enough.

I am continually encouraged by long-time friends Don and Robin Perrero and my college roommate, Jim Krestalude. They wanted to know why it took so long for me to start up again. Inertia was the only excuse I could come up with. I guess Dr. John Kobs, my best friend from high school, put it best: "You're writing again because that's what you do . . . You write."

My personal sounding boards and counselors for decades, I thank George Sewell and Dan Baldwin for keeping me on the less beaten path. We've had a hell-of-a journey together, so far.

Finally, I have to thank Kurt Mueller and the wonderful staff at Speaking Volumes . . . and particularly the fine illustration work by Rick Turylo. Both my works and I have come alive again because of them.

# Prologue

". . . true evil needs no reason to exist.  It simply is
and feeds upon itself."

E.A Bucchianeri

A Compendium of Essays

# Chapter One

Cesar Chamuscado was *El Jeffe*. His domain was small. The Penitentiary of New Mexico, fifteen miles south of Santa Fe, only housed 790 inmates. Level II housed the least dangerous inmates, about 200 prisoners. Level VI, the most dangerous inmates and those on death row, held about 90. The remaining 500 guests were divided between Levels IV and V, dangerous but controllable.

The Hispanics, the Native Americans, even the Whites, were under his thumb. The Arian Brotherhood tried to establish a beachhead. Three of them were gelded by Chamuscado's men. The remaining twenty quickly fell in line and not as reluctantly as Cesar would have imagined. The small cadre of Blacks, fifty to be precise, kept to themselves. The Chamuscados, as Cesar called his followers, didn't bother them. (That was of course until Cesar wanted something.)

The Chamuscados controlled everything. They ran the drugs, the alcohol, even the male-on-male visitations. Through bribery and intimidation, the guards looked the other way.

Chamuscado lay on his bunk, staring at the stained ceiling. This penitentiary was a luxury hotel compared to some of the other facilities he had visited. The two years in a Mexican prison was the worst. Almost as bad was a year in the Phoenix County Tent jail: no air conditioning, baloney sandwiches and really stupid inmates.

Through his twenty years as "El Diablo," the description given to him by the last prosecuting attorney, he had never been intimidated by anything or anyone. That is until two days ago.

Cesar Chamuscado arrived at the Penitentiary of New Mexico three years earlier to begin a twenty-year sentence for drug trafficking. On the first day he was told to avoid Bernardino Chavez. Chavez was a *nagual*.

He was a male witch, a *brujo*, from the moment he was born. His mother was a *bruja*. It was in his blood.

Chavez was serving a 15-year sentence for manslaughter. When he was 18, he killed a rival over a girl. Because he looked so young, the jury passed on the murder-in-the-first-degree. (Some said the jurors were afraid of his mother.)

Bernardino had 10 years left on his sentence. He might be out even sooner for good behavior. He was a loner. He kept to himself and the rest of the inmates left him alone.

For three years Chamuscado left him alone . . . and that got under Chamuscado's skin. Everyone bowed to his every whim, except Chavez. Everyone knew where they stood in the pecking order, except Chavez. Everyone respected him, *El Jeffe*, except Chavez.

Finally, Cesar Chamuscado had enough. He was always afforded first place in the cafeteria line. If others were there before him, they stepped aside.

On Monday, when Cesar arrived at the chow line, the seas parted for him. Every man in line gave way for *El Jeffe,* except Chavez.

This affront was too much.

Chamuscado grabbed the shoulders of the younger, smaller man and threw him to the ground. Once Chavez was on the floor, the older, bigger man began kicking him. He kicked him in the head, he kicked him in the stomach, he kicked him in the groin. Chamuscado had worked himself into such a fit it took three guards to pull him off.

Chavez had to be carried to the infirmary.

Cesar pulled free of the guards and smiled triumphantly at the other inmates. He was finished being intimidated by the *brujo*. From that moment on, the witch would be afraid of him.

That night he began feeling ill.

Tuesday morning Chamuscado woke with fever, followed by chills.

He went to sick call.

The doctor shrugged and gave *El Jeffe* aspirin.

The pills didn't help.

By Tuesday afternoon the fever was higher, and Cesar was becoming delirious. He demanded the doctor visit him in his cell.

The doctor arrived. The prisoner's temperature was 104 degrees. He was checked for appendicitis, but that wasn't the problem. More aspirin was administered, followed by alternating doses of acetaminophen.

Tuesday night was when the nausea hit. Chamuscado was too weak to even crawl to the toilet. His floor was a mess. His last set of clothes was soaked in sweat.

Wednesday morning, he was informed he was the only sick inmate in Levels IV and V.

That's when Cesar Chamuscado realized he was not sick. He was cursed.

Two of his lieutenants were summoned to his cell. He wanted to know where Bernardino Chavez was. He was told the boy was in his cell. Cesar told his men he had been cursed—cursed by Chavez. They were ordered to go to the witch and tell him to lift the curse.

*El Jeffe* stared at the ceiling. For the first time in his life he was afraid. He believed in witches. He believed in ghosts. He believed in Heaven and Hell and he knew his destiny.

Thirty minutes later the henchmen returned. The answer was no! Chavez would not lift the curse.

Chamuscado was desperate. They were sent back with an offer. Chavez could have half of Cesar's empire. They would be partners. All the boy had to do was lift the curse.

While he waited, he sent others out to find a *curandero*, a male witch who could counteract the curse.

The henchmen returned. Chavez still refused.

Cesar's desperation morphed into anger. The men were ordered back to the witch's cell. They would physically persuade Bernardino to lift the curse. They would not leave the boy's cell until he agreed. The prison thugs left for a third time.

Word came back to *El Jeffe*, there were no *curanderos* in the prison.

Chamuscado closed his eyes. It helped with the nausea. It helped with the dizziness. He tried to ignore the sweat dripping from his brow. The seconds beat against his temples. He calmed himself. His men would return. The curse will be lifted and the stupid *brujo* who could have had half of everything would now have all of nothing.

It was an hour before his men returned. When they entered the cell, they were not smiling.

"Did he lift the curse?"

"No, *Jeffe*," the larger of the two said.

"I told you! Do not leave that cell until Chavez lifted the curse!" Cesar screamed.

"We went too far," the second thug squirmed. "He can't lift the curse."

"Why not?"

"He's dead," both men said at the same time.

A look of terror froze Cesar Chamuscado's face. He was cursed. Only Chavez or a *curandero* could lift the curse. Those options were no longer available to him. He was a dead man. He faced a slow and painful death . . . and there was nothing he could do.

***

A hundred miles north, in a small frame house separated from the rest of civilized society, a woman screamed. It was the wail of a mother who had just lost her child. It was a howl of pain. It was a howl of anger. It was a shriek that promised retribution.

# Chapter Two

It had been ten years . . . well, almost ten years, since Pepe Zapata began working for the Gulf Cartel. Juan Garcia Abrego took over the cartel in 1984. After 6 years he was in firm control. His solid contract with the Cali Cartel in Columbia provided him with all the cocaine he could handle. Half of all the cocaine that moved through Mexico was handled by the Gulf Cartel.

Zapata was content to be a part of it. He had grown up on the streets of Matamoros, Mexico. No father. The loving touch of a mother a distant memory. He was scavenging for food from restaurant dumpsters when he was first recruited. He was ten years old.

A teenager, not that much older than himself, needed another lookout. A drug transaction was going down. The dealer needed people watching for the police.

Zapata was posted at one corner. His new acquaintance at the other. The deal went down and Pepe had a career.

At first, he was just a lookout. Each deal put a few pesos in his pocket. He could buy his own food. He could afford clothes from the flea markets. The longer he worked, the more responsibility he was given. Soon, he was a runner. He carried messages from one dealer to another. After a few years, he was carrying product.

By the time he was fifteen, he was a dealer and a full member of the Gulf Cartel.

The higher-ups began to take notice. The boy produced. He was reliable. He never skimmed money off the top. Most importantly, he didn't use the cocaine he was selling. The cartel needed soldiers who weren't befuddled by the drugs they dealt.

Pepe Zapata was given his first gun when he was 16. He had a new assignment. He was now a guard. When the large shipments came in from Columbia, he helped protect them. If they came in by ship, he went to the docks and escorted the bundles of product to the processing centers. If they came in by plane, he was at the airfield, helping load the trucks, then riding in the back, watching for high-jackers.

For the most part, the assignment was mundane. He could see how other soldiers were lured to use the product. They were bored. It helped kill the time. Pepe was never tempted—maybe because he saw how stupid men acted when they were high on cocaine or drunk on tequila. He began to wonder if there might be something more to life than what the cartel offered.

He killed his first man when he was 18.

The Sinaloa Cartel had been studying the Gulf Cartel's operation for some time. They knew the times the cocaine would arrive. They knew the routes the trucks would take.

Sinaloa chose a night operation. That's when Abrego moved his bundles. Fewer prying eyes.

The Sinaloa soldiers set up a roadblock between the airfield and the Gulf warehouses. The convoy of a lead SUV and two two-ton transport trucks came to a halt. The driver of the SUV, the head of the operation, realized too late they were being ambushed. He jumped from his car and started yelling for the trucks to back up. He was gunned down immediately.

The night lit up like *Cinco de Mayo*.

Sinaloa operatives were stationed on rooftops on either side of the narrow street. They opened fire. The noise was deafening. Bullets ripped through the canvas covers of the transports.

Pepe, in the second truck, jumped from the worthless canvas protection and rolled under the vehicle. His AK-47 in hand, he took aim at the muzzle flashes. On his first shot a man fell from the top of a two-story building.

Other Gulf Cartel soldiers tried to engage the enemy, but they were felled almost immediately.

Pepe managed to take out one more of the enemy.

The gun shots became sporadic. Zapata realized the only people firing now were the men on the roofs. If he fired again, they would know he was still alive.

He waited until the gun shots stopped. Leaving his weapon behind, he crawled from the protection of the truck. Then, hunkered down, he scrambled to the protection of the nearest corner. He listened for a moment. No one followed.

He began to run. It felt like he ran all night.

When he finally reached the cartel warehouse it was still dark. He pounded on the door. Once inside, he reported the ambush. The lieutenant in charge of the warehouse already knew. One of the truck drivers reported the attack over his radio. A cadre of Gulf soldiers were dispatched to waylay the Sinaloa men before they escaped with the cocaine. Another gunfight ensued. The trucks were recovered.

Abrego and his top lieutenants wanted to know how Zapata was the only survivor. The young soldier stood in front of the inquisition and told his story. Cartel investigators confirmed they found two dead Sinaloa attackers—the ones Pepe claimed to have killed. In fact, they were the only two dead attackers found at the ambush site. Pepe's version held up.

It was time for him to join the inner circle.

He could have women. He could have booze. He could have all drugs he wanted.

The women were satisfying, but each encounter left him feeling empty. The alcohol made him sick. The drugs he left alone.

And then there was the recurring nightmare of the man falling from the roof. He had killed a man and it seemed to bother him. He had never felt guilt before. He didn't understand it.

It was nine months later when he was given a special assignment. Pepe and Rodrigo Abrego, Juan Garcia's nephew, were dispatched to Monterrey. Zapata was in the dark about their mission. Pepe had known Rodrigo for some time. He was loud-mouthed; he was mean; he was cruel. Rodrigo, who Pepe could not stand, would fill him in on their trip when they got there.

This was Zapata's first visit to Monterrey. It was bigger than Matamoros, and dirtier. They drove through the crowded streets and busy boulevards until they reached the south side of the city. They stopped in front of an upscale house, brightly painted pink.

"This is the home of one of my uncle's accountants," Rodrigo explained. "*Tio* Juan is not happy with his work. We are going in to talk to him."

Rodrigo got out of the sedan he was driving. He signaled Zapata to follow him. They walked to the rear of the car. Abrego had already popped the trunk. Inside was an assortment of lethal weapons. Rodrigo picked up two Beretta 93Rs. Each machine pistol held 20 rounds. He handed one to his companion.

"Do you know how to use these?"

Pepe nodded. "I thought we came here to talk?"

"These are to make sure he listens." Rodrigo laughed at his own remark.

Abrego knocked. Mrs. Diaz opened the door, smiling. As soon as she saw the guns she tried to slam the door shut. Rodrigo stopped her. He pushed his way in. Zapata followed.

"Call your husband," the gunman ordered, grabbing her by her throat.

"David," she whimpered. Then louder, screaming, "David!"

David Diaz came running to the entryway. He stopped at the sight of his wife being choked by armed strangers. "Who are you? What do you want?"

Abrego pushed the woman to her husband. "Get inside," he ordered the couple. Over his shoulder he told Zapata, "Close the door."

In the living area, Rodrigo told the Diaz's to sit.

"Who are you?" Diaz demanded.

"My name is Rodrigo," the gunman said. "I am here because you have been stealing from my uncle."

"No. No. I never . . . I would never steal from Juan Garcia!"

"How many children do you have?"

Maria Diaz mumbled an answer.

"How many?" Abrego screamed.

"Four," the husband blurted. "Listen, take me to Juan Garcia. I'll show him my records. I can prove I didn't steal."

"It's too late for that. Where are your children?" the gunman demanded.

"Away," Maria whimpered. "At their *abuelita's*."

"Search the house!" Rodrigo ordered.

"Why?" Pepe asked.

"Because we can't leave any witnesses behind. Go!"

Zapata hesitated. It was one thing to kill a man in self-defense. But to kill a family? A defenseless family who had never done anything wrong? He had that pang in his gut again. It was the feeling of guilt He didn't know the name for it, but it was there.

Abrego shot him a dirty glance. "I said, 'Go!' "

At that moment, Pepe Zapata made a life altering decision. He pointed his Beretta at the nephew of Juan Garcia Abrego and fired.

\*\*\*

Brother Esteban Fuentes sat up with a start.

The monastery bell was sounding. It was 3:40 am. Vigils began at 4:00.

The good monk was troubled. At one time that dream vexed him nightly. But it hadn't afflicted him for years. Why was it tormenting him now?

He would pray to the Virgin for solace, for forgiveness, for answers.

# Chapter Three

Memorial Day weekend started in two days. Summer vacation would begin the next week. Tina Morales was as anxious for school to end as the 23 students seated in her room. They all stared out the window yearning for freedom.

Las Palmas Middle/High School was a far cry from the gang and drug infested schools of Albuquerque. A typical Tenth grade in the big city usually had 300 students. Class sizes were typically 35 to 40 kids. Ten of them might even pay attention.

Las Palmas M/H School only had 152 students for grades 7 through 12. The entire school district, that stretched from O'Keeffe Ranch in the south to Cohino in the north, had less than 400 students in K through 12.

A year earlier, Morales knew she had to get out of Albuquerque. She had to get away from the schools. She had to get away from an abusive relationship. She had to fulfill her calling.

Scrolling through vacancies listed by the state board of education, she kept coming back to Las Palmas and San Phillipe County. The salary was barely livable. The town looked mostly old and used up, though there were promises of a new school building and higher wages in the future.

Farmington looked more promising. So did Taos and Las Cruces. She even considered out of state, but that would have required a new teaching certificate.

Morales taught general science and chemistry. Few teachers were qualified in those subjects. She could practically write her own ticket. The only thing that stopped her was the attraction of Las Palmas.

She thought about that. It wasn't an attraction. It was more of a compulsion. Something was drawing her to the small community, but she didn't know what.

After nine months, she had few friends. As attractive as she was, she had no suiters (which, at the moment, didn't bother her). She still didn't know why she was there. She went to Saint James Catholic Church twice a week and prayed for guidance. She knew her purpose would be revealed when God was ready.

In the meantime, she was preparing for Summer vacation. There would be a short visit to her grandparents in Nogales, Mexico. She wasn't sure if that would be before or after her retreat to *Saint Anthony's Monastery in the Canyon*. Maybe a week of peace and reflection at the monastery would unfold God's intentions.

"Miss Morales," the student interrupted her thoughts.

"What, Sally?"

"Are you going to be teaching here next year?" the eighth grader asked.

"Yes, as far as I know . . ."

The entire class broke out in smiles. She had become one of their favorite teachers.

"But it won't be any of you. Only eleventh and twelfth graders can take chemistry."

There was a communal, "Aw-w-w!"

The bell rang, signaling the end to another school day . . . and one day closer to freedom.

# Chapter Four

Sheriff Cliff Lansing sat at his desk staring at his new cell phone. It flipped open like Captain Kirk's communicator. There was a small, one-inch tall antenna. Some versions had antennas that could extend. It had a small screen that lit up. The screen showed you the number you had just dialed.

That word, dialed, didn't seem appropriate. The term should have gone the way of the Dodo when rotary dials were replaced with push buttons. "I just buttoned a number into my phone" didn't sound right. "I just pushed a number" didn't sound right either.

He heard someone say: "punch the numbers into your phone." That seemed a little violent.

It was less than two years to the new millennium. Maybe by the year 2000 an enterprising, bright word-specialist would replace "dialed" with something more appropriate.

Meanwhile, he had to write down a new set of phone numbers. Everyone he knew had acquired a cell phone.

Everything was changing. His new ranch house was finished. He had already moved out of the trailer he had been using and into his new home.

Cliff Junior was turning 15. Carol had already signed the permission slip for him to start Driver's Ed. All she needed was $100 to pay for the course. Of course, C.J.'s visit that summer would be brief. He had to stay in Albuquerque because of the lessons.

The Sheriff's office, too, was adjusting to its own changes. Two of the old heads, Rubin Menendez and Carlos Diaz, had retired. After three years, Deputy Gabe Hannah finally joined the Highway Patrol. There wasn't a motorcycle division, yet. But Hannah wanted to be on the ground floor when the unit launched. By then, with enough years on the force, he might even be named division commander.

Three new deputies had been hired to fill the vacancies. Lansing had yet to form an opinion on any of them.

For years, the 9-1-1 Call Center had been housed in a double-wide trailer behind the courthouse. A new addition had been added to the Law Enforcement annex and the Call Center had moved in.

The sheriff was certain he was ready for the new century. Then ten days ago Dr. Margarite Carrera hit him with her news. They were having dinner at *Paco's Cantina* when she made the announcement.

"I can't think of any way to put this gently, Lansing, so I'm just going to blurt it out . . . I'm leaving."

"What?" the sheriff almost choked on the food he was eating. "What do you mean you're leaving?"

"I've been offered a position at the University of New Mexico School of Medicine."

"In Albuquerque?" Lansing made it sound like a dirty word.

"That's where the school is."

"Doing what?"

"I'll be one of the two core instructor/physicians at the Center for Rural and Tribal Emergency Medical Services. Cliff, they sought me out. And I'm perfect for the job. I had five years as an Emergency Room doctor and another six handling medical services for the Northern Pueblos. It's like I've been training for this position all my life"

"You know, John Tanner's leaving Las Palmas in six months," Lansing offered. "You could take his spot at the clinic."

"They hardly pay him anything."

"That's because the county paid for his medical school. You could negotiate for a higher salary. Plus, the county needs a coroner. You could fill both slots and make twice as much."

"They could offer three times as much and I still wouldn't make as much as the university is offering.

"Besides, my folks are getting old. I need to be closer to them. I can't afford to drive two-and-a-half hours every time one of them falls. I'm leaving in a week. I thought you should know."

That ended the dinner conversation—and their relationship.

Lansing was roused from his trance when the cell phone "rang" its sing-song: "Too-da-loo-doo. Too-da-loo-doo. Too-da-loo-doo-doo." It was catchy and annoying at the same time.

He flipped open the phone, "Lansing."

"Sorry to bother you, Sheriff," Marilyn said from the dispatch desk. "I wanted to check out my new cell phone."

"I was the only one you could call?" the sheriff growled.

"Well, no," she admitted. "But I thought you would want to see the fax we got from the Department of Corrections."

"I'll be right there."

\*\*\*

Sheriff Department
May 21, 1998
San Phillipe County
Las Palmas, NM

Sirs,

This letter is to inform you of the death of Bernardino Chavez, Inmate #190145, at the Penitentiary of New Mexico, on May 20, 1998. The body is being held pending notification of next of kin. Disposition of remains will be as per family desires.

The Department of Corrections requests your office's assistance in contacting the family.

Our records show next of kin: Mrs. Berta Chavez, 1092 RR 182, Las Palmas, NM.

Thank you for your cooperation in this matter.


The rest of the fax provided all the necessary contact information.

Nowhere in the letter did they mention how Bernardino died. Lansing considered that a glaring omission. That told him the boy didn't die from an accident or an illness. He was dead by the hands of another inmate or, worse, prison officials.

Lansing remembered the case well. It happened during his first full year as sheriff. The Chavez boy had been nothing but trouble his entire tenure at Las Palmas Middle/High School.

If he wasn't being expelled, he was being truant. When he was in school, he was fighting.

Deputy Rivera investigated the last fight. Bernardino and another boy had been vying for the affection of another 12th grader. Chavez wasn't satisfied with pushing and shoving or fists. He escalated.

One day after school, Chavez caught his rival alone when he was walking home. Bernardino came armed with a baseball bat. His intention might have been to intimidate . . . maybe even just to leave a few bruises. But he went way beyond a simple beat-down.

Chavez administered at least ten blows to the head and face. One arm, one leg, and most ribs were broken. The boy could only be identified by the clothes he was wearing.

It was no problem identifying the assailant. Rivera found Bernardino Chavez walking down the road carrying the weapon, covered in the other boy's blood.

The trial was straight forward. Chavez was guilty. However, even with the shocking photos of the victim, the jury only opted for manslaughter, even though the prosecuting attorney pressed for more severe punishment.

Lansing was sure the jury had been intimidated.

Berta Chavez attended every minute of the trial. She never spoke. She only glared.

She glared at the judge. She glared at the prosecutor. She glared at the jurors.

In her younger days she might have been beautiful. But years of anger and bitterness had taken its toll. People said she was a witch, a *bruja*. No one knew for sure. But everyone in the courtroom was convinced she was giving them the evil eye.

Every person in attendance was relieved when the trial was over, including Lansing.

Now he had to face her again and tell her about her son.

# Chapter Five

Deputy Jack Rivera stood at the Las Palmas IGA Western Union counter filling out the request. He already had the $300 cash. He was sending it to Denver. His wife had requested the money. Sue and their daughter needed it to buy bus tickets. They wanted to come home.

He desperately wanted to see his daughter, DeeDee. She'd been gone for a month.

He had mixed feelings about Sue.

Sue had cheated on him . . . Not only had she cheated, she had run off with a smooth-talking car salesman from Segovia. She had taken their daughter and the three of them ended up in Denver. The fling barely lasted four weeks.

Sue called up crying. She was so sorry. She didn't know what got into her. She was ashamed. Could Rivera please forgive her. She and DeeDee wanted to come home, but they didn't have any money.

In all the blubbering, Rivera couldn't tell if Sue had walked out on the new boyfriend or he had abandoned her. He suspected the latter.

It didn't matter.

He wanted DeeDee home. Husband and wife could work out their problems once the family was together.

He handed the attendant the form and the cash. He had instructed Sue to relay her departure and arrival times through the sheriff's office. Dispatch would pass the information to him. Everyone in Las Palmas thought they were off visiting relatives.

That was Deputy Rivera's story. That's all anyone needed to know.

# Chapter Six

Lansing stopped his Jeep on Route 182, five miles outside of Las Palmas, and looked up the dirt and gravel road. The small frame house sat alone, a quarter mile away. The building had a weathered, corrugated tin roof. The exterior hadn't been painted in years. The road leading up was almost completely over-grown with grass and weeds. One side of the track was worn more than the other, indicating a footpath. Pine trees dotted the fields on either side. A single power line stretched from the highway to the shoddy abode.

The sheriff knew little about Berta Chavez. She lived alone. Berta and Bernardino had moved into the hovel twenty years earlier. She owned the property, but had no apparent means of support.

Those were the facts as Lansing knew them. Everything else was rumor. Berta had once been married to a Jicarilla Apache man. She may have been responsible for his death. Even though her son was half Apache she was driven from the reservation. People feared her because she was a *bruja*. People came to her for evil potions and even more evil curses to be used against enemies. Gossip had it that's how she eked out a living.

The sheriff turned his steering wheel and started up the seldom used road. Even in bright sunlight, he couldn't dismiss the feeling of gloom enveloping him as he grew closer to the house. He stopped when he reached the "yard." A half dozen, scrawny chickens pecked at the ground, looking for insects and seeds. Lansing suspected the foraging wasn't to supplement their diet. That was their diet.

When he got out of his Jeep, he heard the plaintive bleat of a goat coming from behind the building. Other than the chickens and the goat, there were no signs of life.

Lansing walked up to the weathered front door and knocked.

"Mrs. Chavez. This is Sheriff Cliff Lansing," he said loudly. "Can we talk?"

He waited for a response. When he didn't get one, he pounded on the door.

"Mrs. Chavez, are you in there?" This time he shouted.

Still no answer. He tried the door knob. The door was locked.

He stepped back from the door and looked to either side. There was a single window to the left. He tried to peer inside. Between the filthy panes of glass and the tattered drapes he could see nothing.

He decided to survey the abandoned property.

The house faced south. On the east side were piles of wood, some gathered limbs and branches, some stacks of split logs, all presumably for heating and cooking. On the west side was an herb garden. Half of the patch contained perennials. The other half had neat rows of tiny spouts, struggling to survive the still cool Spring nights.

Behind the home was the plaintive goat, tethered to a stake in the ground. She had devoured every weed and blade of grass within her reach. She complained because she wanted food or water or both.

Not far from the goat was a *horno,* a dome shaped, dried-mud oven, popular with Pueblo dwellers and Old-World settlers alike. Spanish for furnace, its operation was simple. A wood fire was built inside on the flat surface. Once the structure was heated to the right temperature, the ashes were removed, and bread or tortillas were baked inside. For meats, the embers were pushed to one side, the food placed in the middle, then the oven completely sealed. Depending on the size and type of animal being cooked, the *horno* would remain closed from two-and-a-half to four hours.

Judging by the piles of ashes accumulating behind the oven, the *horno* was used often.

Lansing walked back to the front of the house. He considered knocking on the door again, but suspected the effort would be futile. He retrieved a pen and business card from his Jeep. On the back he wrote: *Llamada, por favor. Urgente.* (Please, call. Urgent.)

He wedged the card between the front door and the frame. Berta would see it when she returned. That's all the sheriff could do for now.

He got back in his Jeep and left.

Inside the hovel, the drapes were pulled aside by a bony hand. Its owner watched the sheriff depart. Plans had already been formulated. It was time to put them into motion.

# Chapter Seven

"*Jeffe*," Cardenas said, entering the palatial room. "Both Raul and Oscar were just arrested by the police! They won't be any more trouble."

Humberto Garcia Abrego leaned back in his chair and breathed a sigh of relief. For two-and-a-half years he had been fighting for control of the Gulf Cartel. Ever since his brother, Juan Garcia, was captured and sent to the United States to stand trial, the cartel had been in turmoil. Besides himself, a half dozen, senior lieutenants thought they should control the empire Abrego had built. Humberto decided it belonged to him by right of birth. Others felt differently.

The internal struggle was bloody, not to mention disruptive to daily operations. As the dust settled, forty soldiers and four high ranking members of the inner circle lay dead.

Oscar de Leon and Raul Valladares Del Angel, the last two surviving lieutenants, were too well protected for outright assassination. But Humberto knew their movements. The Mexican government had targets on all their backs. Putting a bug in the right ear brought the *Federales* swooping in. They sank their talons deep into Abrego's adversaries and he was the survivor.

Humberto now had two missions in life. Bring the Gulf Cartel back to its former glory and, more importantly, track down the man who killed his son!

Abrego's anger had festered. It burned inside him, a white-hot ember that wouldn't extinguish.

It had been eight years since Rodrigo had been murdered. His body had been found in the trunk of his car on the north side of Monterrey. David Diaz and his entire family had escaped the cartel's justice. And Pepe Zapata, the man who killed his son, still breathed.

# Chapter Eight

Lansing parked in front of *Paco's Mexican Cantina*. In all of San Phillipe County, there were only seven "bars," and they were all consigned to eating establishments. There were no quiet, little, neighborhood taverns to escape to for a quick beer or an even quicker shot of bourbon. This was a blessing and a curse. As sheriff, he didn't need to assign patrols to monitor for drunks stumbling to their cars. But, as sheriff, everyone in the county also knew when he stopped in for a beer. That's why he long ago established a personal, two beer, limit.

The sheriff stepped out of his patrol SUV and closed the door. As soon as he did, he felt and heard the unmistakable splat of bird dung on his Stetson.

"Crap!" he said, loudly, not appreciating the irony of the word.

Human nature being what it is, he immediately looked up. The culprit was gone.

He turned and looked behind him, toward the west. Even with his sunglasses on, the setting sun was glaring. He had to squint. A large bird was flying away. He couldn't make out exactly what it was, though.

He removed his hat to examine the damage. It was a direct hit, as though he was the intended target. Perturbed, he carried the hat into the restaurant. Instead of asking for a table he went directly to the men's room to clean up the bird mess before it dried.

As he dampened paper towels to wipe off the filth, he hoped the felt wouldn't stain. He prided himself in his appearance. The way he looked in public represented the entire Sheriff's Department. If he needed to replace his hat, he would have to travel to Santa Fe. The trip wasn't that bad. It was the thought of forking over $150 for a new hat that bothered him.

Satisfied he had done his best, he went back into the restaurant.

"Where would you like to sit, Sheriff?" Paco's receptionist/daughter asked.

"Along the wall is fine," he said, indicating the smaller tables that seated two.

He sat so he could watch the entrance, mostly out of habit. Not because he was expecting anyone.

"*Una cerveza, por favor*," he said. He would wait to order dinner.

It was while he was sipping his beer that he realized he was sitting in the same seat when Margarite said her goodbye. He kept telling himself he didn't miss her, but he knew that was a lie. They'd had a solid professional relationship. He had thought their personal relationship was just as solid—something more than casual dinners and casual sex. He had taken her for granted. He had assumed Margarite would be around forever. He was wrong and he was alone—again.

Before he realized it, he was halfway through his second beer.

"You're Sheriff Lansing, aren't you?"

Lansing looked up, startled.

"Oh, I'm sorry. I didn't mean to scare you."

"That's all right," he said, embarrassed at being caught off-guard. An attractive Hispanic woman in her early thirties stood next to his table. He stood. "Yes, I'm the sheriff. Can I help you?"

"Am I interrupting anything? Are you waiting for someone?"

"No, I'm very much alone," he admitted.

She extended her hand. "I'm Anna Menendez. My uncle used to work with you."

Lansing shook her hand. "Sure. Rubin. We miss him a lot. How does he like Santa Fe?"

"He loves it," she said, smiling. "Do you mind if I sit?"

"Not at all." He indicated the chair opposite him. "I'm glad for the company."

The lady pulled out the seat, discovering Lansing's wayward hat.

"Oh, let me get that." He retrieved the Stetson, setting it to one side of the table. He did a cursory examination. No stain. Things were looking up. He smiled at the new arrival. "Can I order you anything?"

"No, no. I'm fine."

The two sat.

"Do you mind if I finish my beer?"

"Please, do," Anna said, still smiling.

"Can I help you with anything?"

"I grew up around Carlsbad. I've been working as a secretary with one of the little oil companies down there."

"What brings you up here?"

"Have you ever visited the Permian Basin?"

"I've driven through it."

"It's undeveloped and ugly. At least to me it is. El Paso is the biggest town around, and that's a two-hour drive from Carlsbad. I came to San Phillipe County because I was looking for something different. I have some money saved. I was thinking of opening a little shop of some kind. A boutique, maybe."

Lansing noticed the necklace she was wearing. It was a braided silver chain with a two-inch, tear-drop shaped turquois stone dangling from it. He leaned forward to look at it. "That's a beautiful piece you're wearing."

She looked down at her decoration. "Oh, this? Yes. I love it. I've had it for years." She touched it gently with her finger tips. "I call it *Lagrima de la Madre.*"

"Tear of the Mother," Lansing translated. "Very nice."

"You have something on your shoulder." Menendez observed.

Lansing tried to look.

"Some white paint or something . . ."

"No," Lansing said, disgusted with himself that he hadn't checked his clothes before he left the bathroom. "I had an altercation with a bird on my way in here."

"I can take care of that."

She picked up a paper napkin and indicated Lansing's glass of water on the table. He nodded in agreement. She dipped the end of the napkin into the water. Indicating he should lean forward again, she attacked the problem with vigor. She scrubbed the spot on his shoulder, dipping the napkin again and again to make sure the job was complete. After a few minutes she sat back.

"All done!"

"Thank you," he said, twisting his neck, trying to see the spot.

"Don't worry," she said, reassuringly. "It's gone."

He finished his beer. "Do you mind if I have another?" he asked, setting aside his long-time custom of just two beers.

"Of course, not."

"Are you sure you don't want anything?"

"Positive."

He ordered a third *cerveza*.

"This boutique you're talking about . . . will it carry other religious items?"

"Religious items?" she asked

"Yes, like your *Lagrima de la Madonna*."

"Oh," she said, realizing Lansing's misinterpretation of what she said. She didn't correct him. "Of course, of course. Obviously, those won't be the only things I'd sell."

"Obviously," Lansing agreed. He knew Las Palmas couldn't support the kind of boutique she wanted to open. Initially, he was going to encourage her to try Taos, or even Eagle's Nest. Taos had a lot more tourist traffic, but it was already saturated. Eagle's Nest was tiny, but it saw a lot of highway business.

His beer was delivered, and they continued talking. He suggested Cohino or Segovia as possible locations, pointing out the advantages and disadvantages.

They continued to talk. The conversation meandered through a dozen topics: possible store locations, San Phillipe weather, New Mexico politics, just to name a few.

Eventually, Lansing glanced at his watch. It was almost ten o'clock. He had been there for three hours. *Paco's* was getting ready to close and he hadn't eaten. What was worse, he had lost track of how many beers he had. He had been distracted by the pleasant conversation and the even more pleasant companionship. He settled his tab, then stood. He was unsteady on his feet.

"Do you need some help?" Anna asked.

"Just walk with me out to my car," he requested.

When they got outside, the parking lot was almost empty. The brisk evening air did little to revive him. Anna put her arm around his waist to steady him.

"Do you have far to drive?"

"Too far," Lansing admitted. He knew he shouldn't try the fifteen-mile drive to his ranch. He was too embarrassed to ask for a lift from one of his deputies.

"Why don't you let me drive your Jeep?" Menendez suggested. "We can get a room at the motel. It's only a mile away."

Reluctantly, he agreed.

# Chapter Nine

"What are you going to do?" David Diaz asked Pepe after they stuffed the body of Rodrigo Abrego into the trunk of the sedan.

"I am going away—as far from this place as I can," Zapata admitted. "You need to take your family and leave, as well. When Rodrigo and I don't return to Matamoros, someone will come looking for us. I am not safe. You are not safe."

Diaz nodded. "Where will you go?"

"I don't know—but I wouldn't tell you. And you shouldn't tell me where you're going."

Zapata got into the car, started the engine, and backed out of the driveway. He went down the street, the direction they had come in. He reached a busy boulevard and tried to retrace their route. It wasn't long before he was lost.

Pepe Zapata knew his education was lacking. He was nineteen years old and had never learned to read or write. He knew the letters that formed the word MATAMOROS. He had seen them all his life. He knew if he was heading in that direction, he needed to turn around.

He had to get out of Monterrey first. His knowledge of geography was limited. The sun came up in the east and set in the west. If he faced east and turned to his left, he was facing north. To him, north meant the Rio Grande and Brownsville, Texas. He guessed, if he dumped Rodrigo's car on the north side of town, far away from the Diaz house, Abrego and his men would think Zapata would continue north and escape to the United States.

It took him two hours to reach the northern end of Cerro del Topo Chico Nature Preserve on the outskirts of Monterrey. Rodrigo always carried a large amount of money. Pepe retrieved it from his former partner's body. Abrego wouldn't need it. In the trunk, he also found a small canvas bag full of ammunition clips. He emptied the bag. He put his Beretta along with half the money inside. The rest of the money he stuffed in his pocket. He closed the trunk and walked away.

Typically, assassins burned the bodies of their victims in their cars, dead or alive. Pepe wanted Rodrigo found. He knew Abrego and the Gulf Cartel assumed he was just another, stupid foot soldier. If they thought he wasn't smart enough to cover his tracks, that was fine with him.

He walked for thirty minutes before he reached a busy road. It took another thirty minutes to flag down a taxi. He needed to get to the bus station.

He found himself delivered to *Omnibus de Mexico* in downtown Monterrey. The terminal was busy. People were in line, buying tickets. Others were lounging around, sipping on colas, smoking cigarettes, waiting for buses to depart or arrive.

He got in a ticket line and waited. After fifteen minutes he reached the counter.

"Destination?" the clerk asked.

"South," Zapata replied.

The tired, bored ticket seller was not amused. "South, what?"

"I don't know," the young man admitted. "I just want to go south."

"What town?" the clerk pointed at the large map of Mexico behind him. He put his finger on Monterrey. "We are here." He waved his hand. "Almost all the rest of Mexico is south of us. What town do you want to go to?"

Pepe pointed to the largest town to the south.

"Mexico City?" the man asked. "You want to go to Mexico City? Are you sure? That will cost a thousand pesos. Do you have that much?"

Pepe nodded. He pulled a wad of money from his pocket and began pealing-off hundred-peso notes. When he counted ten, he handed the money to the clerk.

The man behind the counter was suspicious. Zapata didn't appear to be the kind of person who would carry around such a large amount of dough. Then again, the clerk had learned long ago, mind his own business.

He handed Pepe the ticket. "The bus leaves at Eight pm. Can you tell time?"

Zapata gave him a dirty look without answering.

This was Pepe's first trip anywhere. He had never been out of Matamoros. It was also his first bus trip. If he could read, he would have discovered for 100 pesos more he could have caught the express bus. The nearly 500-mile trip would have taken 14 hours.

The ticket clerk had a cruel streak. He put Zapata on the LOCAL. It was now a 700-mile trip and would take three days. They would zig-zag their way down either side of Federal Route 57, hitting small and mid-size towns, eventually reaching the final destination.

When it came time, Pepe found a seat at the back of the bus, next to the window. He had hoped to watch the countryside roll by. Ten minutes out of the station he was asleep.

An hour later they stopped in Saltillo. A few people got off. A few people got on. The seat next to Zapata was taken by a young man about Pepe's age.

"*Buenos noches*," he said.

Zapata nodded suddenly realizing it was dark outside.

"I'm Eduardo," the new arrival said, extending his hand. "Eduardo Fuentes."

Zapata took the offered hand. "Pepe," he said.

"I'm going to San Miguel de Allende," he announced. "I'm going to *Monasterio Benedicto de Santa Maria Magdalena.* I'm going to be a monk."

He kept talking and talking.

The former cartel soldier's first impression was that Eduardo Fuentes was a simpleton. He was in the body of a man, but he talked like a child. He had the excitement of a child. He had the inability to be quiet. Like a child.

The second thing Zapata realized was Fuentes was talking about things he didn't understand. He knew nothing of saints or monasteries or monks or Mary Magdalene. To his knowledge he had never been in a church. When he was a child, a filthy waif on the streets, he remembered following a procession. As it entered a small sanctuary, someone grabbed him by his collar and tossed him to the ground. He was informed his kind was not allowed in God's House.

He had no idea who God was. But if this God didn't want anything to do with him, the feeling was mutual.

"I have a letter from Father Iglesias." He indicated the flimsy, cardboard folder he was holding. "It is to Abbot Pedro. I don't know what it says. My reading is not good. I grew up in the orphanage. There were too many of us. The Sisters didn't have time to give me special lessons. Father Iglesias said maybe in the quiet of the monastery I'll be able to learn.

"He said in the letter my heart is with God. I think he said he hoped the monastery can find a use for me. I'm too old to stay at the orphanage."

Pepe listened to what Eduardo had to say. He knew if his new comrade was raised in an orphanage, he didn't have parents, either. In a way, they were more alike than different.

Within a day, they were friends. Eduardo shared the three flour-tortilla, bean tacos he was given for the trip. After that, Pepe paid for their meals.

There was a very young mother traveling with her two-year-old son. She was trying to get to her parent's home. She spent all her money on their tickets. Pepe and Eduardo adopted the two and the former henchman for the Gulf Cartel bought their meals as well. They said their goodbyes that first evening.

After one day of travel, Fuentes was one day from his destination. It was two in the morning. The bus was again on one of the back roads, six miles from San Diego de la Union, when they, suddenly, came to a stop.

Outside there was gunfire and a lot of shouting. The doors of the bus opened and two men jumped inside. They were armed. They announced they were *banditos* and everyone on the bus would hand over their money and anything else of value.

Pepe was wide awake. So was his sense of injustice. He had been with most of these same travelers since Monterrey. They were quiet, friendly people who just wanted to live their lives. Cartel foot soldiers he'd known had bragged at how easily they had robbed busses just like this. The rabbits inside were too frightened to put up a resistance.

Pepe would be one rabbit too many.

Zapata unzipped his bag and pulled out the Beretta. He had no idea how many men waited outside. He was only concerned with the two men coming down the aisle. The man in front held a large duffle bag to retrieve the loot. The second man brandished his rifle to ensure compliance.

The bus had twenty-two rows of seats. Pepe had to wait until they were closer before he did anything. He wanted to avoid any collateral damage.

"What are you doing?" Eduardo asked in a whisper.

All Pepe said was, "Sh-h-h."

The robbers were six seats away when Zapata jumped up. He fired immediately, killing the gunman with the bag of booty.

Women started screaming. Children were crying.

The second gunman turned his rifle in Pepe's direction and fired. The bullet went wide.

Zapata fired a second time and dropped the man with the rifle.

There was a single bandit waiting for his compadres outside. When the gunfire started, he didn't wait for the results. He ran to the pickup truck blocking the road and sped off.

The bus driver didn't hesitate either. He closed the doors and stomped on the gas. They wouldn't stop until they reached the San Diego de la Union police station.

Pepe Zapata sat down, shaking from all the adrenaline surging through his body. He turned to his new friend. "Eduardo . . ."

His companion said nothing. The gunman's bullet had found a mark. Eduardo Fuentes was dead.

*\*\**

Four a.m. Vigils again.

For Brother Esteban it was another bad night. The dream was worse than ever. He would pray. He would ask for guidance. He was afraid.

He was afraid the dream was not about the past. He was afraid the dream was a warning about things to come.

# Chapter Ten

Lansing's eyes popped open. It was still dark. He was in an unfamiliar room, fully clothed. His gun-belt and boots were the only things he had removed. He was on his back, on a bed. He must have slept that way. There was a person next to him under the bedspread.

He closed his eyes and tried to remember. He had gone to *Paco's*. He was drinking a beer when a beautiful woman joined him. They talked for a long time.

He carefully sat up, trying not to disturb his bedmate. Looking around, he realized he was in a motel room.

That's right, he thought. They drove to the *Las Palmas Inn*. He drove? She drove? He couldn't remember. He vaguely recalled checking in.

He got up and went to the bathroom. He closed the door before turning on the light. After emptying his bladder, Lansing looked at himself in the mirror. His uniform was wrinkled. There was still bird-crap on his shoulder. He was a mess.

Lansing washed and dried his face. Leaving the bathroom light on with the door open, he found his boots, gun belt and keys. He scribbled a message on a bedside notepad: "Call me if you need a ride. Lansing." The note included his mobile number.

Anna Menendez was completely covered. He couldn't even see her face.

The sheriff quietly left the room. He needed to go home, take a shower, and find a clean uniform. It was 5:00 am.

# Chapter Eleven

Roger and Eileen Porter looked at each other from across their breakfast table and smiled. Life had been very good to them . . . No, God had been very good to them and they couldn't remember when they had been happier.

It hadn't always been that way. Roger Porter had been a successful engineer with Sandia Labs in Albuquerque. Eileen had been an equally successful homemaker, a domestic engineer, if you will. They had raised two sons and two daughters, all of who had completed college and were raising families of their own. It had been a hectic thirty years: business trips, trips to the hospital for a broken arm; little-league games, little broken hearts over the end a girl's first crush; baptisms, funerals; all the highs and lows, trials and tribulations that weave the tapestry of our lives.

When their youngest daughter got married and waved goodbye, they turned around and walked back into their big, empty house. They didn't say a word. He went to the den and fixed a bourbon on ice. She went to her separate bedroom and took a Xanax. Thirty years together and they were strangers.

Roger was rapidly approaching retirement. Eileen was rapidly approaching insanity. After six months of silence between the two of them, she seriously considered divorce.

At one time, they had been devout Catholics. All their children had been baptized and gone through confirmation. But their church attendance grew less and less. Eight years earlier they had quit going all together.

One evening, before Roger started another round of silence and whiskey, Eileen made a request. She had an appointment to visit their parish priest the next afternoon. Could he take time from work to go with her? He asked why they should go.

She put it in terms he, as an engineer, could understand. Their marriage was in severe retrogression. It needed a major reset. If not, the whole thing might have to be jettisoned.

Roger allowed himself a small, grim smile. He had forgotten how smart his wife was—and how wise. He put the bourbon bottle down, turned to his bride and pulled her close. It was the first time they had touched in months.

"Of course, I'll go."

They held each other and cried.

The visit with the priest was helpful. He, of course, suggested returning to the church, and attending regularly. He also suggested a couple's retreat, sponsored by the parish

Once home, they agreed to attend church every week. But they were both turned off at the notion of a "couple's" retreat. They would look for something better.

Within a week, Eileen discovered a brochure at the church. It discussed "personal" retreats to *St. Anthony's Monastery in the Canyon.* It was a Benedictine Monastery, 50 miles north of Santa Fe on the Rio Cohino, near Artiga. There were no organized or supervised retreats. Visitors were invited to enjoy the peace and solitude of monastic life. They could enjoy as much or as little of a monk's daily routine as they wanted.

The Porters agreed to try a few days in the north. After lifetimes in the big city, they were overwhelmed at the beauty of the canyon and the quiet of the monastery life. All thirteen guest rooms were spartan: a table, a desk, a chair, no electricity. Vigils began at 4:00 am, followed by meals, work time, and six other opportunities to pray and meditate.

A month later they stayed for a week. The third visit was the month after that.

After the three retreats, they were not only ready to recommit to their marriage: They wanted, in some way, to commit to *St. Anthony's* and a Benedictine lifestyle. Abbot Christopher suggested they become Oblates, essentially, lay-members of the Monastery. The Monks were restricted to the Abbey's grounds. Oblates, who could be married, could be a conduit to the greater world. They had a gift shop in Santa Fe Village, the arts and crafts part of Old Santa Fe near the capitol building. It was called *St. Benedict's Rialto*. The shop sold votive candles, rosaries and other religious items along with hand-made statuettes and icons from the Monastery's craftsmen. All proceeds needed to go to the Monastery, which had to be self-sufficient. The current managers were leaving. Would the Porters be interested?

That suited the Porters. He was retiring, and they would be quite comfortable on his income. They didn't need a salary.

It took a month to sell their long-time home in Albuquerque. They bought a lovely apartment off Sawmill, only five miles from Santa Fe Village. Parking was a half-block from the shop.

They leaned across the kitchen table and kissed. Their ten-year-old Yorkshire Terrier, Auggie, barked to go out. That was the signal. After his constitutional, it was time for the three of them to go to work.

After a year in Santa Fe, there was no place else they wanted to be. The Porters knew they were blessed, and they were grateful.

# Chapter Twelve

Juan Garcia Abrego had been captured by Mexican Federal agents in January 1996. He was immediately shipped to the United States to stand trial for drug trafficking.

The trial was held in Houston, Texas, eight months after his capture. DOJ had been building a case against him for years. Eighty-four witnesses came forward to testify against him. One of the most crucial testimonies came from David Diaz, Juan Garcia's former accountant. He had contacted the U.S. authorities in 1990, seeking protection for himself and his family. In exchange, he would provide the authorities with all the information he had on the inner workings of the Gulf Cartel. Even six years later, the testimony was relevant—it pertained to three of the 22 counts of drug trafficking Abrego was charged with.

Juan Garcia was awarded with 11 consecutive life-sentences.

David Diaz and his family remained in witness protection.

That was the reason the Abregos, both Juan and Humberto, could never hunt down the accountant. He was under the protection of the United States of America.

Humberto Garcia Abrego downed another tequila. He was angry with his brother. A lot of effort was spent looking for Diaz. Juan Garcia hardly gave Rodrigo's murder a second thought. It was no secret that Juan Garcia despised his nephew. But, dammit, Rodrigo was family and should have been treated better.

Six months earlier, when it looked like Abrego was gaining the upper hand in the struggle for cartel control, he hired a private investigator to look for Pepe Zapata. He didn't care if it had been eight years. If Zapata was dead, he wanted unconvertable proof. If he was alive, Abrego wanted to know where he lived.

Today was Friday. The investigator would deliver his report the next morning.

The Gulf Cartel had its own death squad. They would be dispatched to handle the problem. They would take care of Pepe Zapata and anyone who got in their way.

# Chapter Thirteen

It was already 9:00 am. Lansing had lost track of how many cups of coffee he'd had. Kind of like losing track of the number of beers the night before. It was late enough. He thought he would call the motel and check on Anna Menendez.

"Las Palmas Inn," the receptionist said on the other end.

"Yes," the sheriff responded. "Please, connect me to room eleven."

"Certainly."

The phone began ringing. It rang for some time. No one answered. Lansing hung up, then called the motel again.

"Las Palmas Inn."

"Yes, this is Sheriff Lansing. I called a moment ago. I spent last night in room eleven. Did the lady I was with check out?"

"I came on at Seven. Unless she left earlier, no one's checked out. Do you want housekeeping to look at the room?"

"I left something there," he lied. "I'll be over in a few minutes."

True to his word, he showed up at the motel reception desk ten minutes later.

"I left the key in the room. Could housekeeping let me in?"

He met the motel maid at the door and she let him in. Lansing surveyed the room from the entrance. It looked like no one had spent the night there.

"Did you already clean this room?" he asked.

"No, *señor*," she said. "Not yet."

He walked into the room. The bedspread was smooth. Not a single wrinkle. It looked like no one had used the bed, at all. It certainly didn't look like he slept on it.

The note he left was missing.

He checked the bathroom. The towel he used to dry his face hung in its original position, unsullied. Even the paper sanitation strip was still stretched across the toilet seat.

He turned back to the room. He was beginning to suspect he was losing his mind.

Then he saw it. The necklace Anna Menendez wore the night before. It lay on the floor, next to the bed. What did she call it? *Lagrima de la Madonna? Lagrima de la Madre?* Something like that.

He picked it up. Menendez would probably want it back.

But, where was she? She had obviously been there. The necklace was proof.

He put the necklace in his pocket and thanked the housekeeper for her help. He went back to the front desk.

"I did spend last night here at the Inn, didn't I?" he asked.

The receptionist turned and checked the room sign-in cards. She pulled up the card for room eleven. "Yes," she said. "You checked in at Ten-O-Five."

"Was that for double occupancy?"

"No. Just you."

"Okay, thanks. You can check me out now."

Lansing had a choice. He could leave the necklace at the motel. That would be the first place Anna Menendez would look for it. Or, he could take it back to the office, where he knew it wouldn't accidentally "walk-off."

"I was with a lady, last night," he told the receptionist. "She forgot her necklace." He held it up. "If she stops by looking for it, tell her I have it at the Sheriff's Office . . . for safe keeping."

"Sure thing, Sheriff."

It was 9:30. Prep-staff was already busy at *Paco's*.

Paco Garcia was a jolly, rotund, chef-entrepreneur, who nearly lived at his restaurant. He was there for the 8:00 am deliveries and stayed until nearly midnight when the last dish was dried and stacked. No one at the motel seemed to remember Ms. Menendez. Maybe Paco could recall something.

Paco saw Lansing trying the locked, front door to the *Cantina*. He hurried and opened it.

"Good morning, Sheriff," Garcia said. "Can I help you with anything?"

"Yeah, Paco. I was here last night . . ."

"Yes," the owner pointed at the tables along the back wall. "Right over there."

"Right . . . There was a lady sitting with me . . ."

Garcia gave him a funny look. "No, Sheriff. There was no one with you. You came in, sipped on three beers for nearly three hours, then left. You didn't even eat."

"Are you sure?"

"Absolutely. I saw you. You came in, went straight to the restroom . . . You said you had to clean your hat. When you came out, you sat down and ordered a beer."

"What time was that?"

"Six-thirty. Six-forty-five. Something like that."

"Do you remember what time I left?"

"Nine-forty-five. Just before closing."

That fit closely with his check-in time at the motel.

"And there wasn't an attractive woman sitting with me?"

"That is something I would have noticed."

"You said I had three beers?"

"Yes . . . Everybody working here noticed it, too. That's the first time any of us could remember you having more than two beers."

"So? I wasn't tipsy or drunk when I left?"

"No, Sheriff. That's something else I would have noticed. If you were drunk and by yourself, I would have called one of your deputies to take you home."

Lansing was glad to know other people had his back. But he was rapidly becoming upset, confused, and a little unwound about the Anna Menendez issue. He knew she existed. He had her necklace. He couldn't understand why no one else remembered her.

"Thanks, Paco." Lansing turned and left, more confused than ever.

# Chapter Fourteen

At Las Palmas M/H School, classes started at 8:00 and lasted until 3:30. The day started with 15 minutes of Home Room, followed by 3-4 hours of class, one hour for lunch, then 2-3 more hours of class. Generally, Middle School students had lunch first, then High School. Las Palmas only had 13 teachers for all 152 students. Each teacher taught 5 classes every day. With an average of 25 students in every grade, when a teacher taught English I, the entire ninth grade was in the classroom.

A teacher's free hour was spent grading papers or monitoring the lunchroom. If you pulled lunchroom duty, then you ate during your free hour. Teachers ate in their lounge. That's also where the smokers smoked. (They weren't allowed to smoke where they could be seen. It was a bad influence, though there were no secrets.)

Memorial Day seemed to fall a week early this year. It fell on Monday, May 25th. There was another week until the end of the month. The two days of school after the holiday were used for awards ceremonies and graduation.

Tina Morales was on her way to the lounge for lunch. She passed the front glass doors and glanced at the parking lot. There were 60 spaces. On a typical day, staff took up 20 slots, students another 15. Anything extra was noticeable, especially a bright, red Ford F250 with rooftop lights.

The truck was way too familiar to the Science teacher. It belonged to Poncho Chamorro. She hadn't seen either one of them, him or his truck, in almost 10 months.

She hid behind the nearest corner, hoping she wasn't noticed. Slowly, she allowed herself a peek. The sun glared on the windshield. She couldn't tell if the truck was occupied.

Hurrying from the safety of her spot, Morales reached the other hall-way, and access to the front office.

"Hi, Miss Morales," Halley, the office secretary said, smiling. Halley Basa was the lynchpin that held the Las Palmas School District together. She knew all the teachers and all their "needs." She engaged the PTA and School Board with equal deftness, ensuring the needs of the students came first. She always managed to cut through any politics without ruffling feathers. She also knew everything that went on.

"Hey, Mrs. Basa. Has anyone stopped by asking about me?"

Halley Basa jabbed her thumb in the direction of the parking lot. "Are you talking about 'Big Wheels' out there?"

Tina nodded.

"He pulled in about ten this morning. He's just been sitting there ever since. A friend of yours?"

"Not exactly," Morales admitted.

"Do you want me to send out Coach Moran? He can ask what he's doing here."

"Oh, don't worry. I know exactly why he's here."

"Coach or Principal de la Cruz can run him off, if you'd like . . . or should I call the Sheriff?"

Tina considered the situation. Chamorro was a threat to her. She wasn't sure if he was a threat to others. Things might escalate if Poncho was confronted.

"Let's wait," the teacher said. "Maybe he'll get bored and leave."

Before her last class, Morales would check the lot. If Chamorro was still there, something would have to be done.

# Chapter Fifteen

It was Friday, May 22$^{nd}$—the commencement of Memorial Day Weekend.

For most people this was the beginning of a three-day holiday and the start of Summer.

For the San Phillippe Sheriff's Department, this was the season for long days, double shifts and a constant look-out for vacationing drunks. The county boasted four recreational lakes, two-dozen campgrounds and tourist meccas like O'Keeffe Ranch, the Chisum and Aztec Scenic Railroad and the Jicarilla Apache Reservation. San Phillipe also had two National Forests—Carson and Santa Fe. Lansing's office handled the law enforcement for the entire area. The only exception—the Jicarilla Apache Reservation. Their police handled their own business.

It was up to the State Police and the sheriff's office to monitor the traffic to and from these locations . . . and there was always a lot of traffic.

Lansing got back to the department after his visit with Paco. He was perturbed with himself. His mind should have been on law enforcement business and the upcoming weekend. Instead he was concerned about a woman who didn't seem to exist and her necklace, which did.

"What's going on, Sheriff?" Marilyn asked, noticing the perplexed look on her boss' face.

He held up the necklace. "I met Rubin Menendez's niece last night. Somehow, she got separated from her jewelry. I was just trying to track her down."

"What's her name?" Marilyn seemed curious.

"Anna," he said. "Anna Menendez."

"Her last name was 'Menendez?' "

"That's what she said."

"That would make her the daughter of Rubin's brother, wouldn't it?" Marilyn asked.

"I suppose so," the sheriff nodded.

"Rubin doesn't have a brother," the dispatcher observed.

"What!" Lansing almost exploded.

"He has three sisters, all younger than him. But he never had a brother."

The sheriff realized he had been scammed. He stared at the necklace. What the hell was going on? He went from being confused to being angry. That was it! He was finished with Anna Menendez and her necklace.

He walked back to the small room they called the "Evidence Locker." From a cabinet he grabbed a large manila envelope along with a felt-tipped pen. He wrote the name "Menendez" on the outside, then dropped the necklace into it. The envelope was placed in one of the file cabinets.

Lansing locked the room and walked away. He wasn't going to give "Anna Menendez," or whatever her name was, another thought. If she wanted to claim her jewelry, she would have to explain who she really was and what game she was playing.

He walked back to the reception area.

"If anyone comes in looking for that necklace," he announced, "they see me first."

Marilyn and Clem Montoya, the desk sergeant, nodded.

Lansing went back to his office, still pissed at being flimflammed.

# Chapter Sixteen

It was almost 5:00 pm when the Honorable Jason Mateo finished writing his opinion. The defendant, Ramon Para opted for a bench trial, rather than face a jury of his peers. He was charged with molesting his own daughter. In conservative San Phillippe, Para could face 25 to life if his fellow citizens had a say. Mateo was notoriously lenient, especially with fellow Latinos.

Five years earlier, the judge had manipulated a jury into giving an 18-year-old murderer a manslaughter sentence, because he was "just a boy." The entire county thought Bernardino Chavez should have gotten the needle. Mateo thought otherwise.

When word came down that Chavez had died in prison, the judge was upset. He knew other people in the county would think justice was finally served. He didn't think it was . . . but, it really didn't matter to him. He shrugged it off. Such things were beyond his powers to prevent.

Mateo put his hand-written verdict into a manila folder, then placed the folder in his top, left desk drawer and locked it. He didn't want anyone to know he threw out the charges. In his opinion, there was insufficient evidence to convict. (The ten-year-old daughter was too distraught to provide reliable testimony.) He would give the folder to his secretary on Tuesday for typing. Everything would be ready for the Wednesday hearing.

He could now enjoy the three-day weekend with nothing hanging over his head. As he walked to the parking lot, he felt like he didn't have a care in the world.

From the top of the courthouse, two yellow eyes watched the judge get into his car. Soon, whatever cares the Honorable Jason Mateo thought he had, wouldn't matter.

# Chapter Seventeen

When school let out at 3:30, Poncho Chamorro's F250 was nowhere to be seen. That gave Tina Morales only partial relief. He drove two-and-a-half-hours from Albuquerque to track her down. He looked for her for 10 months. He wasn't the type to give up.

Tina's dark-blue Chevy Cavalier was parked in front of the school. Chamorro surely saw it. He would wait until she was off school grounds, then follow her home. Once she was isolated, he would approach her. She wasn't sure the restraining order she took out in Bernalillo County applied in San Phillippe, not that it mattered much in Albuquerque, either.

When the school busses pulled away from the building, Tina joined the other teachers as they headed to their cars to escape for the holiday. The school sat alone, west of town. The caravan reached Highway 15 and split up. Some cars went north. Others south.

To go directly home, Morales needed to go north. She opted for the more indirect route, following the southbound cars. When most turned onto the 146 Bypass, she followed. A mile behind her was the red, Ford truck.

Tina tried not to panic. Las Palmas was not ideal for getting lost in a crowd. She was far enough ahead, though, she could safely duck down one of the side streets. Then she would serpentine her way through town until she got to her small, rental house. There was enough room that she could park her car in the backyard, and it wouldn't be seen from the street.

She took her time, watching behind her, then the side streets when she crossed an intersection. She thought she saw the F250 on a parallel track.

She quickly pulled into an empty driveway and hunkered down—after a time venturing a peek. No red truck.

She backed out onto the street. Hoping it was safe, she proceeded directly home, parking in back. This time, she did start to panic. What if he followed her? What if he pulled into her driveway? She was trapped now. There was no escape.

Tina waited, expecting Poncho to start pounding on her window any moment.

After several minutes, when nothing happened, she unlocked her door and got out. She held the keys in her hand, so they stuck out between her fingers. It wasn't much of a weapon, but it was something.

She unlocked the back door and slipped inside. Quickly locking the door again, she pressed her back against the wall and took a deep breath.

Poncho Chamorro was a psychopath. He had literally charmed the pants off Morales. He made her feel special. Then he went out of his way to make her think he was special. They moved in together. Within a day, he began the manipulation. He had to know her every move. She had no private phone conversations. He checked her phone daily to see who she called or who called her.

The relationship was over the first time he hit her. She had seen too many friends break up, then go back together, in spite of the abuse. That wasn't going to happen to her. She called the police, had him removed, then filed a restraining order. The entire problem with restraining orders was they were just pieces of paper. He kept coming around, kept getting arrested, then come around again once he was out of jail.

That's how she ended up in Las Palmas. She had to be responsible for her own protection. She glanced at the narrow space between the refrigerator and the counter where she kept her twelve-gauge shot gun. It was there, and she knew it was loaded.

The small, wood-frame house had a kitchen, a living-room and one bedroom with a bath. She stashed a Smith and Wesson .38 caliber snub-nosed pistol in a desk drawer in the living room. Her nightstand was where she kept a .25 caliber Beretta. The bullets were hollow-point, so they could do some damage.

Tina Morales wasn't paranoid. She was prepared.

She was also angry she had to live like this.

For nine months she felt safe. Now, at the sight of one, red truck, she felt her world starting to crumble again.

Tina kept peeking through the front curtains, looking to see if she had been discovered. The thought of eating didn't cross her mind.

After three hours, she started to feel safe.

Then she saw it—the red, F250. It slowly cruised by, the driver in-specting each house he passed. He didn't stop. He proceeded around the corner.

Tina hid herself behind the wall, next to the window. She held her breath, as if that would keep the boogey-man away. She remained motionless.

She kept thinking "Please, keep going! Please, keep going!"

Then she heard the crunch of gravel. She dared a peek through the window. Chamorro's truck was pulling into her driveway.

She ran to the kitchen and grabbed the shotgun. With the weapon cra-dled in her arm, she picked up the receiver from the wall phone and dialed.

"Nine-One-One, what's the nature of your emergency?"

"My ex-boyfriend is getting ready to break into my house. I need the police here, now!"

# Chapter Eighteen

Sheriff Lansing spent all afternoon putting out brush fires. When one issue was doused, another would flare up. It was nearly 7:00 pm when he got into his Jeep. The horses needed to be watered and fed. He needed to get some rest. He and all the deputies were on duty for the 3-day holiday.

"Sheriff Lansing, this is dispatch," Marilyn's voice crackled over the radio.

"This is Lansing, go ahead." He'd only seen her a minute earlier.

"Sorry, but, we have a break-in. Four-O-Eight Dollar Street. You're the closest."

"I've got it. Lansing, out."

He started his engine, then threw on the lights and siren. Dollar street was six blocks away.

As he turned the corner onto Dollar, a red, Ford F250 came swerving down the street toward him. Lansing's SUV and truck barely missed each other. As they passed, the truck tried to speed up, hit a parked car, then continued around the corner.

The sheriff was only a block from the reported break-in. He suspected the truck and break-in were related. He did a quick U-turn on the street and headed after the Ford. It hadn't traveled far. It had plowed into yet another parked car.

Lansing parked behind the stalled vehicle. Pulling his gun, he approached cautiously.

Grabbing the handle, he swung the door open. The driver tumbled out, falling on the ground. The lawman bent down to check for vitals. He was immediately struck by the stench of alcohol. Bourbon. The man's face and shoulder were also bloody, peppered with bird-shot from a shotgun. The wounds weren't severe enough to kill him. He was simply passed-out-drunk.

"Dispatch, Sheriff Lansing. I need an ambulance, Three hundred block of Cuello. I also need a unit to Four-O-Eight Dollar to get a statement."

It was dark by the time Lansing was finished with the wreck on Cuello Street. Poncho Chamorro was spending the night at the Las Palmas Clinic, handcuffed to a bed. As a minimum, he faced DWI and reckless driving charges. The sheriff headed to Dollar Street to see if there were any more charges he could heap on.

Deputy Sid Barnes' patrol unit was still parked in front. As the sheriff approached the abode, he noticed the front door had been kicked in. He also saw the door had been liberally salted with birdshot. Inside, the sheriff found Barnes, Mrs. Halley Basa, the High School secretary, and a very shaken High School Science teacher. The two women were seated on the sofa.

Lansing pulled his deputy aside. "What do we have, Sid?"

"The lady's name is Tina Morales, age 29." He referred to his notes. "She's been a teacher at Las Palmas High for the last nine months. Evidently moved here from Albuquerque to get away from an abusive boyfriend. His name is Poncho Chamorro. He found out where she was teaching and followed her home. The long and short of it is, he tried to break in . . . she didn't let him."

Lansing nodded. "Looks like she was ready for when he did show up. Good for her."

He gestured toward the door. "It's going to be a long weekend, Sid. Head on home. I've got this."

Before turning to the two women, he inspected the door. Ms. Morales would need a new one. She shouldn't spend the night there.

"Ms. Morales, I'm, Sheriff Lansing," he said, introducing himself. "I was going to handle your Nine-One-One call, but I ran into Mr. Chamorro on my way here. I had to stop him before he did any more damage."

"Where is he?" she demanded. She appeared more angry than anything.

"He's in our custody. He'll spend tonight in the hospital, then tomorrow we'll transfer him to jail. He won't bother you for a long time . . . Would you like to tell me what happened?"

"Sheriff, I really wouldn't. Not tonight. I told your deputy everything. I'd like to just get some rest."

"Sure." He gestured toward the front door. "Do you have a place to stay?"

"She's spending the weekend with me and my husband," the secretary said.

"That's great, Mrs. Basa." Lansing had known her for years. "I'm sure Ms. Morales appreciates it."

Tina nodded.

"Where's your shotgun, Ms. Morales?"

She gestured to the living room desk. The gun was on top.

"I need to confiscate it until all the paperwork is finished. It's procedure. You'll get it back". He picked up the shotgun. "Do you have any more weapons?"

She pointed at the desk. "There's a .38 in the top right drawer. Then there's a Beretta in my nightstand."

Lansing retrieved the guns. "Is this it?"

She smiled sheepishly. "I ran out of rooms."

# Chapter Nineteen

It was 8:00 pm when Jack Rivera clocked off his shift. His wife, Sue, had contacted Marilyn, and the dispatcher passed the info along to him: Sue and DeeDee were catching the 4:00 Greyhound out of Denver. With all the little stops along the way, they wouldn't reach Albuquerque until midnight.

Usually, after a 12-hour shift, Rivera looked forward to a hot shower before doing anything else. Tonight, that wasn't the case. He was too excited. His family was coming home. After parking his patrol unit in his driveway, he ran inside to change. He draped his uniform over a chair, threw on a sweatshirt and blue-jeans, and headed out again. This time, in his own car. The drive to Albuquerque was two and a half hours. He'd get there a bit before eleven. He didn't mind a little wait at the bus terminal.

Ever since he wired the $300 to Sue, Rivera wondered if he had done the right thing. When and if Sue and DeeDee got home, could he ever trust his wife again. For that matter, what had he done to drive her away? All of those concerns, though, seemed to melt away as the moment of their reunion grew closer.

It was dark by 8:30. As the deputy headed south, he kept fiddling with the radio dial, trying to find a station that didn't disappear in five minutes. He had just passed through Santa Fe and onto Interstate 25 when he finally picked up a clear station. It was almost 10:00.

He needed to pay closer attention to the road. This was Friday evening and the beginning of a 3-day holiday weekend. The traffic was terrible, though he noticed more cars leaving Albuquerque than arriving.

The newscaster's voice dripped with genuine concern with her next bulletin. "New Mexico State Police have just reported a tragic start to this

Memorial Day Weekend. Reports are just coming in of a tanker truck-Greyhound bus collision on Interstate 25, just outside of Raton, New Mexico. The fiery collision happened at 9:30 pm, Mountain Daylight Savings Time. There are no reports of survivors."

Interstate 25 ran from Denver to Albuquerque, directly through Raton, New Mexico.

Rivera pulled onto the shoulder and slammed on his brakes. He stared at the radio with tears welling up in his eyes. He began pounding the steering wheel. "NO! NO! NO! NO!"

Sue and DeeDee were on that bus!

He checked the traffic in his mirror. Pressing on the accelerator, he picked up speed so he could merge. A moment later he was on the highway again. Going to Albuquerque made no sense now. A mile ahead was the exit for La Cienega. He would do a flip-flop. Start heading north. Raton was 180 miles away.

With any luck, he'd be there by 1:00 am.

He had no idea what he would do when he got there.

# Chapter Twenty

Sheriff Cliff Lansing stood holding his refrigerator door open, looking for something to eat. When the Chamorro/Morales incident was finally settled, it was past 9:00. By the time he drove home and fed the horses, it was after 10:00. The animals were bedded down for the night before he realized he hadn't had dinner.

He opened the milk carton. Its contents had gone rotten a week earlier.

A plastic container contained something green and fuzzy.

He thanked the good Lord that beer didn't spoil.

It looked like it was going to be a slice of ham on whole wheat—again.

He sat on the sofa with his sandwich and a cold beer. He took a bite. While he chewed, he tried to list all the things he needed to get done the next day. He'd swing by the office first, make sure everyone was on patrol as scheduled. He'd then head out on his own patrol, going where he was needed.

He took a sip of beer.

Sometime during this long weekend, he needed a quick stop at the Las Palmas IGA to restock his barren shelves.

Boy, he thought, the sofa sure was comfortable. He took another bite of his sandwich. As he chewed he started to doze off. He vaguely remembered swallowing. His last thought was, he needed to get out of his uniform.

He woke with a start when the phone began ringing. He was still on the sofa, a half-eaten sandwich lying on the cushion next to him. His watch read 12:08.

All he could think of was: What the Hell!

The sheriff picked up the receiver. "Lansing."

"Sheriff, you need to get down to the courthouse," Phil Peters shouted, almost in hysterics. "The Nine-Eleven Call Center's on fire!"

"I'm on my way," Lansing said, jumping up, knocking over what was left of his beer.

"Crap!" he groused. His living room would smell like a brewery. At the moment, he didn't care.

He grabbed his Stetson and locked the door as he left.

His siren and flashing lights notified everyone he was on his way.

*** 

The 9-1-1 Call Center serviced all of San Phillippe County. Five operators manned stations during the daytime and evening shifts. From ten at night until 6:00 am, only three operators were on duty.

After twenty years, the Call Center moved from the "temporary" double-wide trailers, into permanent facilities adjacent to the Sheriff's Office. The Center was attached to the rest of the courthouse by phone-lines only. Its plumbing, heating and cooling were independent from the rest of the courthouse complex. That saved the expense of expanding existing facilities to accommodate the new addition.

Also, the thinking went, if something happened to the 86-year-old courthouse, the 9-1-1 Center would be spared. No one even considered the opposite might happen.

When Lansing arrived, two fire trucks and their crews were battling the blaze. The Call Center looked gutted. The firefighters were chiefly concerned with making sure the fire didn't spread. The sheriff's annex, along with the rest of the courthouse, had been spared.

Phil Peters stood outside.

"Was anyone hurt?" Lansing asked the night dispatcher.

Peters shook his head. "No, thank God."

"How much damage did our office sustain?"

"We got a little smoke. That's it. The Fire Chief wanted everybody out of the building until he gave the 'All Clear.' "

"Makes sense," the sheriff agreed. "Do you know how it started?"

"I don't have a clue," the dispatcher confessed. He pointed at a woman standing by herself. "There's Melissa Raphael. I think she's the one who pulled the alarm."

To Lansing, the 9-1-1 operator looked upset. She needed support more than an inquisition.

"Can I get you anything, Melissa?" he asked.

She shook her head, trying not to cry. "No, thank you, Sheriff. I'm fine."

"Just let me know." He turned back to Peters. "As soon as we get back in that office, I need to contact State Emergency Services. We need personnel up here stringing new Nine-One-One lines by daybreak."

He went over to the Fire Chief. "How soon can we get inside?"

"Give us thirty minutes, Cliff. I'll do a walk-through while my men check the roof."

# Chapter Twenty-One

Abbot Pedro reviewed the documents: Birth Certificate, Baptismal Certificate, Letter of Confirmation, School Records.

Then there was the letter from Father Iglesias. It essentially said:

Eduardo Fuentes is a good boy. His heart is with God. He is nineteen years old. He can barely read and write. We tried. Maybe there is something wrong with his head. The orphanage can no longer care for him. It is our prayer that he can be of service to your monastery. He has a strong back and will work hard.

The Abbot looked up at the young man and sighed. The *ADO Platino* bus driver had delivered him personally to the gates of the monastery. He told the story of the attempted highway robbery and how the friend of Eduardo Fuentes stopped the *bandidos,* but lost his life doing so. Eduardo was upset over the whole ordeal. Also, the boy had trouble reading his ticket. The driver agreed to help him get to his destination.

"We will let you stay for a month," Abbot Pedro told the man who said his name was Eduardo Fuentes. "After that, we will see."

After the shoot-out with the would-be robbers, Pepe Zapata made another life-altering decision. If he wanted to escape the Gulf Cartel, what better way than to be dead. The interior of the bus had been dark. Other riders only knew someone fired a weapon from the rear seat. They couldn't tell who.

He put the gun into Eduardo's lifeless hand. He also stuffed the money he had left into Fuentes' pockets. Then he took the cardboard folder that contained the life history of the dead man and slipped it into his canvas bag. From then on, Pepe Zapata would be known as Eduardo Fuentes, the not too bright orphan from Saltillo.

Of course, when the bus stopped at the San Diego de la Union police station, everyone on the bus was questioned. The new Eduardo Fuentes told what he knew of the gunman. They had only known each other for 24 hours. He said he believed the man's name was Pepe Zapata. He claimed to be from Matamoros.

No, he didn't know the man had a gun. No, he didn't know what the man did for a living. No, he didn't know why he had all that money. He was very sorry he couldn't be of more help.

He, himself, Eduardo Fuentes, was on his way to San Miguel de Allende. He was going to join a monastery there. The police examined the papers from his bag. Satisfied he was who he said he was, they sent him on his way.

That night was the last time he heard the name Pepe Zapata spoken.

\*\*\*

Brother Esteban Fuentes stared at the blackness of his ceiling.

He couldn't sleep. The previous eight years played like a documentary in his mind.

Poor, dim Eduardo Fuentes was treated like an idiot when he first arrived at *Monasterio Benedicto de Santa Maria Magdelena*. They expected him to at least know how to say his "Hail Mary's" and his "Our Father's." It was as if he had never heard of them. After a week, though, he had them down pat.

They soon discovered Eduardo Fuentes was an eager learner and an even harder worker. He tackled each chore with gusto. The brethren and the oblates of the monastery took an immediate liking to their new charge. They took turns teaching him how to read and write. They taught him church liturgy. They gave him, for the first time in his life, a home and a purpose.

In his heart, the new Eduardo Fuentes came to love the Mother Church, the traditions it held to and the beauty of its ceremonies. He felt like he was becoming to know God's love and he wanted to worship him with all his being.

One month turned into two. Eduardo had been living in the visitor's quarters, though he now participated in all the same activities as the "professed monks." Abbot Pedro was surprised how wrong Father Iglesias had been. There was nothing wrong with Eduardo Fuentes' head. It was probably the orphanage's fault he didn't know his catechism or how to read. They never took the time to properly teach him.

At the end of the second month the Abbot invited Fuentes into his office.

"Eduardo, do you like it here?"

"Very much, Abbot Pedro."

"What are your intentions?"

"What do you mean?"

"Do you want to stay here?"

"Oh, yes, sir."

"I have talked with the other monks. You have been in what we call an 'Observership.' They all agree, if you chose, they would gladly accept you as a Postulant. Your vow would only last a year. You can renew the vow for two years after that before making a permanent decision. But you would wear a black cassock with a leather belt and move into the cloister. You would live with the other novitiates and participate in all monastic activities."

Eduardo bowed his head, respectfully. "Father, I am not worthy."

The former Gulf Cartel foot soldier hadn't given much thought to his future. He would hide out at the monastery for a while, until he could come up with a better plan. From the beginning, though, he had become caught up in the monastic lifestyle. At first, the silence was overwhelming. Then he realized, the peace and quiet was intended to bring the participants closer to God.

He appreciated the effort of the monks to teach him. He looked forward to the fellowship when they ate together. No one spoke, save the brother assigned to read the liturgy. But it was fellowship, nonetheless. He even enjoyed the work assignments. Keeping busy with his hands he found to be a blessing.

But to become a monk? He was at the monastery under false pretenses. This incarnation of Eduardo Fuentes was a lie.

"And why, my son, do you think you are not worthy?"

Eduardo Fuentes/Pepe Zapata knelt before Abbot Pedro and made a confession. It was the first true confession he had ever made in his life. He revealed everything. Who he really was. What he had done. How he had assumed the life of the real Eduardo Fuentes.

Abbot Pedro studied the supplicant. In all his forty years as a monk, the good father had never heard such a confession. He was unsure of what should happen next. All he knew was, the man kneeling before him, the man he had come to know, was a good man.

"Get up . . ." The Abbot hesitated. "Get up, Eduardo. Do not say anything to the other monks. I need to pray for guidance. Come back tomorrow."

***

Eduardo returned the next day.

Abbot Pedro instructed Fuentes to kneel.

"Do you, Eduardo Fuentes, accept Jesus Christ as your savior? Accept that he was born of the Virgin Mary, died on the Cross for our sins, and was resurrected three days later?"

"Yes, with all my heart."

Abbot Pedro made the Sign of the Cross on Eduardo's forehead and sprinkled him with Holy Water.

"Eduardo Fuentes, I baptize you in the name of the Father, the Son, and the Holy Ghost."

Tears streamed down Eduardo Fuentes' face. "What does this mean?"

"To become a monk at a Benedictine monastery the rules are simple: you must be male, unmarried, baptized in the Roman Catholic Church and receive the Sacrament of Confirmation."

"What about everything I did before?"

"To accept Christ is to be washed of your sins. Through God's grace we are born anew. Tomorrow, you will begin learning your catechism so that you can receive the Sacrament of Confirmation. After that, you may take your vows. From then on, you will be known as Brother Esteban, named after the first martyred Saint."

\*\*\*

Brother Esteban was a novitiate for three years before he took his vows of Obedience, Stability, and Conversion of Life. After his Solemn Profession, he lived one more year at the monastery, concentrating his studies on philosophy and church doctrine. He applied to visit their parent monastery, *Saint Anthony's Monastery in the Canyon* in New Mexico. The intent was to study there for a year. That had been four years ago.

He fell in love with the monastery. The monks of *Saint Mary Magdelina's* were exclusively Latino, though not all were Mexican. *Saint Anthony's* had monks from not just the U.S. There were brothers from Germany, Africa, the Philippines, England, Vietnam, and India, to name a few.

Esteban always felt like an outsider in his own monastery because he hadn't been raised in the faith. At *Saint Anthony's,* nearly everyone was an outsider, coming together under one roof, to worship the Lord.

He had truly found a home.

But now . . . Why now was his past being resurrected?

After Vigils, Brother Esteban remained in the church. Most of the other monks returned to their cells for solitary prayers. He studied the paintings on the walls. Above the votive candles were icons of the Virgin Mary, to the left, Saint Anthony, the monastery's patron saint, to the right, Saint Benedict depicted with a Raven on his shoulder.

It was said, a Raven once saved Saint Benedict's life. The bird had protected him from being poisoned. To the Benedictine Order, the Raven was sacred.

Brother Esteban bent his head and closed his eyes. He asked the Virgin Mary to pray for his sins. He asked Saint Anthony to intervene on his behalf that God grant him wisdom. He implored Saint Benedict for the Lord to give him strength for the gathering storm.

As Pepe Zapata, Brother Esteban had seen true evil.

He now understood his dreams.

Evil was on its way.

# Chapter Twenty-Two

By the time the Fire Chief and his men were finished, it was 2:00 am. Once they were back into their offices, Sheriff Lansing and Deputy Peters began making phone calls. That time of night, the New Mexico Office of Emergency Management only had the switchboard available. But the operators knew who needed to be contacted.

Within the hour, essential personnel were arriving at the Santa Fe offices. This was the kind of emergency the office was created for. By federal mandate, the 9-1-1 System was established in 1968. It had taken 30 years for it to be implemented in 98% of the country. But once it was in place, it became as vital to a community as the police and fire protection it represented.

The county commissioners were contacted. A location for a temporary call center was needed, immediately. With Summer Vacation eminent, the school library was selected. The phone company now had a starting point.

The day room at the sheriff's office would be the temporary home, but it would still be hours before 9-1-1 calls could be routed there. Phones were borrowed from other courthouse offices to meet the need.

The line to the sheriff's office continued to ring all night. People were complaining they got a busy signal when they dialed 9-1-1. Peters was constantly routing patrol units to complaints and ambulance services to emergencies. He did his best to keep his call-log up to date.

During a lull in the action, Lansing reviewed the dispatch log to see where the hotspots had been that night. Curiously, he noticed a call from Sue Rivera.

"What was that call about?" he asked the dispatcher, pointing at the 8:30 entry.

"That was Jack Rivera's wife. She wanted him to know they got off their bus in Trinidad, Colorado, when their kid got sick."

"Did you let him know?"

"He had already checked out for the day. I figured she'd reach him at home."

Lansing let the matter drop. He didn't give it another thought until another call came in at 5:30. Peters answered, then put the caller on hold. "Sheriff, you need to take this."

Lansing was still in the front office. He picked up another phone.

"Hello, this is Sheriff Lansing."

"Cliff. It's Jack." The two men had been deputies together. Rivera always addressed him as "sheriff" in public. In private, he was allowed to be more informal.

"Yeah, what's wrong?" Lansing could hear the stress in the man's voice.

"I'm not going to be in today."

"Why? Where are you?"

"I'm in Raton . . . There was an accident last night . . . A bus accident. Sue and DeeDee were killed." He started choking up so badly Lansing could barely understand him. "I'm waiting to see if I can identify the bodies."

Lansing signaled Peters to bring him the call-log. "What time was that accident?"

"They said it happened around nine, nine thirty. Why?"

"Sue called dispatch here at Eight-thirty. She said your daughter was sick. They had to get off the bus in Trinidad, Colorado."

"What!?" Rivera choked, joy in his voice. "They're alive . . . You're telling me they're alive!"

Lansing had no idea what his deputy had been suffering over the previous eight hours, but he was glad he was delivering good news. "Let's hope so. At least, they weren't on that bus."

"Cliff, I gotta go! I need to get to Trinidad. I'm sorry about today . . . I promise, I'll be in tomorrow."

Rivera hung up the phone before the Sheriff could say, "Have a nice day!"

# Chapter Twenty-Three

The Honorable Jason Mateo thoroughly enjoyed his country living. His 3500 square foot log cabin rested in the foothills, overlooking the Rio Cohino Valley. He and his wife of 35 years, Gail, had no plans for the Memorial Day weekend. They hated the traffic and despised the crowds associated with such holidays.

Besides, the judge argued, he couldn't find any place more peaceful or pleasant than his own back yard. He surveyed his domain and thought how much he enjoyed being in control. He ruled over his little acreage. His wife catered to his every whim. And in the courtroom, even God didn't have more authority than him.

He sat on the rear porch sipping a fresh cup of coffee and reading the *Santa Fe Sentinel*. The front page had the photo of a burning Greyhound bus. The fiery crash had occurred south of Raton. At one point, traffic had been backed up for nearly twenty miles.

Mateo shook his head. He was very familiar with the media's propensity for exaggeration. If the paper said the traffic was backed up for twenty miles, he would have bet 20 bucks it was only backed up for ten.

Still, he thought, what a tragedy.

He turned the page to read the rest of the story.

That's when he noticed the hum. He couldn't identify what it was, specifically, but it seemed familiar . . . and it was growing louder. He squinted his eyes in concentration, listening.

The hum grew louder and closer. Then it was no longer a hum . . . It was a buzz! The buzz of a hoard of bees.

He pulled the paper down. That's when he saw the cloud. A black swarm of hundreds of bees, thirty feet away, coming right at him. He jumped up. His feet tangled with the legs of his wrought-iron chair.

He fell.

"Gail!" he began yelling as he scrambled to his feet. "Gail! Help! Help me!"

He was reaching for the handle of the screen door when the swarm engulfed him.

Gail rushed to the back door. She watched in horror as her husband ran down the steps and into the yard, screaming and swatting at the insects as they pursued him relentlessly. The back porch was littered with the bodies of dozens of bees who had sacrificed their stingers and their lives.

Mateo ran, swiping futilely at his attackers. He got fifty feet into the yard before he stumbled and fell.

Gail rushed to the phone and dialed 9-1-1.

Instead of a reassuring voice on the other line, all she got was a busy signal!

"No!" she shrieked. She dialed the emergency number again. Again, the busy signal. "No! No! No!"

All she could do was watch in terror as her husband's body convulsed from the injection of venom from hundreds of tiny barbs that remained imbedded in his skin.

It was another hour before the temporary 9-1-1 system was up and running.

By then it was much too late for the Honorable Jason Mateo.

# Chapter Twenty-Four

Clinton Campion was ushered into the plush offices of Humberto Garcia Abrego. He carried a briefcase. *El Jeffe* of the Gulf Cartel, currently the most lucrative drug operation in Mexico, stepped from behind his hand-carved desk to greet his visitor.

"*Señor* Campion," he said extending his hand. "I am impressed, you personally, are delivering the results of your company's investigation."

"When a client is willing to spend a half-million dollars to find a couple of people, the least I can do, as owner and chief investigator, is meet with that client."

"This is my senior lieutenant, Osiel Cardenas Guillen," Abrego said, introducing a man seated apart.

Guillen merely nodded.

"Would you care for a drink?" Humberto Garcia indicated a fully stocked bar along one wall.

"*Gracias*, no. It's a little early for me."

Humberto walked back to his seat behind the desk. "Your Spanish is very good, *señor*."

"Thank you. CC Investigations and Surveillance International, does a lot of business in Central and South America. It helps our work if we can blend in."

"I trust we are meeting today because you have results?" Humberto said, not smiling.

"I do." Campion gestured to the top of the expansive desk. Abrego nodded. The investigator placed his briefcase on top, then opened it. He pulled out a leather-bound portfolio and handed it to *El Jeffe*.

Humberto Garcia opened the folio. Each document, the result of six months of investigation, was inserted into a plastic page protector.

"I can walk you through what we've uncovered, if you'd like?"

"*Por favor.*" Abrego nodded.

"Mr. David Diaz was the easiest to find. It was public record that he testified against your brother two years ago. Obviously, he and his family were in witness protection. Bribing government officials gets more expensive every year, but it can still be done.

"His new name is Diego Carrillo. He and his family now live in Oklahoma City. I believe their address is in Document Four. He works for a small CPA firm in the suburb of Britton.

"Pepe Zapata was more of a challenge."

"Is he in the U.S., as well?"

"I don't think so."

"But we know he was heading that way. We found my son's car on the north side of Monterrey, miles from the Diaz house."

"And that's the assumption we made, as well.

"You had two photos of Zapata. One taken when he was sixteen. The other when he was eighteen. Unfortunately, they were group photos. My people scanned them into a computer, then isolated and enhanced Zapata's images. We made copies from those images.

"They were shown to every coyote operation we could find. After eight years, no one could be sure."

"So, that was it?" Humberto sounded angry.

"No, no, no," Campion said quickly. "On a hunch, our investigators thought, what if he didn't go north. What if he headed south instead?"

"And . . . You found . . .? What?"

"Your son's body was found the day after he went missing. That same night, there was a shoot-out on a bus heading to Mexico City, outside San Diego de la Union. Two bandits and one of the passengers were killed. Reportedly, the name of the passenger was Pepe Zapata."

"So, that's it? The murderer of my son is dead?"

"My offices aren't so sure."

"What do you mean?"

"You paid us five-hundred-thousand dollars. My company has a reputation. We are very good at what we do. We are also thorough. We wanted to make sure there was no doubts Mr. Zapata was dead.

"My investigators went to the San Diego de la Union police station. They had a file on the attempted bus robbery along with the passenger interviews. One passenger was a young man from Saltillo. Eduardo Fuentes. He and Zapata rode together for a day.

"In the interview he seemed to know a lot about his traveling companion. Maybe too much. If I was Zapata and I was running from a cartel, I certainly wouldn't be advertising my name or where I was from."

"So, where is this young man?"

Campion held up his hand, indicating he had more to tell.

"The police files had the name and address of the bus driver. My men tracked him down. He absolutely remembered that night. And he remembered the young man who rode with Zapata. We showed him the photo we had. He said, yes, that could be the man.

"The poor soul couldn't read. The driver personally escorted the man to his destination: *Monasterio Benedicto de Santa Maria Magdelena* outside San Miguel de Allende. So, that was our next stop.

"Only the Prior was permitted to speak to us. He claimed he had never heard of Eduardo Fuentes or Pepe Zapata. He said he didn't recognize the man in the photo and that he was sorry he couldn't be of more help.

"My men thought we had hit a dead end. On the way out of the monastery, though, they noticed a series of pictures on the wall. They were group photos of the monks of the monastery. They were taken annually, going back fifteen years.

"Pepe Zapata appears in one photo taken four years ago. My men are sure of it."

"So, the good Prior was lying?"

"Maybe. I don't know. The old Abbot might have known him, but he passed away two years ago."

"Where is Zapata?"

"I don't know, nor do I know what name he goes by, now. When a monk takes his initial vows, he is given a new name. The Abbot, himself, selects the name.

"But whatever name he goes by, Pepe Zapata was definitely at that monastery four years ago. And wherever he is now, the Prior probably knows, but he's not talking to my people. Maybe your folks will have better luck."

Abrego thanked Campion for his good work. As the two men said their goodbyes, Guillen interrupted, breaking his silence.

"I have just one question, *Señor* Campion. Do you have any concerns about how your information is used?"

"No, I don't. All I do is provide information. Sometimes very expensive information. How it is handled is ultimately up to the client . . . *Adios, señores.*"

Once Humberto Garcia was alone with his lieutenant, he began punching his fist into his palm and walking back and forth. He was more than a little agitated.

"Get me de los Santos," he growled at Cardenas. "I have work for him!"

"*Si, El Jeffe,*" Guillen stood and left the room.

In his own office, Osiel Cardenas Guillen made two phone calls.

The first was to Santiago de los Santos, the head of *Peloton de la Muerte,* the Gulf Cartel's death squad. Humberto Garcia had an assignment.

The second call was very short.

"We need to meet!  Abrego's out of control."

# Chapter Twenty-Five

By 9:00 am Saturday morning Sheriff Cliff Lansing felt the situation was under control. The temporary 9-1-1 Call Center was operating out of the Day Room. The phones were already ringing at a steady pace. The phone company assured him the high school library would be operational by Monday morning.

All available deputies were carrying on their assigned duties. Even Marilyn was giving up her weekend to help squash any more emergencies that might arise.

The loss of the Call Center was bad enough, but they got the report thirty minutes earlier that Judge Mateo had been stung to death by bees in his own yard. Lansing was ambivalent at the news. He didn't care much for the judge and he was sure the feelings were mutual. But the sheriff wanted Gail Mateo to know he was sorry for her loss.

Coffee wasn't helping any more. He said he was going to knock off for a few hours and try to get some sleep. No one should bother him at home unless there was a real emergency. He would check back in after 3:00.

The horses got his attention first. He turned them loose in the corral, so they could get some exercise. He made sure they had oats and water.

His uniform was getting rank. He'd worn it for over 24 hours. Inside the house he hit the shower. Wearing his shorts, he cleaned up his spilt beer and threw away the old sandwich.

When he stretched out on his bed, he fell asleep as soon as he closed his eyes.

"This better be good!" Lansing muttered when his bedside phone rang at noon.

"This is Lansing! What is it?"

"Yeah, Cliff, sorry to bother you . . . but I thought you should know . . ."

"Know? Know what? Who is this?" he snapped.

"It's Richard . . . Enriquez . . . Carol's husband!"

Lansing knew exactly who Richard Enriquez was. He was an ex-boyfriend from Carol's high school. He started sniffing around as soon as Carol and C.J. moved back to Albuquerque. It took him three years to wear her down. They had been married for two years now. Lansing kept his opinion of the man to himself. So did Cliff Junior.

"What's wrong? Why are you calling?"

"There was an incident this morning. . ."

"Incident? What kind of incident?" Lansing was wide awake now.

"Some gang members . . . at least, we think they were gang members . . . Anyway, some teenage thugs. . ."

"Spit it out, Richard!"

"Carol and C.J. were carjacked this morning. . ."

"Carjacked!" the sheriff yelled. "Are they all right?"

"Yes, they're fine . . . They're fine . . ." Enriquez sounded like he was having a hard time holding it together. "It was at a gas station . . . These kids pulled up and blocked them in . . . Carol and the boy managed to jump out and get away . . . They ran inside the station. . .

"Some idiot shot at them, but missed. . ."

"You're sure they're all right? Do I need to come to Albuquerque?"

"No, no. You don't have to come here. They're all right, I'm telling you . . . Carol said you taught her a purse, a wallet, a car isn't worth getting killed over . . . But they called the police from the gas station. They managed to stop the car three blocks from the scene. . ."

"Where are they, now?" the sheriff demanded.

"On their way home . . . Carol said she was too upset to talk any more. She asked me to call you. . ."

"I'm glad you did, Richard," he said, relieved. He thought for a moment. "Tell her and C.J. I'll check on them later."

Lansing lay back on his pillow. He was too tired to think straight. Why did Enriquez call him now? Couldn't Carol have called when she got home? Would he have been pissed off if they called him later instead of immediately? Of course, he would . . . Carol knew that. That's why she had Richard call. Carol still knew Cliff Lansing pretty well.

It was after 4:00 when the phone rang again.

"Lansing," he said, still groggy.

"Sorry to bother you, Sheriff." It was Marilyn. "There's been an accident. Deputy Grant. He's at the clinic!"

# Chapter Twenty-Six

"I can't believe all the equipment you have," Tina Morales said, marveling at the traveling home repair tools Marcus Galban brought. "I'm even more impressed you have a door already."

"When you own ten properties like I do," Tina's landlord observed, "you have to be prepared for almost anything."

Tina had called Mr. Galban the evening before, explaining what happened. First, he wanted to make sure she wasn't hurt. Second, he needed assurance she had a place to stay. Third, he promised she would be back in the house the next night . . . provided she felt safe.

If she had a new front door, Tina was sure she would feel protected.

Morales spent most of Saturday at Halley Basa's house. By mid-afternoon she was getting antsy. She wanted to see how her own place was coming along.

Galban had the driveway blocked with his truck, saw-horses, and various power tools necessary for the job—heavy-duty sander to plane the door for proper fitting, hand-held power saw for cutting the wood for a new door frame and jambs, a drill for installing hardware.

Tina parked on the street. It appeared most of the work was done.

Approaching the doorless entrance, the owner was attaching hinges to the frame.

"Is there anything I can do?" the tenant asked.

Galban sized her up. He guessed she was 5'1" and might weigh 110 pounds. He didn't want to tax her with too much. "I will hold the door in place. I need for you to mark where the hinges go."

"I can do that!" she said confidently.

The landlord/maintenance man retrieved the door from the saw-horses and maneuvered it into the correct position. The Science teacher, using the pencil provided, marked where hinge-holes needed to be drilled.

Even though the door weighed nearly what she did, Tina managed to steady it long enough for Galban to get the screws in place. Once the hinges were secure, the door swung freely. All that remained was installing the doorknob, dead-bolt, and strike plates.

The landlord was going to fit the strike plates with 3-inch screws. That would eliminate almost entirely the chance of the door getting kicked in again.

Tina stood in the front yard watching Galban finish the project. She was unaware of the glaring yellow eyes fixed on her.

From the rooftop across the street, a Great Horned Owl spread her wings. She saw an enemy that needed to be eliminated. She began her dive. At the last moment, as she maneuvered her talons to make a strike, she emitted a blood-curdling screech.

Tina turned just in time to see the claws aimed for her head. Instinctively, she ducked, putting an arm up to defend herself.

Talons, as big as her own hands, dug into her flesh. The bird flew off, emitting another screech, leaving Morales with deep gashes in her arm.

Galban saw everything from the doorway. He ran to his tenant. Tina was bleeding profusely.

"What can I do?" he asked desperately.

"I have some towels in my bathroom," Morales instructed. "I'll wrap this. Can you get me to the clinic?"

"Absolutely," he said, running into the house.

A minute later they were speeding down the street in his truck. Galban would worry about the door and his tools later.

# Chapter Twenty-Seven

*Saint Benedict's Rialto* occupied the southern corner of Santa Fe Village. The shop was spacious and, being on a corner, had large windows on two sides, offering lots of natural light. It sold handcrafted crosses, icons, and other keepsakes created by the monks of *St. Anthony's Monastery in the Canyon.* The store also offered religious themed books, rosaries and music CDs of Gregorian Chants. One of the CDs, a very good seller, was a recording of the *St. Anthony's* monks.

Roger Porter stepped onto the sidewalk outside *Saint Benedict's Rialto* and locked the door behind him. It was Saturday evening. The *Rialto* was closed for the Lord's day. They didn't open again until Monday morning.

Eileen waited for him. Auggie also waited, on his leash, a bit less patiently. There was a tree and a hydrant half a block away. One of the two was going to get his needed attention.

The three strolled down Don Gaspar Avenue, past the parking lot and stopped at the corner. To the left was West Water Street. To the right was East Water Street. Within 4 blocks were 20 places to dine. Over half knew Auggie and welcomed him.

The problem was not deciding where to eat. The problem was finding a place that wasn't packed. It was Memorial Day weekend. The Summer tourist season had started with a vengeance. The shops and cafes were busy, the narrow streets were crowded, and the locals knew better than to hang around.

"What are our plans for tomorrow?" Roger asked, after they crossed Water and headed toward San Francisco Street. "The Cathedral for ten o'clock mass?"

"I was thinking of a drive. Leave early, catch breakfast in Segovia, then attend mass at *Saint Anthony's*."

"It has been a while since we've been to the canyon," Roger admitted. "At least a month."

"I'm sure they'll see a holiday crowd but Auggie told me earlier he needed a break. Maybe a little road trip."

"He did, did he?"

Their Yorkshire Terrier stopped and stuck his nose up in the air. The smell of seasoned, shredded pork and hot sopapillas fresh off the grease had wafted his way.

Eileen bent over, as if listening for something the dog was saying. She stood up.

"He also said he was hungry!"

"That makes two of us. How about *Tia Sophia's*? It's right around the corner."

Eileen held up her hand, as if listening again. "Auggie says that's good, but can we pick up the pace?"

"I'll try to remind him: he has to learn to slow down. He's seventy in 'dog years!'"

# Chapter Twenty-Eight

"So, Art," Lansing said to his deputy, "tell me what happened."

Arthur Grant was sitting up, his legs dangling off the exam table, shirtless. He had scrapes on his back that had been treated. He still wore his uniform pants. They had a small rip. X-rays indicated no broken bones.

"I was patrolling Highway Fifteen, just north of O'Keeffe Ranch. There was an SUV pulled to the side of the road. It was two ladies with five or six kids and they had a flat.

"I forget where they were going . . . that really doesn't matter. They didn't know what they were doing. They had a full-sized spare pulled out and the jack, but they didn't have a clue what to do next.

"We 'Protect and *Serve*', right? So, I offered my services.

"Of course, the flat had to be road-side. Everything was going fine . . . Got the car jacked up, flat off, spare on. I was tightening the lug nuts when some idiot . . . I'm pretty sure he was speeding . . . swerved and hit me. I'm positive it was on purpose!"

"You had hazard lights going on your patrol unit, right?"

"Yes, sir," the rookie said. "I know I've only been around four months, but I know enough to do that. . ."

"Did anyone get a look at the vehicle that hit you?" the sheriff asked.

"No, not really. It was a car . . . a small sedan of some kind . . . white, I think. It just grazed me. But it hit me hard enough that I rolled on the shoulder two or three times. Ripped up my uniform . . ." He showed his now bandaged arm. "Got a few scrapes. According to the doctor I'll probably have a few bruises tomorrow."

Lansing studied his deputy. "How'd you get to the clinic?"

"I drove myself. I called dispatch. Danny Cortez showed up. He followed me into town to make sure I got here okay." The deputy noticed the worried look on his boss' face. "I'm going to be all right, Sheriff. Like I said: a few scrapes and bruises. I'll be at work tomorrow."

"Don't be so sure," Lansing said, shaking his head. "Did you play sports in high school?"

"Sure."

"Did you ever finish a game and think you were fine . . . then realized the next day that you hurt all over?"

"Yeah, once or twice."

"I guarantee, Arthur, that's the way you'll feel in the morning. I'm going to talk to the doctor." The sheriff stopped at the exam room door. "If he gives the okay, fine. But if you need a day or two off to recuperate, take them. San Phillippe can survive a couple of days without you."

"Yes, sir."

At the reception desk, Lansing asked for Dr. Tanner.

Tanner, he was informed, was with a patient. He also learned Poncho Chamorro was being kept a second night. Dr. Tanner would explain.

Lansing stood to one side, keeping clear of foot traffic. For a Saturday on a holiday weekend, there was a lot of traffic. Tanner had two Physician Assistants and three nurses to aid him at the clinic. It appeared all hands were on deck.

Tanner finally emerged from one of the exam rooms. He spotted the sheriff immediately, even though Lansing had opted for civilian clothes.

"Afternoon, Sheriff," John Tanner said when he approached.

"Hi, Doc. You look busy."

"We've been scrambling around here since noon."

"So, what's your opinion on Deputy Grant?"

"He's banged up, but nothing's broken. He can report to work when he feels ready. I'd say, give him a couple of days . . ."

"I told him the same thing . . . Listen," the sheriff said, changing the subject, "what's this about keeping Chamorro in the clinic another night?"

"He was still drunk this morning and pretty combative . . . He didn't like being handcuffed to his bed. The P.A. on duty last night got most of the buckshot out. We sedated him this morning and I finished cleaning out the rest. We pulled out twenty pellets, total.

"I'm keeping him here for observation. I put him on antibiotics, but he can still come down with an infection. If he looks better in the morning, I'll release him to you."

"I'm more worried about him trying to escape than I am about his health," Lansing confessed.

"He's still cuffed to the bed. I don't think he'll get away."

Over Tanner's shoulder, the sheriff noticed Tina Morales emerging from the exam room the doctor had just vacated.

"What's Miss Morales doing here?"

Tanner turned and looked. "Oh, the lady coming down the hall? She got attacked by a bird . . . A really big bird, judging from her injuries."

She approached the two men. Her right forearm was bandaged.

"How are you feeling?" Tanner asked.

"I'll be honest," Tina said. "It hurts."

"Those pills we gave you will get you through the night. Your skin was ripped, and you have puncture wounds. Those are going to hurt for a while."

"What happened, if you don't mind me asking?" Lansing asked.

Morales shot him a look that said, "None of your business!" Her expression changed when she realized who asked the question.

86

"I'm sorry, Sheriff," she apologized. "I didn't recognize you without your uniform."

"I get that a lot," he admitted. "If you don't want to talk about it, I understand. However, as sheriff, I need to know if there's a wild animal out there attacking people."

"Sure . . . but can we go somewhere else to talk?"

"Absolutely. Would you care to meet me at the diner?"

"I got dropped off here. My car's at my house."

"I think I can squeeze you into my Jeep."

# Chapter Twenty-Nine

Sheriff Lansing and Tina Morales found themselves seated across from each other at the Las Palmas Diner. It was after 6:00 pm. She hadn't eaten since breakfast. He couldn't remember the last time he'd had a decent meal.

Lansing was genuinely interested in her bird attack. She told him what happened. The Science teacher was positive it was done by a Great Horned Owl. They were indigenous to the area and were the largest owls around. She didn't think they were that big, though.

Tina couldn't come up with a single reason for the bird to attack. She admitted she was a small person, but that, seriously, couldn't be the bird's excuse.

"Maybe, he didn't like your looks," the sheriff suggested. He didn't think his own encounter with a bird outside *Paco's* was worth mentioning.

"I guess we can go with that," she agreed, taking a sip of iced tea.

"So, what do you teach?"

"General Science to the middle-schoolers. Chemistry to juniors and seniors. I think I'm pretty good at it, too. I, at least, try to make it interesting."

"Why Las Palmas?"

"What do you mean?"

"Why are you teaching here?"

"You met the reason yesterday."

"No," Lansing corrected. "Chamorro was the reason you left Albuquerque. But . . . A science teacher? I'll bet you could have taught anywhere. Why choose Las Palmas?"

She still didn't know the answer to that question. She shrugged. "Why not?" She turned the tables. "Why are you here?"

"Born and raised in San Phillippe. I grew up on a ranch, fifteen miles south of here. Graduated from Las Palmas High. Lived in the big city for a while. Didn't care for it much.

"I moved back here when my dad got sick. That was fourteen years ago. Came back, never left."

Lansing couldn't understand why he found himself talking so readily with this stranger. Margarite had barely been gone two weeks. Was he that desperate for a woman to talk to? Or was Tina Morales the kind of person that just drew you out. Then again, how did he behave around the non-existent Anna Menendez a couple days earlier? He hoped this was a different situation.

"No family?" she asked, noticing the ringless finger.

"I have a son and ex-wife. Country living didn't appeal to her. They live in Albuquerque."

The teacher's cell phone rang. She retrieved it from her purse. "Excuse me," she said. Then, "This is Tina . . . Yes, Mr. Galban. I'm finished with the doctor . . . No, I'm at the Diner, now . . . Yes, I'll be here. You can drop them by . . . Okay. Bye."

She looked at the phone, found the "off" button, then closed the device.

"That was my landlord," she explained. "He hung a new front door. He's dropping off my keys."

The keys were delivered.

They finished their meal, then talked for another hour.

Lansing assured her, Chamorro would not bother her any longer. He was still in the clinic, but would be moved to county lock-up in the morning. They wouldn't use the cells in his office because of the fire.

She'd heard about the blaze. The 9-1-1-Call Center, wasn't it? One of Halley Basa's neighbors was a firefighter. He told the whole story about what happened.

He asked if she could come by Tuesday. His office needed a victim's statement. He could let her have her guns back then.

Yes. She could come in. No problem. Tuesday was Awards Day at school. They didn't need her for that.

The couple was totally unaware of the old, Hispanic woman in the booth behind them. They hadn't noticed her at the clinic. They had no idea she had followed them to the Diner. She quietly sipped her tea and listened to every word they said.

It was 8:00 by the time he dropped her at home. He offered to walk her to the door. She thanked him but pointed out she needed to move her car off the street. They said their "good-nights" and Lansing drove away.

Tina Morales waved at him as he headed down the street. She wondered if he was involved with anyone. She hoped not. Cliff Lansing was the first nice guy she'd met in a very long time. It didn't hurt that he was tall. In her opinion, good looking. And he was a sheriff, which meant he was responsible.

She wondered if Lansing was the reason she had been drawn to Las Palmas. Surely there was another explanation.

She hadn't made the connection yet.

The attack by the Great Horned Owl was not a random act of errant Nature. It was inexorably entwined with her compulsion to be in Las Palmas and her ultimate destiny.

# Chapter Thirty

The only light in the room came from the hallway, leaking through the cracks that outlined the closed door. Chamorro laid in the hospital bed seething. He was ticked at being arrested. He was pissed the hospital didn't give him something stronger for his pain. Mostly, he was consumed with "taking care of" the Tina Morales situation, once and for all.

He treated her like a queen! He treated her like she was the only woman in the world! What did she do to in return?

She called the cops on him just because he got angry . . . one time! She got a restraining order and had him arrested at least three times. Then Morales ran out on him . . . It took him most of one year to track her down. When he finds her, all he wants to do is talk . . . What does she do? She blasts him with a shotgun and puts him in the hospital! (The ex-boyfriend didn't realize Tina's shot was not a direct hit. He was lucky to still have a head.)

Still, he had every reason in the world to hate the woman. He hated her with every aching inch of his being.

He thought about yelling at the nursing staff again, but he was hoarse from previous rants. He wanted more morphine . . . more Demerol . . . more something.

He couldn't sleep. He hurt too much. He was too filled with rage.

Chamorro didn't see when the hallway lights dimmed. He barely noticed the dark figure entering his room. He became very aware of his surroundings when the cuffs came off his left wrist.

"Put these on!" a raspy voice ordered.

A small bundle of clothes and a pair of shoes were shoved into the prisoner's arms.

"Hurry up!"

Chamorro couldn't tell if he was being addressed by a man or a woman. It didn't matter to him as he tore off the hospital gown and began dressing.

The right side of his face, neck and shoulder were bandaged where the buckshot had been removed. Despite his haste, he was careful not to do more damage. The shirt, at least, buttoned down the front. He didn't have to pull it over his head. The pants were snug and too short. The shoes were a half-size too big. The ensemble would have to do for now.

He stood, a little wobbly on his feet.

"Follow me!" the figure ordered.

At the door, Chamorro's rescuer looked both ways, then signaled him to fall in behind them. In less than a minute they were down the short hallway and into the crisp, night air of the high desert.

In the parking lot, the freed prisoner was led to a car. The dark figure signaled for him to drive. Soon, they were heading north, away from Las Palmas.

# Chapter Thirty-One

"He WHAT!" Lansing practically screamed into the phone.

"Chamorro escaped," Deputy Paul de Jesus, weekend dispatcher, repeated. "We just got the call from the clinic."

"When did it happen?"

"They only have one, night nurse . . . She checked the prisoner at three a.m. That's when she found that the bed was empty . . . She called Nine-One-One. They notified me."

Lansing glanced at his bedside clock: 3:15. He'd been asleep since 11:00.

It had been a short night. After leaving Tina Morales, he called Albuquerque to check on Carol and C.J. They were shaken, but all right. No one got hurt and the car was recovered.

Back at the ranch, he had to make sure the horses were bedded down.

For himself, he took a shower to help unwind. It felt good to lie down clean and with a full belly of food.

"I'm coming in, Paul. Dispatch a unit to Four-O-Eight Dollar Street. Have them check that the resident, Tina Morales, is all right. After that, I want them parked in front of her house till I get there."

"Yes, sir, Sheriff."

Lansing threw on his uniform, not sure if he'd be back to the ranch that day. He'd call Juan Vega, one of the neighboring ranchers, later. He used Oscar, one of Vega's sons, as a ranch hand regularly when he was tied up with office duties.

Driving into town, Lansing checked to make sure someone had gotten to the Morales house. Jerry Lopez was stationed outside. Tina Morales was shocked at the news, but seemed to handle it well when Lopez reassured her he would be posted there in his Jeep.

The sheriff's first stop was the clinic. The night nurse was still there, even though her only patient was gone.

"You did your check at Three?" Lansing confirmed as he examined the now empty hospital bed.

Tilly Ortega nodded, holding back the tears.

"Before that, when did you look in on him?"

"It was midnight. He was still awake. He was yelling because he wanted something for the pain. I gave him a shot of Demerol at Eleven. He couldn't get another shot 'til Three. I told him that.

"I dimmed the hall lights for him. I thought that might help him sleep."

"Where were you between midnight and Three?"

"I was sitting at the reception desk up front . . . I had a book to read . . ." She paused, a worried look on her face. "Am I going to be in trouble?"

"Did you turn him loose?"

"Of course not!" she said, indignantly.

"Then, no, you're not in trouble . . ." He looked around the room. Chamorro's hospital gown was tossed on the floor. "Did he have any clothes in the room?"

"I don't think so."

"I can't believe he left here naked . . ." He examined the open cuffs. Someone unlocked them with a key. "You didn't see anyone come in the front door or Chamorro sneak out?"

"I would have noticed . . . The book isn't that good."

Lansing walked into the hall, then proceeded toward the back of the clinic. The nurse followed. The back door opened from the inside with a push bar. Otherwise, it remained closed and locked.

Lansing pushed the door open, then stepped outside. He let the door close, then tried to open it. It remained locked. It was dark outside, but light enough he could tell there were no tool-marks on the door. He knocked on the door and Ortega let him in.

"Someone must have had a key," the sheriff guessed, walking back down the hallway. Again, the nurse followed. "Today's Sunday. The clinic's not open, is it?"

"No . . . But it will be open Monday, even though it's Memorial Day."

"I'll send forensics over later to see if they can get any fingerprints."

"If you don't need me here, I'd like to go home. I'll lock things up, but there's custodial number on the front window. They can let your people in later."

"That's fine. Thank you for the help. I'll get in touch if I need any-thing else."

*** 

The sheriff's next stop was his offices. He checked with Deputy de Jesus on the calls that came in during the night. For a Saturday night it was normal, even for the holiday weekend. The only hiccup was Chamorro's escape.

He then headed for the Evidence Locker. Signing the property log, he removed the shotgun, and the Smith and Wesson .38 Cal and the Beretta .25 Cal pistols belonging to Tina Morales. They were doing her no good being locked up.

The lights in the little house were on when Lansing parked behind Jerry Lopez's Jeep.

"It's been quiet," the deputy reported. "Do you want me to stay here?"

"I'll let you know."

Lansing knocked on the front door.

"Who is it?" Morales demanded.

"It's Sheriff Lansing."

"What do you want?" She sounded tired and angry.

"I brought your guns back. . . I thought you might need them!"

She unlocked the door and swung it open, none too gently. "You think, so? Really?" the teacher snarked. She gestured to the desk. "You can put them over there."

Lansing did as he was ordered. "Miss Morales, I'm really sorry about Chamorro," he said, turning back to her.

"I am, too," she snapped, still holding onto the door. "I thought you told me I didn't have to worry about him anymore?"

"I know I did."

"How'd he get away?"

"I don't know, but he didn't do it on his own," he said, trying to calm her.

"You mean, he had help?"

"It looks that way . . . Does he know anyone around here?"

"I don't think so . . . Just me," she said softening her tone. "Why would anyone help him?"

"I thought you might know."

All the Science teacher could do was shake her head.

"If I had the manpower, I would have posted someone at the clinic. But I don't. Besides, I thought he would be in county lock-up by now."

"What's going to happen?"

"We'll put out a BOLO for him: a 'be on the look-out' notice," he explained. "I'll get a bench warrant. So far, he'll be wanted for DUI and reckless driving, breaking and entering, plus destruction of property."

He paused. "Do you feel safe staying here, alone?" He walked over and closed the door she was holding.

"Yes . . . No . . ." She shook her head. "I don't know." She sat on the loveseat she jokingly called her sofa. "I thought I was safe because Poncho didn't know where I was. But he knows now . . . and he can't be too happy that I shot him."

"I wouldn't think so," Lansing admitted. "Is there someplace you can go? Someone you can stay with?"

"I suppose I could go back to Halley's, but that's not a long-term solution."

"What would be a long-term solution?"

"Leave Las Palmas. Move . . . again."

"When are you going to quit running?"

Tina Morales made the sign of the cross. "Forgive me, Lord . . . I'll quit running when Poncho Chamorro is dead!"

# Chapter Thirty-Two

Rivera closed the bedroom door as quietly as possible. Sue was still asleep.

Jack, Sue and DeeDee got home late the previous afternoon. Both parents had been up for nearly 36 hours by the time they reached the house. DeeDee had encountered a 24-hour bug of some type. She recovered in the car on the drive back to Las Palmas.

They snacked during the trip. By the time they pulled into the driveway, all three were ready to crash.

The deputy slept for twelve hours straight. When he woke, he tried not to disturb his wife. He showered, then dressed in the bathroom. He would grab a bite to eat after he started patrol.

He opened his daughter's bedroom door a sliver. Peeking at her tiny body, it took all his strength not to scoop her up and hug her within an inch of her life.

Jack Rivera was 34 years old when he got married. Sue was ten years his junior. He couldn't help but wonder if she wanted one last fling before she turned 30. They hadn't talked it out yet. They would, soon.

The one thing he knew for sure was the day DeeDee was born was the happiest day of his life. The past four years were filled with nothing but joy. He didn't know he could love another human being as much as he loved his daughter.

He eased the door shut, then proceeded to the living room to put on his boots. He wished he could take a day . . . a week . . . a month off . . . just so he could spend time with his family. He suspected every husband and father felt that way. He would call and check on them later.

\*\*\*

Weekends were special for the Cortez family. Everybody got up early to have breakfast together, especially if Danny had weekend patrol. Evelyn (she went by Ebbie) cooked. James, their nine-year-old son, as usual, got up complaining he needed more sleep. He changed his tune when he smelled the bacon cooking.

"Isn't it great!" Deputy Cortez observed. "Summer vacation starts next week. We can have breakfast like this every day."

James groaned. "Do we have to?"

During the school year, James was down the street, waiting for the school bus by 7:00. So, he usually had breakfast before his dad. For the youngster, eating breakfast after 7:00 should have been a treat.

"If Daddy says we eat together," Ebbie reported, "then we eat together." She started filling the table with hash-browned potatoes, bacon, refried beans, eggs and tortillas. Included was a jar of salsa for extra kick.

The deputy started digging in. Despite the complaining, so did his son.

Ebbie filled two coffee cups before sitting to join her men.

"What are your plans today?" Danny asked, sipping on his coffee.

"We're going to ten o'clock mass. I'm packing a lunch and a group of us are taking the kids to Wild Duck Reservoir for a picnic."

"You think that's a good idea?" the husband observed. "It's a holiday weekend. The place is going to be packed."

"We'll be fine. A couple of the girls are going down early to grab some tables. Besides, James and I needed to do something while you're working.

The deputy turned to his son. "Are you going swimming?"

"Yes," James replied, with a mouth full of food.

"Well, please, be careful."

"He's a good swimmer," Ebbie said, reassuringly. "Aren't you?"

James nodded, spooning salsa onto his beans.

Conversation faded as all three concentrated on their food.

"Well, I'm off," Deputy Cortez announced, finishing his coffee and wiping his mouth.

He stood and kissed his wife. "Thank you for another wonderful meal!"

"You're welcome," she said. "Don't forget your lunch. It's in the fridge."

"Got it!" he said, grabbing his lunch box. "I'll see you two tonight."

A minute later he was in his patrol unit, checking in with dispatch. He was on patrol.

# Chapter Thirty-Three

"Tomorrow is an American holiday," Santiago de los Santos observed. "*Señor* Diaz and his family may be out for the long weekend. I have a team driving up from Houston today. They'll watch the house beginning in the morning. When the family is home . . ." the henchman shrugged. "No more problem."

"They are not a problem," Humberto Garcia snarled. "They are an annoyance."

He finished his tequila. He picked up the bottle and poured himself another round. He offered a refill to de los Santos. The "problem solver" held out his glass.

Osiel Cardenas Guillen sat in his usual seat, off to one side, not partaking of any beverage. And, as usual, simply observing.

"And what about the monastery?"

"Campion's documents were very thorough. He outlined where the monks would be at any given hour of the day. They are in the church in the morning at Four for Vigils. Again, around Six for Lauds and Mass. They have their meals and work duties throughout the day. They gather back in the church at Three-thirty for what they call 'None' then again around Six for Vespers."

"We will make our visit when they're gathered for Lauds."

"How far away is San Miguel de Allende?"

"Four hundred miles . . ."

"When will you visit?"

"Tomorrow." He noticed his boss' questioning expression. "We're flying into Guanajuato Airport this afternoon. That's thirty minutes from the monastery."

"How many men?" Guillen asked.

De los Santos turned to the senior lieutenant. "There will be five of us."

"Why so many?" the lieutenant pressed.

"If Zapata is there, extracting him will be simple." De los Santos swirled the tequila in his glass to melt what little ice he had left. "If he is not, and the good monks choose not to discuss his location, we may have some lengthy conversations.

"Three men will be posted to ensure the congregation does not leave the church. I will do the questioning. If necessary, Flores will do the persuading."

Osiel Cardenas looked concerned. "How much persuading?"

"As much as necessary!" Abrego stormed. "This is the murderer of my son we're talking about!" He downed his drink.

"I have had to wait too long . . . Zapata has been a free man for too long . . ." He stabbed the air with his index finger, emphasizing every sentence. "It is time he paid for his sins!

"You don't have a son, Osiel. You don't know what it's like to lose one!

"It nearly killed his mother . . . To me, it was like losing a hand or an entire arm. And you can't imagine the pain . . . Don't you dare sit there and ask stupid questions about 'how much persuasion.' Don't you dare presume you can pass judgement on me!

"Santiago will do what's necessary. He was given an assignment. He will complete it!"

Both Guillen and de los Santos nodded grimly.

The henchman nodded because he had a job to do.

Guillen did so because he knew Humberto Garcia Abrego's days as head of the Gulf Cartel were numbered.

The Gulf Cartel's top lieutenant had thrown his support to Humberto out of loyalty to Juan Garcia. But Juan Garcia was no longer in the picture. As the younger brother's control grew more secure, the more erratic he became.

The Cartel was not operating as a business, now. It had become Abrego's piggy-bank to finance his vendettas against enemies, real and imagined.

To usurp Abrego, Guillen needed firepower and foot soldiers not loyal to the current *Jeffe*. He couldn't turn to the Sinaloa, the Juarez, or any other cartel. That would be a bloodbath. However, he found a ready supply of men already trained to fight, who's loyalty could be bought: the Mexican army.

Abrego would be gone in two weeks . . . maybe sooner.

# Chapter Thirty-Four

*Saint Anthony's Monastery in the Canyon* was nestled on the broad banks of the Rio Cohino. In 35 years it had grown from a single building and a half-dozen monks to a dozen buildings and nearly forty monks, including the novitiates.

Surrounded by high, sand-stone cliffs, the entire complex was built in the familiar pueblo/adobe style, with edifices stained to match the canyon walls. The cloisters, refectory and church had all been rebuilt in the early Nineties. Ready to embrace the 21st Century, the monks were connected with the outside world through a satellite dish that provided access to the new internet plus telephone communications. As funding became available, the tiny settlement was transitioning from generator-supplied electricity to solar-panels.

The monastery was self-supporting, with vegetable gardens and chicken coups. All water came from the river. They received no aid from the Vatican. Financial support came primarily from donations and the sale of religious items from the Abbey store and *St. Benedicts Rialto* in Santa Fe.

Saint Anthony's Church dominated the surrounding buildings. A 60-foot tall bell tower with a cross on top greeted visitors. The bell rang seven times daily, to prompt the monks' activities from Vigils in the morning to Vespers at night.

Entering the church through double-wooden doors, one is greeted by a stone altar on a slightly raised platform. The building is comprised of eight "walls." Four of the walls are really alcoves. The entry is the first alcove, with seating for 24 visitors. The alcoves to either side of the altar provided seating for four dozen brethren. The final alcove, behind the altar, contained the Tabernacle and entry point for the monks.

The other walls were 40 feet high. They extended over the alcoves as 20-foot high windows, which gave the illusion the church was much larger than it actually was. The entire structure was a celebration of light.

Through the windows behind the altar, overlooking the church, were three crosses mounted atop the canyon rim. Illuminated, it was the only light visible in the entire canyon at night.

The only access to the monastery grounds was by National Forest Road 262. The road started at Highway 15, near Artiga, and stopped at the monastery. For most of the way, the 15-mile, dirt and gravel, one-lane track paralleled the Rio Cohino. On a good day, it took thirty minutes to cover the distance.

Roger and Eileen Porter turned off the main highway at 8:15. They reached the parking area by 10 'til 9:00. It was still another 200 yards to the church. The Sunday Mass would begin at ten after, so there was plenty of time.

As they suspected, the holiday weekend attracted a larger crowd than usual. Eight other cars were already parked in the small, gravel parking zone.

Auggie jumped down from the car, ready to stretch his legs.

He looked around, seeming to recognize the surroundings. He remembered there would be a short walk, then he would have to wait outside, his leash tied to something. His folks would go inside the place. That gave him a chance for a nap. Maybe a quick visit with the three resident monastery dogs. Then his parents would come out, they would get back in the car, and go for another ride. Life was good!

The Porters found only two seats left when they entered the visitors alcove. A couple of people were asked to move so they could sit together. They were readily accommodated.

Brother John Mkubu, a monk originally from Kenya, was the Guestmaster. He greeted each visitor with a broad smile and a warm welcome.

Perhaps it was the smiles, as much as anything, that attracted the Porters to the monastery. In their solitude, the brethren exuded a joy for life and for the love of God, greater than any other place the Porters had ever seen.

Despite the smile, Roger and Eileen noticed a worry in Brother John's eyes. Their questions would have to wait.

The mass, as always was beautiful. The Gregorian Chants delivered by the monks were as haunting and enthralling as ever. Each visitor took communion.

Again, Brother John engaged the visitors as they departed.

The Porters lingered behind, hoping to find out what was bothering their friend.

"It is so good that you drove up from Santa Fe," Brother John said in his thick, Kenyan accent. "I trust the bazar is doing well."

The Porters had to smile at Mkubu's colloquialism. In Kenya, people shopped at bazars. They sold items for the monastery so, obviously, they operated a bazar.

"The bazar is doing very well," Eileen said, returning the smile. "Is anything wrong today?"

"What do you mean?" The worry seemed to flicker in the monk's eyes.

"I don't know," she admitted. "The service seemed more . . ." She looked at her husband in search of the right word.

"Subdued?" Roger offered.

"Yes," Eileen agreed. "Subdued."

"Oh, no," the Kenyan said, shaking his head. "Nothing is wrong. I assure you."

They shook hands, said their goodbyes, and the Porters retrieved Auggie, unconvinced something wasn't bothering the monk.

Brother John Mkubu retreated to the cloister. He was concerned, as was the rest of the community. Brother Esteban Fuentes had attended Vigils at 4:00, then disappeared. No one could find him anywhere. He hadn't attended Lauds. He missed breakfast, then Mass.

A cassock was found draped on the cloister wall. If it was Esteban's he must have left.

Things like this simply didn't happen . . . and Brother John was not the only one concerned.

# Chapter Thirty-Five

Typically, Sunday morning at the San Phillipe Sheriff's Office was quiet. Not this holiday weekend. The 9-1-1 Call Center was temporarily parked in the Day Room. That would be its home for another 24 hours. People were constantly in and out of the offices delivering food, coffee, soft drinks, whatever was needed to keep the operators placated.

The 9-1-1 operators were busy. That meant Lansing's deputies were busy.

Ray Blanco called in. He was hurting too badly to handle his duties. The sheriff understood, but that put them a man down. Traffic monitoring, speeding tickets and regular patrols were handed over to the Highway Patrol.

Again, Marilyn came in to handle dispatcher duties. Leroy Ramirez was pulled from his normal rotation as weekend dispatcher and placed on patrol.

Even Lansing found himself answering calls when all his deputies were busy. A minor traffic accident sent him north to Cohino.

Driving back to Las Palmas, he realized he hadn't heard anything from Berta Chavez, yet. He had left his card on Thursday. Surely, she had seen it by now. Route 182 was not that far out of his way. He decided it wouldn't hurt to swing by Berta's place to see if she got his note.

Ten minutes later he came to a stop in front of the Chavez house. His business card was still wedged into the door frame. The old woman was either gone or she was in the house and, for whatever reason, couldn't open the door.

The sheriff debated over what he should do. He could go about his day and assume Chavez had gone somewhere. Or he could do a wellness check—she could be hurt, even dead.

He decided it was his duty to check on the old woman.

Getting out of his Jeep, the first thing he noticed was there were no chickens scratching out a subsistence in the front yard. He peered around the back. No more goat.

At the front door, he pounded and yelled, "Mrs. Chavez. This is Sheriff Cliff Lansing. I came by to see if you're all right!"

He listened for a moment. No response from inside.

Pounding on the door again: "Mrs. Chavez!"

With his ear against the door, there was still no response.

He tried the door knob. The door was unlocked.

Pushing the door open, he said, "Mrs. Chavez?" This time he didn't shout. "Are you in here?"

When no one answered, he stepped inside. It was dark, even with the bright sunlight seeping through the dirty window and the open front door. It smelled musty. He was grateful he wasn't assaulted by stench of decaying flesh.

The house was tiny, not more than 400 square feet. It had a front room, bedroom with small bath, and a kitchen nook. No phone.

Lansing tried the light switch. No electricity.

He inspected the residence. It had been abandoned, but he couldn't tell for how long. There had been animals outside four days earlier. Chavez disappeared with all her possessions, including the goat and chickens, after his first visit. Why didn't she contact him? She must have seen his note.

Closing the door, he decided Berta Chavez was no longer his concern.

Behind the camouflage of a nearby pine, the Great Horned Owl watched as Lansing drove away. A moment later she took to wing.

Barely two miles away was her new roost, an old abandoned barn. Nestled in a knot of pines and junipers, the forgotten structure was perfect for her needs. There was so much more to do.

# Chapter Thirty-Six

"Hi, Sheriff," Ebbie Cortez said, approaching the church parking lot. Lansing had just emerged from his Jeep. "You're late for Mass."

"Won't be the first time, Ebbie," he confessed. "You two doing anything special today?"

"We're going swimming down at Wild Duck Lake!" James said, excitedly.

"Isn't the water still cold?"

"The water's always cold," Ebbie observed. "But it's supposed to get over eighty, today, so, we should be all right."

"Watch out for the crowds. They can trample you, even if you're in the water . . . And be careful. There's no lifeguard."

"Oh, we know," Ebbie nodded. "The kids use a buddy system . . . That way they can watch each other."

"That's good. You two have fun."

Lansing turned and headed toward the church. As he approached, Tina Morales emerged through the open doors.

"Sheriff Lansing," Morales asked, "what are you doing here?"

"I needed to take care of some business," he said, tipping his hat to her. "Have you decided? Are you going to stay at your house?"

"No. I'll be at Halley and Joe Basa's until school's out. That's Wednesday. If Poncho is still on the loose, I'm leaving town—at least, for a while."

"If there's anything my office can do, let me know."

"Thanks. I will."

She watched as Lansing continued into St. James Church. It was absolutely none of her business, but she was curious about the real purpose of the sheriff's visit. Acting as if she forgot something, she went back into the building.

To the left of the entrance was the devotional area. A statue of the Virgin overlooked the votive candles. Standing near the entrance, Morales watched as Lansing stood with his head bowed. A moment later, he lit a candle, did the sign of the cross, then turned to leave.

Tina ducked out the entrance before he saw her. She waited for the sheriff outside.

When he emerged, he was surprised to see the teacher still standing there.

"I didn't know you were Catholic," Morales said.

"Not a very faithful one, I guess," Lansing shrugged.

The two fell in step and proceeded to the parking lot. "I've never seen you at Mass."

"I've been remiss," he confessed. "What can I say?"

"I noticed you lit a candle."

They continued walking, but Lansing gave the woman a sidelong glance that told her to back off.

"I'm sorry," she said. "It's none of my business."

He was satisfied with the apology and let the subject drop. They reached her car first.

"I guess I'll see you Tuesday," Tina said.

"Tuesday?"

"The victim's statement?"

"Oh, yes. Guess I forgot." He tipped his hat, again. "See you then."

Morales got in her car and started the engine. As she drove off, Lansing got into his own vehicle.

"Dispatch, Patrol One," he said into the radio mic. "I'm back up."

"Sheriff! Thank, God . . . There's a disturbance at Jack Rivera's place . . ." Marilyn reported. "Can you get over there?"

"I'm on my way!" The sheriff flipped on his siren and emergency lights, and practically peeled out of the parking lot.

Rivera's driveway was empty when Lansing arrived. He parked on the street, drew his weapon, and approached the house cautiously.

The front door was kicked in. It reminded him too much of what happened two nights earlier.

He carefully stepped through the door.

"Sue? Are you in here?" He listened for a response. In the back of the house he could hear sobbing. Hurrying toward the sound, he discovered Sue in the master bedroom, on the far side of the bed. She was on the floor, clutching her daughter. Both were crying.

The sheriff holstered his pistol.

"Are you all right?" he asked, kneeling next to the two.

Sue Rivera nodded her head, trembling.

"Did anyone hurt you?"

This time she shook her head, no.

"Tell me what happened."

"I heard this man knocking . . . He said he needed to come in . . ." She talked in gasps and gulps. "I looked out the window . . . It was some guy I'd never seen before. He was wrapped in bandages. You could see the blood . . ."

She had to catch her breath. DeeDee's face was buried in her mother's chest.

"I told him to go away, or else I'd call the sheriff's office. That's when he kicked in the front door . . . He had a knife . . . He wanted my purse and my car keys . . . He chased us back here!"

She started sobbing even more.

Lansing heard a noise coming from the front of the house. He pulled his gun again. At the front door he found a knot of three people huddled together.

"Is she all right?" a man asked.

"Who are you?" the sheriff demanded.

"We live next door . . . We're the one who called Nine-One-One."

Lansing untensed. He signaled to the only woman in the group. "Can you help me with her?"

"Absolutely." The woman pushed past her husband and followed the sheriff to the back of the house. A few minutes later the victims were sitting on the living room sofa. Mother and daughter would not let each other go.

Neither Sue nor DeeDee had been hurt. Just scared. Sue's purse was gone. The family car was gone. Some clothes had been snatched from Jack's closet.

Lansing had a very good idea who the perpetrator was. He got a corroborating description from the man reporting the break-in. Of all the places Chamorro could have picked, though, why a deputy's home?

Once Sue and DeeDee Rivera were safely placed in the neighbor's house, Lansing contacted dispatch. They needed to pull Jack Rivera off patrol. He had to take care of more important things.

It was 1:00 pm by the time the sheriff got back to his office. He'd been up for 10 hours and the short night was catching up.

The building seemed a bit less chaotic. The operators and the dispatchers were clicking along fairly smoothly.

It wouldn't last.

# Chapter Thirty-Seven

As had been predicted, the parking lot, picnic tables and swimming beach at Wild Duck Reservoir were packed. Families who couldn't afford a trip over the three-day holiday opted for local venues. Since school was still in session Tuesday, most children had to stay close to home, anyway.

Wild Duck Park was 6 miles from Highway 15. It had paved parking for 60 vehicles and boat trailers. The 30 overflow cars and trucks squeezed onto either side of the access road. The narrow entry way now was barely wide enough for a single car to get through.

Pine and juniper trees were scattered around the three dozen picnic tables, giving some shade. Opting for shade, though, meant a blocked view of the beach and swimming area.

"Helen, have you seen the boys?" Ebbie Cortez asked, a worried look on her face.

Helen, sitting in a folding lawn chair and deeply engrossed in a romance novel, looked up. "What?"

"The boys . . . James and Pedro . . . Where are they?"

Helen stood, lifted her sunglasses, and looked around. She pointed at a table not far away. "There's Pedro. I think he's getting a cupcake."

Ebbie hurried over. "Pedro, where's James?"

With a mouthful of food, all the boy could do was mumble. However, he was able to point toward the lake.

"You two were supposed to be watching each other," the worried mother scolded.

The picnic area sat on a rise, above the beach. Depending on the time of year, the reservoir could rise or fall. The beach expanded or shrank, based on the level of the lake. In mid-Spring, the reservoir was still waiting for the snow melt, so the beach was still broad.

It was also crowded with sunbathers, Frisbee throwers and sand-castle builders. Despite the chilly water, an unseasonably high temperature of 81° tempted the adventurous into the lake.

Ebbie surveyed the scene, still perched on the rise. In a swarm of adults and kids, all dressed in swimsuits and shorts, it was almost impossible to pick out a nine-year-old boy wearing dark blue swim trunks.

James' mother scanned from right to left, checking the crowd closest to her, then looking a little further out. Her search reached the water. Children paddle blow-up rafts and splashed each other. Adults stood waste deep trying to keep track of their kids.

Some distance from the shore was a pole with depth markers in feet. When the reservoir was full, that location could be as much as 12 feet deep. The current depth was five and a half feet, hardly enough to worry an adult. For a child of nine, that was another matter.

Near the marker, Ebbie saw the small body, face down, bobbing with the waves.

"JAMES!" she screamed, running to the lake. "JAMES! SOMEBODY HELP HIM!

People on the beach looked toward the commotion. Parents in the water saw the frantic woman yelling and running toward them. They looked around—trying to locate the object of her concern.

As the desperate mother splashed into the lake, a man spotted the boy. He tried to run in the water. He found it easier to swim. A dozen strokes got him to the boy.

The would-be hero grabbed James and turned him over. The boy was blue.

He half-dragged, half-carried the lifeless body to shallow water. As soon as he could, he picked the boy up with both arms.

The anxious mother caught up to him. She brushed the hair from her son's face. "James! James! My baby! *Mijo*, can you hear me!"

The two adults waded/floundered their way to shore.

Someone in the crowd yelled: "Somebody. Call Nine-One-One!"

People cleared a space for them when they reached the beach. James was placed on the ground.

"Does anyone know C-P-R?" the impromptu lifeguard asked.

Another man nearby yelled, "I do!"

The crowd parted to allow the man through. He got on his knees and began working on the boy, alternating mouth-to-mouth resuscitation with chest compressions.

All Ebbie Cortez could do was kneel next to her son and pray.

\*\*\*

Lansing sat in his office, his head leaned back with his eyes closed. He thought he was dozing, but wasn't completely sure. He jerked awake when his phone rang.

"Lansing." He hoped he sounded alert when he answered.

"I thought you should know, Sheriff," Marilyn reported. "I got a call from the Highway Patrol. There's been a six-car pile-up outside O'Keeffe Ranch. One of our units was involved."

"Who?" Lansing demanded.

"Leroy Ramirez."

"Damn," the sheriff swore. "Anyone hurt?"

"I don't know. They're trying to sort things out."

The lawman stood, phone in hand. "If anyone calls, tell them I'm headed that way."

"One more thing, Sheriff. A boy nearly drowned at Wild Duck Reservoir. EMS was dispatched. Danny Cortez is on his way, as well . . . In case they need help."

# Chapter Thirty-Eight

Pepe Zapata had grown up on the hot, humid streets of Matamoros. As a child he assumed the entire world was like his home town. He hadn't realized how miserable the heat was because he didn't know any better.

When he stepped off the bus in San Miguel de Allende he was bathed in dry, cool air. He assumed that was an aberration. Even the Brownsville area had cold snaps, but the hot always came back. At 6000 feet, the monastery and the surrounding hills seldom saw temperatures above 90°. Most of the year, daytime temperatures ranged from 70° to 85°, even in winter. At night, it fell below freezing twice a year at most.

The newly christened Esteban Fuentes spent four years at the *Monasterio Benedicto*. He couldn't imagine wanting to live anywhere else. A year at *St. Anthony's Monastery in the Canyon* changed his mind. The summers were just as mild. The winters were colder, but they had SNOW! He had never seen snow before. He was as excited as a little kid when he first saw it. After four years in the canyon, next to the Rio Cohino, he, once again, couldn't imagine wanting to live anywhere else.

But things had changed.

In his prayers, in his dreams, he had seen the Evil. It was coming there—and he was sure it was his fault. He reasoned, if he left the monastery, the Evil would spare his brothers.

It was spur of the moment. He hadn't thought through his actions—where he was going, what he would do, how he could ever support himself.

After Vigils, he waited for the other monks to go to their cells. Once he was sure the cloister was empty, he made his way to the wardrobe. He found a T-shirt and a pair of jeans that fit. He wore the "borrowed" clothes beneath his robes. The sandals he wore were sturdy. He was positive they would hold up during his trip.

It was still dark. He hoped no one would notice him taking the path, away from the cloister. Eventually the path reached Forest Road 262. He left his monk's robes draped on the cloister wall.

The road paralleled the river for ten miles, then made a sharp turn to the left. It would be 5 more miles before it reached the main highway.

Brother Esteban wanted to make sure he wasn't seen. He knew Sunday worshipers would be arriving not long after daybreak. Once it turned light, he would find a path that followed the road. Keeping out of sight was not a problem. The road varied from 50 to 100 feet above the canyon floor. He would stay close to the river as long as possible— sometimes having to wade and swim when the canyon walls plunged into the water.

Being outside the cloister was a new experience. Of course, he had traveled a few times before. He had traveled to the canyon from Mexico. He had left *St. Anthony's* with a group to visit the *Rialto* in Santa Fe. But those times he had a purpose and a destination.

Today—here and now—he was feeling something new. It was a topic often discussed in his philosophy classes. It was a subject almost foreign to him: Free will.

As a child, free will didn't exist. Eat someone else's garbage or starve.

When he was recruited by drug dealers, his options were to help them and earn a few pesos or go back to eating garbage.

As a cartel foot soldier, the only thing he understood was either follow orders or be another corpse in an alley.

To him, free will was never an option.

As he walked along, he supposed he had made a couple of choices of his own free will. It was his own decision to kill Rodrigo Abrego. No one forced him to assume Eduardo Fuentes' identity. No one made him become a monk.

These had been his choices.

But once he had taken his vows, both as a novitiate and a professed monk, had he surrendered his free will? Saint Benedict had laid out specific rules for his monastic order. To belong, there was no free will regarding the contemplative life. Vigils, Lauds, Terce and any of the other calls to prayer were not options. To be late, or worse, miss a required function meant punishment by the Abbot. To shirk one's work assignment meant punishment by the Abbot. To have a close friendship with another monk, greater than with the others, meant punishment by the Abbot.

To physically leave the cloister, the offender could face excommunication. To rejoin the cloister, the wayward monk would be ostracized. He would eat alone. He would work alone. He would pray alone. During the term of punishment, the offending monk would be shunned by his brothers. The length and severity of the punishment depended on the benevolence of the Abbot. But there would be consequences.

How was any of this free will?

Brother Esteban realized he was thirsty. He hadn't planned his departure. He simply left the compound. He had no water. No food. It took him a moment to realized there was an entire river, 30 yards away.

He knelt on the bank and plunged his hands into the ice-cold water. Using his cupped fingers and palms as a ladle, he drank one mouthful. Then another—and another. He had forgotten how parched a person got in the high desert, even in moderate temperatures.

He sat back and absorbed the beauty around him. It felt good to rest for a moment. In the distance he could hear the Abbey bell calling the faithful to worship. It was time for mass. He wondered how far he had traveled.

Out of habit, he bent his head and gave thanks for the moment.

A red-faced warbler sang to him from a nearby branch. The rising sun warmed the back of his neck. The last, cool breeze of the morning brushed against his cheeks.

In his solitude, away from the demands of the daily monastic routine and alone with nature, Pepe/Esteban felt himself washed in a new revelation. He did have free will.

Since the moment he was baptized eight years earlier, God had given him free will.

He could have walked away any time he wanted. Unlike the cartel, no one held a gun to his head. And not many men had been granted a pardon from the sins of an earlier life. As Abbot Pedro said so many years ago: Through God's grace we are born anew.

Esteban stood, refreshed. He also found his resolve wavering.

Leaving the cloister wasn't an easy decision.

Was it God's will that he should leave monastery? Or was he exercising his own free will? Was he wise enough to make such a decision on his own? Shouldn't he, at least, have sought council with Abbot Christian?

He prayed that God would give him a sign.

National Forest Road 262 finally made it's turn away from Rio Cohino. Esteban still followed a path of his own making, paralleling the gravel track. The small, steep hills he encountered became more difficult. Now, much too late, he realized, his sturdy sandals were not designed for long-haul treks. He kept stopping to remove pebbles and sand.

Two miles from Highway 15, he sat to rest and to clean his footwear. He was tired, thirsty and hungry. He looked at the tiny cuts on his feet. His suffering was nothing. He knew that. Others had sacrificed so much more than him—for him.

As he stood, there came a low, gurgling croak from the branch of a juniper tree ten feet ahead. A raven, the size of a red-tailed hawk, stared at him. Esteban stared back.

Was this God's sign? Was he being told to keep going?

A second raven joined the first in the tree. They began making harsh grating sounds, as if talking to each other. A flutter of wings announced the arrival of four more birds. Two perched in the juniper. Two came to rest in a leafless, scrub, to the left of the monk.

The chattering from the birds became louder and shriller. As the volume increased, so did the number of ravens. A dozen joined the original six. Soon, six more were added.

Their cacophony was overwhelming, and it was directed at the monk.

Esteban realized the flock had not surrounded him. They had positioned themselves in the juniper, in bushes, on the ground, between where he stood and the highway beyond.

He was to go no further.

The sign was clear. He was to return to the cloister. He was to accept whatever punishment he was given—and he was to make his stand, at the monastery, along with his brothers, against the approaching Evil!

# Chapter Thirty-Nine

Any day of the week, a six-car pile-up on Highway 15 would be an issue. But on a holiday Sunday, with ten times the traffic, the ensuing traffic jam was ten times the problem. EMS units from Segovia and Las Palmas parked on the shoulders, behind tow trucks.

Highway Patrol Officer Marty Hernandez directed traffic around the wreckage.

Other than the disabled unit driven by Leroy Ramirez, Lansing's Jeep was the only Sheriff's vehicle on the scene. With Hernandez occupied, the sheriff had to corner one of the EMS technicians to get a sense of what happened.

An over-eager pick-up truck driver tried to pull out from O'Keeffe Ranch. He was watching traffic from his left, attempting to make a left-hand turn. Seeing an opening, he gunned it . . . T-boning the car coming from the right. Unfortunately, that was Ramirez's patrol unit.

Two cars going north, two cars heading south couldn't avoid the collision. The only serious injury was sustained by Ramirez when he was hit broadside. His left leg was crushed. He was already en route to Santa Fe via ambulance.

Lansing helped direct the tow trucks as they maneuvered to remove the wrecked cars. Two vehicles were from Albuquerque. The owners pestered the sheriff over what were they supposed to do without their cars. The best he could offer was his cell phone, so they could contact their insurance companies.

It was after 5:00 before the wrecks were cleared and the highway was completely open. Lansing and Officer Hernandez compared notes. Only one ticket was issued. It went to the driver who caused the accident.

"Dispatch," Lansing finally reported, checking in with his office. "Patrol one. Just letting you know, I'm rolling."

"Roger, Sheriff." Marilyn sounded tired. This was her seventh day in a row manning her desk.

"Who's still out on patrol?" he asked, as he drove toward Las Palmas.

"Just you and Willie Estrada. . ."

Willie Estrada was one of the department's new-hires. Willie was also the only female deputy. She went by "Willie" because she couldn't stand her given name, "Wilma." The deputy served double-duty—regular patrol plus forensics. She replaced Rubin Menendez when he retired.

"Where's Cortez? I thought he was still on duty?"

"He's at the clinic . . . with his son."

"What's wrong with his son?" Lansing was becoming irritated.

"The boy that nearly drowned at Wild Duck . . . That was Danny's son, James."

"Oh," the sheriff said, disappointed in himself over getting angry. "Is he all right?"

"I haven't heard," Marilyn confessed. "Let's hope so . . . Jerry Lopez said he would report in early to take up the slack."

"Good."

Sheriff Cliff Lansing made a quick assessment of his resources. He was down one patrol car. Leroy Ramirez would be gone for God knew how long. Rivera and Cortez were sidelined with family matters. Hopefully, they would be back up in the morning. Deputy Arthur Grant should be healed up by Tuesday. Four deputies were assigned to night patrol.

Lansing couldn't believe the bad luck his office had encountered in the past few days. Two deputies were involved in vehicular accidents in as many days. Jack River's home was invaded . . . apparently by an escaped prisoner. This after the deputy thought his wife and child were killed in a bus accident. Danny Cortez's son nearly drowns.

He had forgotten to include the 9-1-1 Call Center fire, Judge Mateo's death and the attack on his own family.

# Chapter Forty

"What the Hell is that dog barking at?" Joe Basa griped. "He's been going at it for thirty minutes!"

"Not true, Hon," Halley observed from the kitchen. "I only let him out ten minutes ago!"

Mrs. Basa and Miss Morales were almost finished cleaning the kitchen after Sunday supper.

"Well, he's squeezed a half an hour of barking into those ten minutes . . ."

"I'm sure it's a coyote. You know how The Thing likes to bark at coyotes," Halley laughed.

The Thing was the Basa family dog. A mongrel, he was a mixture of German Shepherd, Pit Bull, Basset Hound, Labrador Retriever, Beagle, Wire-haired Something and a possible non-canine creature. The combined features yielded an animal altogether unattractive, and the most loving pet any family could hope for.

He was also a great guard-dog. For eight years, no one got near the house without the family knowing.

"Should I let him in?" Joe asked. It was getting dark. They preferred The Thing stay inside at night primarily because of his barking.

"I don't think he's done his business, yet," Halley commented, trying to locate the dog through kitchen window. "Give him a few more minutes."

"All right." Joe Basa went back to watching TV.

Somebody's "funny" home videos were playing. To Joe, the videos mostly consisted of men getting hit, kicked or otherwise crunched in the *cojones*. He couldn't figure out why that was funny.

Also, he couldn't understand why Hollywood abandoned the Western. When he was a kid, Sunday night was *Bonanza* followed by *The High Chaparral*. The last "Western" he saw on TV was *Little House on the Prairie*. Sure, it had Little Joe, but it really wasn't a "Western" western. Besides, that had been 15 years ago.

Tina and Halley joined Joe in the living room. They began laughing at the misfortune of others while Joe grimaced at each assault on some other man's manhood.

Meanwhile, The Thing continued to bark. After trying to ignore it for so long, the barking became white noise for the humans in the house. They ignored it, until it came to an abrupt end—punctuated by a loud yelp.

"What the Hell!" Joe jumped to his feet and ran to the back door. The women followed.

The back, porch light only illuminated half the yard. The Thing was further out, in the dark.

"I need a flashlight!" Joe said, turning back into the kitchen,

"Try the 'junk' drawer," Halley suggested.

Basa found what he needed and headed back to the yard. Tina and Halley watched from the lighted porch.

The beam of the flashlight swept back and forth as Joe looked for their pet. Basa was nearly to the fence when he found The Thing.

"Son of a bitch!" he cried.

"What's wrong, Joe?" Halley was worried. She hurried to where her husband stood.

Basa turned the light away so she couldn't see what he had just seen. "Don't, Hal!"

He held her back.

"Why? What happened?"

"Go inside. Call the Sheriff's office."

\*\*\*

It was over an hour before Deputy Jerry Lopez arrived. Basa had covered The Thing with an old bed spread. The pet owner lifted the covering to show what someone had done to his dog.

The throat not only had been cut, the head was nearly severed. (That's what Joe didn't want his wife to see.) But the assault didn't stop there. The animal had also been disemboweled.

Whoever killed the animal wanted to make sure the homeowners knew this was intentional. It wasn't someone defending themselves from a rabid pet

"Do you know who might have done this?" Lopez asked.

"No." Basa shook his head. "I've had neighbors complain about the barking, but I didn't think they would do something like this."

"You didn't see anyone in the yard?"

"They were gone by the time we got back here."

"What time was that?"

"Close to Nine."

While Basa filled in the details for the deputy, Tina sat on the sofa with Halley, trying to comfort her.

"That stupid dog," the school secretary sniffed. "He never hurt anyone. Why did they have to kill him, Tina?"

"I don't know, Halley," Tina said, rubbing her friend's back. "I don't know."

Despite her words, Tina thought she had a very good idea why The Thing was killed. She also knew who did it.

If she hadn't stayed with the Basa's, their pet would still be alive. They were being punished because they offered to give her sanctuary. In the morning, she would find another place to stay—or just leave La Palmas all together.

# Chapter Forty-One

Compline, the final office of the day, was drawing to a close. The final hymn was being sung to Our Lady. When the song was completed, The Great Silence would commence. All unnecessary conversation between the monks would cease until after Mass the next morning.

The church was almost empty. Abbot Christian was about to retreat behind the Tabernacle to the cloister when he saw a movement in the shadows. He wanted to ask who was there, but he knew the rules.

As if sensing the Abbot's dilemma, the figure stepped forward. It was a hungry, dirty and haggard Esteban Fuentes. He stepped closer, his head bowed in penance.

"I know I've done wrong in the eyes of the order," the monk admitted in a whisper. "I know I must be punished—but there was a reason for my absence.

"Father, we need to talk!"

Abbot Christian sensed the earnest fear in Esteban's voice. It wasn't fear over the coming punishment. It was much more profound. Desperate.

"Go to your cell, Brother," the Abbot said quietly. "We will talk after Mass—and I expect you to attend."

Esteban nodded, and did as he was told.

# Chapter Forty-Two

The *Monasterio Benedicto de Santa Maria Magdelena* was located only 500 feet from *Rio Laja*, 5 miles north of San Miguel. Unlike its parent monastery, it was not isolated in the countryside. A half mile to the west, across the river, was *Los Ricos*. A mile to the north *Monticello de la Milpas*. A mile to the east, the hotel *Atotonilco el Viejo,* where Santiago de los Santos and his four henchmen spent the night.

The monastery church and cloister were quite spacious for the number of brethren. There were only 7 professed monks and 6 novitiates. The operation was only able to function because of the two dozen oblates that worked the grounds, the kitchen and the rest of the facilities on a daily basis. The oblates often attended Terce, the "little hour" when the Gregorian Chants were conducted, around 9:00.

De los Santos chose Lauds for his visit. This was the time of chants conducted to welcome the new day, just before Mass.

The Gulf Cartel hit squad entered the church when the chant began at 5:45. They were all armed with automatic rifles. However, de los Santos instructed his men not to use them. Too many people lived too close to the monastery grounds. They didn't want the police alerted over gunfire.

The foot soldiers spread out, blocking the exits. Prior Philip, the head of the monastery, immediately stopped the chant.

"What are you men doing here? This is God's house! How dare you bring weapons in here!" the prior protested.

"Shut up, *Padre*," Santiago ordered. "We are looking for someone."

The monks stood in pews to either side of the altar. They looked to each other, not fully grasping what was happening.

Miguel Flores held a computer rendering of Pepe Zapata's face. He stepped from one monk to the next, comparing faces. Some men had beards. Others did not. He lingered at little longer with the bearded faces, just to make sure he didn't make a mistake. When he finished, he looked at his leader and shook his head.

De los Santos raised his voice. "I am looking for the man in that photo."

Flores held it up, so the brethren could see.

"His name is Pepe Zapata . . . He is a murderer! He assumed the name of a dead man, Eduardo Fuentes. We know he came here eight years ago." He pointed at the closed doors behind him.

"You have a picture in the hallway from four years ago. He is in that picture.

"I want to know where he is and what name he goes by . . ."

"My son," Prior Philip pleaded. "We do not know this man you seek . . . If he is not here with us now, I don't know where he could be."

De los Santos waved his hand. Flores immediately stepped to the man closest to him. He pulled out a knife and slit the man's throat. As the novitiate crumbled to the floor, the rest of the monks cried out in protest and anguish. Six of the men tried to rush for an exit only to be shoved back to their group.

"Shut up!" De los Santos shouted, pointing his gun and making it clear he would use it. "Every one of you will remain in this room." He turned back to the prior. "*Padre*, I am not a patient man . . ." He signaled to Flores. "Show him the picture!"

Flores held the picture up, inches from the prior's face.

"Do you recognize him?" Santiago demanded.

"I'm . . . I'm not sure," Philip said, trembling.

De los Santos waved his hand again. A different soldier stepped forward, grabbed an older monk from behind, and slit his throat. He let the body drop.

"No!" the prior shrieked.

"How long have you been at this monastery?" Santiago growled.

"Fifteen years . . ." the clergyman was beginning to cry.

"Then you know him!" The henchman was face to face with the man, yelling. "You were here! You know who he is!"

The prior nodded. "He is now Brother Esteban . . ." he whispered.

"What? What did you say?" de la Santos screamed.

"Esteban!" Prior Philip yelled. "Brother Esteban . . . Fuentes . . . But he's no longer here. He left!"

"What do you mean 'he left?'"

"Monks do that! Sometimes they've had enough, and they just leave . . ."

De los Santos flicked his wrist. Flores nearly decapitated the next monk.

"Where did he leave to?"

"He went to the States!" another monk yelled. "He went to the United States . . ."

The new confessor had Santiago de los Santos' complete attention. "The United States is a big country. Where did he go in the United States?"

"He went to our parent Monastery," Prior Philip finally confessed. "*Saint Anthony's Monastery in the Canyon*, in New Mexico. That was four years ago. I don't know if he's still there."

"And how do I learn if he's still there?"

"I suppose you'll have to go there and find out for yourself!" Philip said defiantly.

None of the men in the hit squad wore face coverings. Too late, Prior Philip realized exactly what that meant. They were not afraid of being identified. There would be no witnesses.

# Chapter Forty-Three

Maybe it was the nearly 10 hours of sleep, but Cliff Lansing felt amazingly refreshed Monday morning. No one called him at 3:00 am to report another tragedy in the making.

He had talked to C.J. before going to bed. His son and his ex-wife were doing fine. The boy would start Driver's Ed on June first. It would end the middle of July. Could he come for his summer visit then? Any time C.J. could visit was fine with his father.

After putting the horses in the corral, he headed into work. It wasn't 7:00, yet. He would check the overnight logs, try to get an update on Leroy Ramirez's condition, then sneak over to the Las Palmas Diner for a quick breakfast.

The one report he found disturbing from Sunday night concerned the Basa household. Somebody killed their dog. Not only killed it, but according to Jerry Lopez, mutilated it. The sheriff immediately suspected the incident had to do with Tina Morales.

He honestly doubted Poncho Chamorro was involved. The man stole a car and had to be hundreds of miles away by now. But who else had a reason to kill the animal? It must have been done as a threat against the Basa's—and a warning to Morales.

Trying to get information about Deputy Ramirez was impossible. The information desk at Christus St. Francis had no record of the deputy being admitted. He was transferred to the Emergency Room. Yes, they did treat him. Yes, he was transferred to a room, but it was after midnight. Possibly, the information desk didn't have his room number, yet.

Back to Information. Yes, it turned out he did have a room number, but he had been moved. He was scheduled for surgery because the injuries were so severe. He was connected to the surgical unit. Was

Lansing immediate family? No, then they couldn't release any information. No, it didn't matter if Lansing was the man's boss.

Back to Information. He would have to talk to hospital administration—but no one was available. It was a holiday, for God's sake! What did he expect?

Lansing's only recourse was to contact the Santa Fe County Sheriff's Office. He and Glen Juarez had a good working relationship. Maybe Sheriff Juarez could send a deputy to the hospital and find out how Ramirez was doing.

It was after 8:00 when Lansing walked out to the reception area. Clem Montoya was already manning the Sergeant's Desk. Marilyn was just walking in, late, at least for her. She looked drained.

"Marilyn, is anything wrong?" the sheriff asked.

She looked at him through blood-shot eyes. Her face was flushed. She had been crying.

"Oh, Cliff!" she cried, almost collapsing in his arms.

He helped her to one of the reception area chairs.

"What happened?"

"My little cat . . . Misty . . . Somebody killed her . . ."

"What?"

She nodded. "They wrapped a coat hanger around her neck and hung her on my front door!" She dug in her purse to retrieve a tissue. Her tears began all over again.

"Clem, see if there's a bottle of water in the Day Room fridge," Lansing suggested.

Montoya went down the hall, then immediately came back. "Can't get to it, Sheriff. Those operators are still in there."

Lansing swore under his breath. "Rinse out a cup and get some water from the fountain," he ordered.

A minute later, Marilyn was sipping from a spare coffee mug. She was soon calming down. The tears had stopped.

"Are you going to be all right?" the sheriff asked.

Marilyn nodded.

"Do you need the day off?" he asked.

"The last place I want to be right now is at home," she admitted.

"Where's Misty now?"

"She's still on the door . . . I couldn't touch her . . ."

Lansing helped the dispatcher to her feet. "Do you want me to do something with the body?"

"Could you put her in a small, cardboard box? I want to bury her in my flowerbed."

"I'll take care of that. Don't worry."

The weekend, night dispatcher left, and Marilyn assumed her regular spot.

Not particularly hungry, Lansing knew he should eat something. In his office, he grabbed his Stetson and was about to leave when his phone rang. It was Marilyn. Jack Rivera called in. He needed the day off . . . to fix his house.

# Chapter Forty-Four

After Mass and breakfast, Abbot Christian and Brother Esteban met in the Abbot's office. The daily chapter meeting didn't start until 8:30, but Esteban had a lot to say.

Before going to bed, Esteban showered. Despite his exhaustion, his sleep was troubled. In the morning he felt as though he had not slept at all. The hike the previous day seemed like a dream. He started to believe his encounter with the ravens was only in his imagination.

During Vigils, Lauds and the subsequent Mass, the other monks gave Brother Esteban sidelong glances. The impression was they didn't understand why he was allowed to participate in the daily rituals.

Once the two men were alone, Esteban first had to describe his life before his baptism and how he came to monastic life. Abbreviated though the description was, that previous life was the backdrop to his current and disturbing dreams. It was his dreams that drove him to leave the cloister—He hoped his departure would ensure the safety of all the other brethren.

He only returned to the monastery after being confronted by the flock of ravens blocking his path. He knew, in his heart, God wanted him to return.

Abbot Christian listened in silence. He waited until Esteban was finished before asking any questions.

"When you saw the ravens yesterday, when was the last time you had eaten?"

"The evening meal . . . the day before."

"And what time was you're encounter?"

"I think it was after noon."

The Abbot nodded. "I see . . . Were you hungry?"

"Yes."

"These ravens you encountered . . . Did one of them call your name?"

"No . . . Would that matter?"

"It could very much . . . How do you know those ravens were sent by God, specifically for you?"

The Roman Catholic church took a very dim view of any reported "miracle." Especially if that miracle was only witnessed by one person. Miracles, specifically miracles performed by nominated saints, were investigated thoroughly. The investigator had a designated title. He was called The Devil's Advocate. That was the role Abbot Christian was playing now—Devil's Advocate.

Esteban sat in silence.

"I ask you again, Brother Esteban . . . How do you know those ravens were sent by God?"

Esteban shook his head. "I don't know—I mean, I prayed that God give a sign. I needed him to tell me what I should do. Then the ravens came. I assumed they were sent by Him."

"You said you were hungry . . . We have four Hermits in the canyon. They have eschewed living in the Cloister, so they can better seek a personal relationship with God. Often, they fast. When they do, they have visions of the Virgin, of our Christ, even of God, himself.

"Perhaps in your hunger, you imagined a flock of ravens—Or you saw a few birds and interpreted their presence as a sign. Do you think that's a possibility?"

"Of course," Esteban agreed, frowning. The suggestion fit with his own doubts about his experiences the previous day.

"I'm not saying I doubt that you believe you saw a flock of ravens. In your heart, I'm sure you thought God was speaking to you. But be honest, Brother. Do you really believe God needs to speak through you?"

Esteban felt deflated. Abbot Christian made perfect sense. Still. . .

"What about the dreams I've been having?"

"Delayed guilt," the Abbot said, shrugging. "All the things you said you did before coming to the church . . . Did you really repent?"

"I thought I did. I pray for forgiveness every day."

"We all do, Brother Esteban. We are born into sin." The Abbot thought for a moment. "Now that you bring them up—You say, in your dreams, a Great Evil is coming. What is this Great Evil?"

"I don't know," Esteban admitted.

"I mean, it must be something, if you've had all these dreams," the Abbot pushed. "Is it a man? Is it a plague? Is it a great storm?"

"I don't know!" Esteban cried out. "I don't know. I don't know. I don't know!"

Abbot Christian put his hand on Esteban's shoulder. "I think you are troubled, Brother Esteban. Very troubled.

"You should have talked to me. You shouldn't have just walked away from our cloister—but I don't think you did it for selfish reasons. Nonetheless, you have broken your Vow of Permanency, to not leave the order.

"For the next week, you will not participate in our daily offices. You will dine apart. You will work apart. You will pray apart from the rest of us—and we will pray for you—that God will see fit to ease your troubled mind."

Abbot Christian made the sign of the cross. "Now, go in peace, my brother."

# Chapter Forty-Five

It was Memorial Day. The Las Palmas High School Band was going to gather at the flagpole in the town square and play a few marches. Father Roberto from St. James Catholic church would do the invocation. Mayor Salido would say a few words. The veterans would be happy that someone took notice of their fallen comrades . . . and the day, like so many others, would be forgotten.

Sheriff Lansing wished he had time to enjoy the observance. The good mood he started the day with had dissipated by 9:00 am. The Basa's dead dog, Marilyn's dead cat, the missing Poncho Chamorro were all itches he couldn't scratch.

He had Clem Montoya contact the phone company. When could they expect the 9-1-1 operations to vacate the Sheriff's office and move to the high school library? Maybe Tuesday, if they could get the right equipment. After all, it was a holiday weekend. Another itch.

Behind the Sheriff's office, the State Fire Marshall and his minions were banging around, trying to figure out what caused the Call Center Fire. So far, they didn't think it was arson. Most likely electrical. But they couldn't pinpoint exactly where the fire started. It seemed all four walls burst into flames at the same time . . . which, of course, couldn't happen.

For Lansing, the cause of the fire didn't matter to him. That was someone else's itch.

It was the aftermath that he had to suffer through.

The one bright spot that morning was Arthur Grant. He was ready to get back on patrol. That took up the slack when Rivera needed the day off.

James Cortez had fully recovered from his near drowning, so his dad reported for work.

The sheriff had a quick bite at the Las Palmas Diner, across the street from the town square. The gathering that day wouldn't be large, but he wanted to avoid it as much as possible. He was soon in his Jeep, making rounds.

First stop was Marilyn's house. The cat was stiff. That gave him an idea for the size of box he needed. He put the carcass on the back-seat floor.

Jack Rivera had nailed a 4'x8' sheet of plywood over his front entrance. He needed to go to the box store in Segovia to find a replacement door. He asked Lansing if he could borrow the sheriff's personal truck. Lansing swung by to drop off his keys.

Sue and DeeDee were doing fine. He didn't want them to be alone— just in case—so, he was taking them with him.

The final stop was Joe and Halley Basa's place. He accepted the invitation to come in and have a cup of coffee. Even though he had seen the report, he asked them to explain to him what happened.

Joe did, in detail. He even showed the sheriff the poor, dead animal.

Back at the kitchen table, Tina Morales was subdued. She had been angry with the Sheriff and his deputies when Poncho escaped. It was becoming evident to her that her safety was her own responsibility.

"Are you going to stay here?" Lansing asked.

"It's obvious that I can't," Tina said, solemnly. "I don't want anyone to get hurt because of me. Next time, it may not be just a dog." She realized that last statement hurt Halley.

"I'm sorry. I shouldn't have put it that way."

"That's okay, Tina." She patted the teacher's hand. "I know what you meant."

"Maybe it's time for me to leave."

"What do you mean 'leave?' " Halley asked.

"Leave town. The school year is over. I don't need to stay. With that *pendejo* running loose, I'm not safe and neither is anyone near me."

"Maybe it wasn't Chamorro who killed the dog," Lansing suggested.

"Who else could it be?" Tina demanded.

"The Basa's dog wasn't the only pet killed last night." He explained what happened to Marilyn's cat. In fact, he had the animal in his Jeep if they wanted confirmation.

"It's very possible we have a serial pet murderer on our hands," the sheriff concluded. "It may not have anything at all to do with your former boyfriend."

Morales wasn't totally convinced. "I still don't think I should stay with Halley and Joe."

"So, you're going back to your place?" Halley asked.

Tina's doubtful look said, "No."

"If you're looking for a place to hide for a couple of days, you could stay at my ranch,"

Lansing suggested.

The teacher just stared at him. "How is being isolated on a ranch, fifteen miles out of town any protection?"

"I wouldn't leave you out there by yourself."

"Are you going to be there?"

"Not all the time. Of course not."

She gave him a look that said, "Explain to me what you mean."

"My neighbor's son, Oscar Vega. He can stay at the ranch with you."

"I know Oscar. He was in my chemistry class. He's a nice kid and all, but he's not much bigger than me. How is that protection?"

"He's a smart guy, plus he's one hell-of-a shot. He won't let anyone get near you."

"You have two more days until school's out," Halley observed. "If you don't want to be alone and you don't feel safe here, try the sheriff's ranch."

"Besides, I'll bet Chamorro won't be running around much longer," Lansing observed. "There's a 'be on the lookout' order for him and the car he stole . . ."

"He stole a car?" Morales said, shocked.

Lansing nodded. "He needed to get away, somehow. I'm sure he's long gone, by now. But the woman who saw him yesterday said he was bleeding through his bandages. He probably needs medical attention."

Despite her misgivings, Morales agreed to stay at the ranch. Lansing would make a call. Oscar would meet her there.

"I do have one suggestion, though," the sheriff offered.

"What's that?"

"You'd better stop off at the grocery store first. I don't think there's any food at my place—that's edible."

# Chapter Forty-Six

The interior of the barn was dark. The only light came from the cracks between the weathered boards of the walls and holes in the roof. There wasn't a lot of room, either. Two stolen cars took up most of the space.

The first car was used when Chamorro escaped from the hospital. The second, the escaped prisoner acquired during a home invasion he'd done the day before.

Poncho Chamorro didn't understand why he was doing the strange tasks the old woman had him perform.

Saturday night, the old woman freed him from the hospital. She had him drive to a tiny house in the middle of nowhere. He was tired, and he hurt. She handed him a bottle and told him to drink. Whatever it was, it had a bitter taste. But in just a few minutes, he felt invigorated.

He also found he had no will of his own. When the woman told him to do something, he did it, whether he understood the reason or not.

His first task was to load the goat and the chickens into the back seat of the car. The woman loaded her own meager possessions. Soon, they were down the road and across a field.

He pulled the car into the old barn. She closed the door behind him.

Once the car was unloaded, she indicated a pile of rags in a corner. That was for him. He slept until mid-afternoon.

She woke him. Gave him another swig of her concoction. When he first sat up, he was dizzy. When the drink kicked in, he was ready to go. She directed him to drive into town.

Once in Las Palmas, she had him drive by a certain house. At the end of the block, she handed him a hunting knife and gave him instructions.

He walked back to the house, demanded to be let in, then kicked down the door. He was told to scare the people inside, but not to harm them—this time. Take the purse, the keys, the car and follow her back to the barn.

The elixir wore off almost as soon as they reached their hideout.

Again, he slept.

When she woke him again, it was almost dark outside. He wasn't feeling well. He touched the bandages on his face. They were sticky where the blood had seeped through. He hurt where they had removed the pellets.

He tried to push the bottle away when she offered it. She insisted he drink. He did as he was told. Soon, he wasn't hurting.

They slowly prowled the streets of Las Palmas, until the old woman finally pointed at a house. She somehow sensed that was the house she wanted. This time, their mark was in a back yard. A pet. A barking dog.

Once again, she handed him the hunting knife and gave her instructions.

He didn't know why he killed the dog, or gutted it, or decapitated it.

Drenched in the animal's blood, he began driving again. Before they left town, they made one more stop. This time the old woman got out—a wire hanger in her hand. She was gone ten minutes.

When she returned, the smile on her face sent a chill through his spine.

Once they were back at the barn, he had to shoo a chicken from his lowly bed. As he lay on his rags he felt nauseated. He was running a fever. He couldn't remember the last time he ate. It didn't matter. If he did eat, it wouldn't stay down.

He hadn't prayed since he was a child. He wondered if he remembered how.

Lifting his head, he looked around. The old woman was nowhere to be seen. She kept doing that. Disappearing.

Then, when she returned, he would probably have to drink from her bottle and they would be off, doing whatever she commanded.

He made a decision. No more. He was finished being her zombie slave.

Half crawling, half stumbling, he reached the car he had taken during the home invasion. On the seat, he found the hunting knife he'd used on the dog.

When he returned to his nest, he hid the weapon beneath his filthy rags.

He was ready—the next time she got near him—he would be free.

# Chapter Forty-Seven

"The charter we employed is broken down," de los Santos reported. "They've been working on it all morning. The airport mechanic said it could take two days for parts, another day for repairs."

Humberto Garcia Abrego listened to his henchman on the phone. He was not happy. "How long will it take you to drive back?"

"It's noon. We'll be there by Ten tonight."

The plan was simple. De los Santos and his men would go to the monastery, grab Zapata and return to Matamoros. If Zapata wasn't there, it was up to de los Santos as to what measures he would use to get the information. However, even Abrego was taken aback by the hit squad's violence.

"We are getting reports on the television here in Matamoros . . . even the Brownsville stations are talking about the 'Massacre in the Monastery.'" Abrego said. "They say all the monks were killed. They also say no one has a clue about who might have done it."

De los Santos knew there was half a chance Abrego's phone was bugged. "Whoever did it must have been careful. We're about twenty miles from San Miguel. That's where it happened, isn't it?"

"Yes, it is," Abrego growled. "Did you find what you were looking for?"

"No," de los Santos admitted. "But we know where to look now."

"Where?" Humberto demanded.

"In the U.S., at another mon . . ." De los Santos caught himself before he completed the word. "At another town, in New Mexico."

"When will you make the trip?"

"I can start tomorrow," de los Santos considered, out loud. "We will have to drive—plus we can't bring our own 'equipment.' You'll have to make arrangements for us after we cross the border."

"Fine," Abrego snapped. "Come straight here when you get to town."

"I will, *Jeffe*."

Humbert Garcia Abrego slammed the phone down, nearly breaking it. "That ASS!"

Osiel Cardenas Guillen stood across the room, watching the news reports on the TV. He turned to his boss. "Is there a problem?" he asked, casually.

"No!" The cartel chief stomped to the bar and poured himself a tequila. He downed it in two gulps. "Osiel, contact Morgan in Houston. Tell him we need weapons."

"A shipment?"

"No . . . De los Santos is going to the States . . ." Abrego said, indicating his lieutenant didn't need to know any details. "Tell him Santiago will contact him tomorrow. He'll tell him what he needs and when he'll pick them up."

"Where is Santiago going?"

Abrego shrugged. "He's going where he needs to go."

"You don't think he's killed enough already?"

"No, he hasn't!" Humberto stormed. "It's unfortunate those men died, but men die all the time. I will not rest, and he will not stop, until Zapata is dead!" He threw his glass against the wall, shattering it.

"As you wish, *Jeffe*," Guillen said, backing out of the room.

In his own office, Guillen contacted Morgan. To most of the world J.D. Morgan was a legitimate arms dealer. To a select few, he was as dirty as they came. He had been the cartel's go-to weapon supplier for years.

"Santiago de los Santos will call you tomorrow. I suspect he'll need a cache for five men."

"What are they for?" Morgan asked, suspiciously. Promoting violence in a foreign country was one thing. In the United States? That was another matter.

"Simply for protection," Guillen lied. "They are meeting with a Triad out of Hong Kong. The U.S. is neutral ground."

"And just where is this meeting?"

"You're asking too many questions, Morgan."

"If something goes down in this country, and those weapons are traced to me . . ."

"Relax . . . They're meeting in New Orleans . . . You happy?"

"Why aren't you taking a boat over there? It's just as fast."

"Coast Guard . . . They inspect everything coming out of Matamoros . . . Heaven forbid! They might think we're carrying drugs."

Morgan chuckled at the other end. "All right, all right. Have de los Santos call me tomorrow. We'll have what he needs."

Guillen hung up the phone. He opened his office door to make sure the hallway was empty. Closing his door again, he pulled out his cell phone.

"Arturo, this is Osiel . . . How close are you to making a move?"

He waited for the response.

"I don't think we can wait that long. Have you seen the news today? Yes, I am talking about the monastery . . . Yes, that was Abrego's doing . . ."

Guillen paused, listening to the response.

"I don't think it's that funny . . .

"The Gulf Cartel does not kill women, we do not kill children, we do not kill priests and monks. But that's not my concern here. Abrego's taking his vengeance across the border. We don't need the entire U.S government coming down on us . . .

"Move the timeline up. We need to take out Abrego this week!"

# Chapter Forty-Eight

It was still early in the planting season. The young sprouts were just popping up. Sometimes it was tough telling the difference between a new bean plant and a new weed. Brother Esteban did his best. His work assignment was the Abbey vegetable garden. He was the only monk assigned to weeding that morning.

For physical work, the brothers usually wore pants or jeans and a half-cassock. The long robes were too cumbersome for lawn mowing, digging in the garden and other such labor. That's how Esteban was attired for his current chores.

The garden was not laid out in neat rows. It was set up in rock lined patches. Each patch was assigned a single legume, vegetable or fruit— the fruit being tomatoes, melons and squashes. Well-worn paths ran between the plots for easy access. It also made watering easier.

Esteban enjoyed the work. He could concentrate on pesky weeds and didn't have to think about his transgression the day before. He even found himself humming a tune. He didn't know what it was or where it came from, but it seemed to calm his mind.

His pleasant solitude was interrupted by a squawk. From the top of one of the wooden posts used to string up bean vines, a lone raven sat, glaring at the monk. When the monk looked up, the animal squawked again.

"What do you want from me?" Esteban groused. "You told me to come back! I'm back!"

The bird made an "Augh . . . Augh" sound. It was deep and guttural. It almost sounded like it was it was trying to talk.

"I wish I knew what you were trying to say." Esteban was about to return to his chores when he spotted another monk approaching from the cloister. He stopped and waited.

Out of respect to the general silence of the grounds, no one yelled or shouted. The monk waited until he was just a few feet away.

"Brother Esteban . . . Abbot Christian needs to see you."

"What about?"

"I don't know, but he said it is urgent."

Esteban stood and brushed the dirt from his knees. His hands were filthy with grime deep under his nails. He tried to clean them the best he could as he followed his Brother to the cloister offices.

"You wanted to see me, Father?" Esteban asked.

Abbot Christian sat at his desk. He looked up when the question was asked. There was a pained expression on his face.

"Brother Esteban, please sit down."

The monk did as instructed.

"In your dreams . . . did they involve *Monasterio Benedicto*?"

"Yes, I told you they did. I dreamed about how I came there . . . how I was baptized and took my vows . . ."

"I know. I know about that," the Abbot said, cutting him off. "I wanted to know about the Great Evil you talked about. Did it involve the *Monasterio Benedicto de Santa Maria Magdelena*?"

"The Great Evil?" Esteban shook his head. "The Evil was just a feeling I had. A dread—like something bad was going to happen. And it was going to be my fault."

Abbot Christian stood and turned to the window behind his desk. He gazed into the canyon beyond, he hands clasped behind his back. "Evil did come."

"What do you mean?"

"It came to our daughter monastery in San Miguel. Someone attacked our brethren at Mass this morning. All thirteen were killed!"

"What?" The monk nearly fell from his seat.

Christian made the sign of the cross. "One of their oblates called this morning . . . Someone came in while they gathered for Lauds and Mass. No one knows why. The police have no idea who might have done it. But it must have been several men. They trapped Prior Philip and the other monks in the church . . ." He stopped, trying to find the right words, then just blurted them out. "Their throats were cut!"

"Oh, my God!" Esteban said, standing.

"You said you thought it was your fault. Why?"

"I told you, all those years ago that I killed a man."

"Yes, to protect a family."

"That man was the nephew of the head of the Gulf Drug Cartel. The cartel may be coming after me."

"Why? Wasn't that eight years ago? Why look for you now?"

"I don't know. It's just what I feel."

Abbot Christian paced behind his desk. "It may be that cartel you talk about . . . It may be something else." He seemed to be talking himself out of his earlier assumptions. "It may not have anything to do with you at all."

"You're right, Father. Of course."

The Abbot took a deep breath to calm himself down. "I can't imagine the great tragedy that befell our brothers in Mexico had anything to do with your dreams . . . In fact, I shouldn't have even called you in here. I believe I was jumping to conclusions."

Esteban Fuentes could only stare at his superior in disbelief. The man was playing Devil's Advocate again. An entire cloister had been murdered. Fuentes provided a warning that morning, that Evil was coming.

Abbot Christian refused to connect Esteban's dreams and fears with the realities presented to him.

"I will inform the rest of the monastery about the tragedy at Sext, before we eat lunch. That will give each of us ample time to contemplate and pray for our fallen brethren."

"Of course, Father . . . Will that be all?"

"Yes, Brother. You can carry on."

As Esteban headed back to the garden, he wondered if he should have mentioned the encounter with the raven. He decided, probably not. It would be dismissed, just like the ravens the day before and his dreams about approaching Evil.

# Chapter Forty-Nine

Tina Morales stopped at her little house on Dollar Street to pick up a few items a bachelor's place wouldn't provide. Then she swung by the Las Palmas IGA to pick up fixings for at least a couple of meals. She needed enough for three people.

Satisfied no one would starve, even with her cooking, she headed south on Highway 15. The sheriff said the turn-off to his place was on the right, exactly 14.8 miles south of the Las Palmas town limits. There was no mistaking it. The ranch house, barn and other structures were the only buildings within three miles.

Morales was going to comment that the ranch would never need a gate to protect against intruders. The ruts and potholes in the half-mile, ranch drive would deter any sane person from invading his property.

The front of the house actually faced away from the highway and overlooked the "barnyard." The teacher parked her car in front of the house. No other vehicles were present. She grabbed a bag of groceries and proceeded to the door. It was locked.

"Damn," she said under her breath. She had been told Oscar Vega would arrive before she got there. He would unlock the house. "Now what am I going to do?" she thought out loud.

She set down the groceries and retrieved her phone. Before she could dial the number Lansing had given her, someone called to her.

"Miss Morales! Miss Morales!" It was Oscar. He was running from behind the barn.

"Oh, you are here."

"I need to talk to Sheriff Lansing!" he declared as he ran up.

"Why? What's the matter?"

"His horses . . . There's something wrong—They're sick."

"Show me," she said.

Oscar turned and they both ran to the corral behind the barn.

Lansing owned three horses. Cement Head (his favorite), a chestnut stallion with a white blaze on its forehead; Paladin, an all-black gelding; and Little Orphan Annie, a Dun mare with a cream-colored coat with black mane and tail. All three were stumbling and swaying as if they were drunk. The mare saw Oscar and tried to run toward him. After just a few steps she tripped and fell. She whinnied in protest as she tried to stand.

"I don't know what to do. My dad dropped me off, but I don't think he's home, yet."

"I'll call the sheriff with my phone." She indicated her cell.

"Lansing," the sheriff said, when he answered.

"Yes. This is Tina Morales. Sheriff, I'm at your ranch . . ."

"Good. You found it. Is Oscar there?"

"Listen, I'm giving him my phone. He needs to talk to you." She handed the part-time ranch-hand the phone.

"Hi, Sheriff. There's something wrong with the horses . . ."

"What do you mean 'there's something wrong?' "

"It looks like they ate something bad." Vega described their conditions. "What should I do?"

"Go in the ranch house," Lansing instructed. "In the kitchen, next to the phone, is a list of emergency numbers. Doc Beltran, the vet . . . he has a couple of numbers there. Today's a holiday. Call him on his cell. Tell him this is an emergency . . . Tell him I'll meet him at the ranch."

"Yes, sir." He handed the phone back to his teacher and ran to the house.

"Lansing, it's me again. Is there anything I can do?"

"Have you been around horses?"

"No."

"Then, unless you have a vet license up your sleeve, I don't think there's much you can do."

"I'm familiar with herbal remedies . . . and I do have a minor in chemistry."

"We'll see. We have to figure out what's wrong with the horses first . . . I'll be there as soon as I can."

While waiting for the others to arrive, Morales unloaded groceries and figured out where she would sleep. Lansing got there first. He headed straight for the corral where Oscar greeted him.

As Tina stepped outside to join them, the veterinarian pulled in. She indicated that the doctor should follow her to the corral.

The sheriff was on his knees, stoking Cement Head's neck. Upon seeing Lansing, his horse attempted to run toward him. He fell just like the mare. Lansing looked up when the vet approached. "I don't know what they could have eaten . . . they've been in the corral all day."

Rob Beltran came to San Phillipe County in the mid-70s. He had been the primary veterinarian for the Lansing ranch for almost 25 years. He and the sheriff had been friends for 12 years, ever since Lansing moved back from Albuquerque.

"What do they usually eat?" Beltran asked, pulling out a stethoscope and kneeling to listen to the horse's lungs.

"They have oat buckets along the side of the barn. I give them each a couple of scoops in the morning, plus they have their hay in the cradle."

"Cement Head's breathing is pretty labored," Beltran said, standing. "He's also producing too much saliva . . ." He noticed the gelding was still standing, but he was swaying and uneasy on his feet. "Were all three horses like that?"

"Yes," Vega said. "Definitely."

"We need to get them up. We're going to flush out their stomachs. They need to be standing for that. We'll see if that helps."

Oscar dragged a hose from the side of the barn while the two older men got the horses to stand. Cement Head tried to protest as Doc Beltran forced the hose down his gullet. The sheriff held him steady. At the vet's signal, the young Vega turned on the spigot.

The water filled the horse's stomach. Soon, the water was gushing back out the horse's mouth. Beltran continued the flush for two full minutes. He signaled to Oscar to stop.

The process was completed on the other two animals.

All three horses sensed the humans were there to help them. Cement Head even came up to Lansing and nuzzled him, giving thanks.

Beltran handed Oscar a clear plastic bag. "Get me a sample of the oats from their buckets. Dump out the rest in the trash where no animals can get to it." He turned to Lansing. "Do you have some unopened feed?"

"Sure."

"I need a sample from your open oat bag. It looks to me like your food might be toxic. I'd use the new bag till I get some test results back. You also need to take care of their feed buckets. Clean them good before using them again. If there is poison present, you want to make sure it's gone."

"Most definitely." The two men walked to the corral gate. The sun was setting. "Thanks for everything, Doc . . . I trust you'll bill me."

"You can count on it, Clifford."

Lansing and Vega put the horses in the barn for the night. Oscar then retrieved the feed buckets. They would get rinsed that night with boiling water.

They were greeted at the front door by Tina. While they were busy rescuing horses, she fixed what she hoped would be a halfway decent meal. "I hope you two are hungry!"

"We are," the rancher said, stomping the mud and straw from his boots. Oscar followed suit.

"It smells good," the boy admitted, once inside.

"Spaghetti sauce and noodles . . . An all-American favorite. It's ready when you are."

"Let us wash up," Lansing said, "and we'll be right there."

# Chapter Fifty

Poncho Chamorro woke when someone kicked the bottom of his foot. It was dark outside. Except for retrieving the hunting knife from the stolen car, he hadn't left his rag pile the entire day.

He couldn't open his right eye. That side of his face was swollen. He felt feverish and dizzy. His bandages hadn't been changed in over two days. They were hard and stiff from the dried blood. It had also been two days since his last dose of antibiotics.

A staph infection was racking his body. He had neither the strength nor the desire to move.

"Get up!" the old crone ordered.

"I can't." Chamorro whispered. "I need a doctor."

"You had a doctor and walked away . . . Willingly."

"I want to go back . . . Take me back . . ."

"No."

"Then I'll take myself . . ." He felt beneath his tangle of rags. The knife he had hidden was gone.

"Looking for this?" The hag dangled the weapon in front of him.

Chamorro lunged for it but fell flat. His strength was almost gone.

"And what were you planning to do with this, *Mijo*?"

"P-protect myself . . ."

"Protect yourself from me?" She "tsk-tsk-ed." "I know you. I know what kind of man you are. You were going to kill me, weren't you?"

Poncho barely had enough strength to shake his head. "I wouldn't do that."

"It's all right, *Mijo*. You helped enough—just stay here."

As she so often did, the old woman disappeared.

Poncho Chamorro closed his eyes. He fell asleep again, though he didn't know for how long. He was dreaming. In the dream, he heard a baby crying. The sound grew louder and louder until it woke him up

It wasn't a baby crying. It was the goat, bleating in fear.

The barn was on fire. Chamorro, the goat and the chickens were trapped inside.

The former bully tried to stand. He couldn't. He had no strength. The air was filled with smoke. He grabbed a rag from his bedding and held it over his mouth.

His one good eye watered and stung from the smoke. He tried to crawl with one hand. It was almost impossible. In his confusion, he had no idea what direction an exit would be.

The car! If he could get to the stolen car, he could start it and smash through the barn door. To navigate, he had plenty of light from the flames. They now shot up all four walls of the barn.

Nearly blind now, he crawled until he bumped into one of the cars. He reached up to grab the handle. His hand was immediately burned. Using the rag for protection, he attempted to open the door again, this time, successfully.

He was on the rider's side. He had to crawl over the center console to reach the driver's seat.

The car immediately filled with smoke when he opened the door. When he finally reached the driver's seat, he couldn't see as far as the windshield.

He felt for the ignition switch—No key!

He remembered. He put the key above the visor. However, when he pulled the visor down, the keys fell to the floor.

Chamorro panicked. He was being overwhelmed by the heat and the smoke.

Feeling for the keys, he bent over slightly. When he found them he sat up again. It was as though he had just stuck his head in a blast furnace. He took a breath. Every inch of his lungs was singed with searing smoke.

He didn't even have the strength to cough. He tried to gasp for air. There was no air to be had. With no oxygen and no options, Poncho Chamorro collapsed against the steering wheel. He died in seconds—ten long, painful and terrifying seconds.

In a tree, not far away, the Great Horned Owl watched the barn blaze away in the night.

Fire! So purifying. Nature's way to purge.

# Chapter Fifty-One

"Good Morning, it's Tuesday, the twenty-sixth day of May. I am your news anchor, Johnathan Wheeler," the man on the TV announced. "And this is your Six a.m. News.

"Tragedy over the Memorial Day weekend for a family of six in northwestern Oklahoma City. We go to Melanie Vaughn at the scene . . ."

The station switched to an outdoor, remote location. A petite, blonde reporter, doused in camera lights, was looking down at her notes when the director cut to her. She looked up, paused for a second, then began:

"Yes, Johnathan, a tragedy indeed. I am here in the Britton section of Oklahoma City. Five members of the Diego Carrillo family were found brutally murdered in their home yesterday evening. According to police, they were discovered by their eighteen-year-old daughter, who had been away for the weekend.

"The father, mother and three of the four children were found in the living room."

Vaughn turned and looked behind her. The camera followed her gaze and widened the shot. It was still dark outside. Viewers could barely make out the house. The yellow, "police-line" tape was visible.

"This is the home on Berkshire Way where the slayings occurred. Neighbors say they were a quiet family who kept to themselves. Records indicated the Carrillo's had lived in this house for over seven years.

"As of yet, the causes of death have not been released. However, one officer on the scene said the murders could only be described as 'execution-style.' "

The camera shot reverted to a close-up of the reporter.

"At the moment, officials have no idea as to the motive or who is responsible for this heinous crime.

"Meanwhile, this station will keep you up to date on developments as they unfold.

"This is Melanie Vaughn, reporting for KOCT-TV, Channel 3 News.

"Back to you Johnathan"

The shot returned to the anchor desk. Wheeler continued:

"Thank you for that report, Melanie . . .

"Police ask anyone who has information about this crime, please contact 'Crime Stoppers' at the number below . . ."

# Chapter Fifty-Two

Oscar Vega was hired to be Tina Morales' bodyguard. It made sense that he stayed at the Lansing ranch, even when the sheriff was around. That way, they didn't have to make trips to the Vega spread to pick him up. The arrangement was that he would stay until Thursday morning. The teacher would make long term plans by then.

Morales had picked up milk and cereal for breakfast. That was fine with Oscar.

The rancher wanted something more substantial. He had to check on the horses before anything else. After that he needed to swing by the office to view the over-night logs.

Lansing suggested Morales drop Vega at school, then join him at the diner for breakfast.

The horses, fortunately, looked fine after their ordeal from the day before. Lansing put two scoops of oats into the clean buckets. Each scoop held two and a half pounds of oats and the feed came from the newly opened bag.

He turned the horses loose in the corral, while Oscar hung the buckets in the normal spots. As the two walked back to the ranch house, Lansing asked, "You're a junior, right?"

"Yes."

"One more year of school. What are you going to do after that?"

Vega shrugged. "I don't know. Get a job somewhere, I guess. There won't be enough work for me on our ranch."

"Do you like ranch work?"

"It's all right . . . It's something I know how to do."

"Don't want to go to college?"

"No. I don't even like high school . . . I just go 'cause my folks say I have to."

"Yeah," Lansing agreed. "I can understand how they feel . . . How was Miss Morales as a teacher?"

"I might have liked school more if they were all like her. I think chemistry was my best grade last year. She made you want to learn."

Lansing admitted to himself he was impressed.

It was 8:30 when the sheriff showed up at the diner. Morales was already waiting for him in a booth. Kelly filled their coffee cups.

The sheriff motioned toward the town square with his head. "How were the festivities yesterday?"

"About the same," the waitress admitted. "The crowd gets smaller every year. The band managed to play most of the same notes and the mayor talked too long . . ."

"He does like the sound of his voice," Lansing agreed.

"What would you like, Sheriff?"

"I'll take the Denver Omelet," he said, without looking at the menu. "With a side of whole wheat toast and hash browns."

"I'll have a poached egg on toast," Tina decided after looking at the choices.

"Is this together?"

"Yeah, I've got it," Lansing said.

When they were alone, the teacher asked, "Anymore dead animals last night?"

"Nope," Lansing admitted. "It was quiet on that front. In fact, it was quiet almost everywhere. I guess everybody was worn out from the long weekend.

"The only thing I saw in the reports was a fire—some old barn out in the country, about six miles from town."

"Anyone hurt?"

"I don't know. I don't think so. No one even knew the place was out there. The fire department said it was too far gone to try and save it. They just let it burn itself out. Made sure the fire didn't spread.

"After everything cools down, they said they would sift through the rubble. Try to find out what caused the fire. My bet is some teenagers were out there drinking and had a camp-fire that got away from them."

He noticed Tina gazing out the window. "Am I boring you?"

"Oh, no. Of course not," she said, turning back to him. "After everything is over around here—Once Poncho is out of the way—I was thinking, I'd like to stay in San Phillipe County. I like the high school. I like the other teachers."

"You were in Albuquerque before this?"

She nodded.

"I don't blame you for not wanting to go back. I, personally, didn't like living there.

My ex-wife couldn't wait to return."

"Some people like big cities," the teacher observed. "I don't. I grew up in Phoenix. Way too big. I got a scholarship to the University of New Mexico. That's how I ended up in Albuquerque." She took a sip of her coffee. "Do you get lonely out at that ranch with nobody around?"

"I've got my horses."

"It's hard to carry on a conversation with a horse."

"That may be true, but they're great listeners—and they seldom argue."

Tina smiled at that response. "They argue?"

"You'd be surprised," he continued. "As sheriff, though, I don't have a lot of time to be lonely."

"You're not going to be a sheriff forever," she observed.

"Maybe, so," he agreed. "I try not to think about things like that."

Kelly arrived with their breakfasts.

"Do you still want me to come to your office for that victim's statement?"

"We're going to catch up with Chamorro, eventually. Right now, I have him on drunken and reckless driving, escape and evading arrest. I can tack on property damage, breaking and entering, and attempted battery—but I can't do that without your written statement."

"Not a problem."

"Good," the sheriff said, dousing his eggs with Mexican hot sauce. "We'll go to my office right after we eat."

Two bites into his breakfast, Lansing got a call on his cell.

"Lansing." He listened for a moment. "I'll meet you there in half an hour."

"Anything wrong?" Tina asked.

"They want me to come out to the barn that burned. Seems they found something."

He took a bite of his food. "You can still fill out the 'victim's statement,' if you want."

"I can wait till you get back. Give me your phone."

He handed it over. She plugged in a few letters and numbers, then slid it back across the table. "Just call me when you're back."

"What are you going to do?"

"I'll be at the school. I still need to clean out my desk—say some good-byes for the summer."

# Chapter Fifty-Three

Lansing had a fairly good idea where the burned barn was located. It was along Route 182, a couple of miles past Berta Chavez's place. He gave the old woman only a passing thought. He fully expected to get a call from the State Board of Corrections. They would be demanding to know why he hadn't contacted the poor old lady about the death of her son.

He shrugged off the thought of the old woman, just like he would shrug off the state when they started pestering him.

The sheriff slowed down when he got to the approximate location. He saw a patch of trees. Some had been scorched. The Fire Chief's red pick-up truck was parked near them.

He found the track the fire engines had used the night before. A moment later he was out of his Jeep, approaching the senior fireman.

"This is twice inside of a week, George," Lansing said as he walked up. "We have to quit meeting like this."

"Tell me about it, Cliff," Chief Marron agreed.

"What do you have?" Lansing could see where the Fire Chief and one of his helpers had pulled away part of the fallen roof. It looked like they had partially uncovered a car. "Is that a car in there?"

"Actually, there's two," Marron admitted. "And it looks like we need to get an ambulance out here."

"Why?"

"That car we've uncovered has a body inside."

Lansing stepped closer for a better look. The blackened remains of a human could be seen slumped over the steering wheel. "Son of a bitch!"

"Can't tell if it's a man or a woman, at this point," the Fire Chief continued. "We're going to need a few more people out here to clear away the debris."

"I'll see what I can do." Lansing walked back to his patrol unit and contacted dispatch. It took some doing, but he managed to commandeer a county road crew working just outside Cohino. EMS, the road crew and Deputy Cortez were all on the scene within an hour.

An hour after that, both cars were uncovered. Danny Cortez was able to retrieve the license plate and VIN numbers. EMS recovered the charred remains of the hapless driver. Chief Marron made a preliminary judgement that the blaze was arson, citing four separate spots where fires were initiated.

EMS was told to store the body at the funeral home cold room. He would ask the Santa Fe morgue to handle the autopsy.

Deputy Cortez came over from his patrol unit, a notepad in his hand. "We found the owners of the cars. The first one was stolen out of Cohino about a week ago.

"The one with the body—That one belongs to Jack Rivera."

"You have to be kidding me!" Lansing exclaimed. "I'll bet you a hundred bucks that was Poncho Chamorro's body they just hauled off."

"Wouldn't that be convenient," Cortez said.

"It's been a long weekend," the sheriff assessed. "It's about time we caught a break!"

# Chapter Fifty-Four

More and more, Lansing was appreciating his cell phone. No more answering machines. No more notes on his desk to call someone. Many times, no more answering the phone and talking to someone you were trying to avoid. That was the convenience of "Caller ID" and "Voice Mail." Also, he didn't need a landline for someone to contact him if they had news.

The sheriff was driving back to his office when he got a call from Rob Beltran, the vet.

"I suspected some sort of toxin poisoning when I saw the horses stumbling yesterday," Beltran began. "I sent your samples over to the Agriculture Extension office first thing this morning. There's a quick test they can do to check for alkaloids."

"What would alkaloids mean, if they showed up?" Lansing asked.

"They'd be a strong indication of ergot contamination. It looks to me your entire bag of feed oats were spoiled."

"I've never heard of oats getting ergot poisoning."

"It's rare," the vet admitted. "Very rare. But it normally occurs under damp, moist conditions."

"My barn hardly qualifies."

"I know," Beltran agreed. "When did you open that bag?"

"Friday. A fifty-pound bag lasts me six days."

"I think those spores were introduced after you opened your bag. And I don't think those were your run of the mill, household ergot spores."

"What do you mean?"

"I had to do a little research, but your horses looked like they had 'paspalum staggers.' "

"What the hell is that?"

"It's a rye-grass ergot poisoning. Usually shows up in cattle. Occasionally horses come down with it, though. It takes about two days to kick in."

"I've never heard of it."

"I'm not surprised. The 'staggers' is restricted to Australia. But the paspalum toxin is what we call a 'tremorgenic mycotoxin.' You can get the same effects from certain penicillium bacteria."

"What's that in layman's terms?"

"It's related to bread-mold. Someone introduced the mold after you opened the bag. Stirred it around with a couple of cups of water. Left it in your dark barn and let nature take its course."

"So, this was no accident."

"Oh, no," the vet concluded. "Not by a long-shot. The Ag extension is sending your sample to UNM. They'll try to identify the exact culprit."

"Is there a cure?"

"Yep . . . Quit feeding your horses the contaminated grain."

"That's it?"

"That's it."

Lansing was pulling into his parking space behind the Law Enforcement Annex. "Thanks for the news, Doc. I'll talk to you later."

Back inside his offices, he discovered the Day Room had been vacated by the 9-1-1 operators. Clem Montoya at the front desk smiled.

"Sure is quiet around here," the Desk Sergeant observed.

"When did they leave?"

"The last one left about forty-five minutes ago," Marilyn chimed in. "They went over to the school one at a time, so that there was minimal interruption."

"Did anyone tell Jack we found his car?"

"No," Clem admitted. "Not, yet."

"He's supposed to drop my truck keys by. I'll tell him then."

The sheriff went back to his office. Since he hadn't heard from Tina Morales, he took out his cell and dialed the number she'd input.

"This is Tina," she answered.

"Yes, Miss Morales. Sheriff Lansing. I'm back at my office, if you want to stop by."

"That sounds good. There was only a half-day of school. I'm waiting for Oscar."

"All right," the sheriff replied. "I'll see you then."

His next call was Sheriff Clem Juarez. What was Ramirez's status? No operation, yet. Had to wait until the swelling went down

It was nearly noon before Jack Rivera stopped in to return Lansing's keys.

"Thanks for the loan of your truck, Cliff. I still need to do some painting, but we're in good shape, now."

"There's good news and bad news about your car," Lansing said. "The good news is we found it. The bad news is it was destroyed in a barn fire last night."

"Actually, that's good news all the way around," the deputy admitted, after a pause. "The insurance company said I had to wait ninety days after the car was stolen before I could file a claim. All I need now is a police report."

"Danny's going to fill out the report this afternoon. He also has photos, if you need them for your claim."

"Where's the car? My insurance agent can go take his own damn photos. The S.O.B. can earn his money, for a change."

Lansing showed him on a map. Rivera thanked him and left. Ten minutes later, Oscar Vega knocked on Lansing's door sill.

The sheriff looked up. "Oh, hi, Oscar. Where's Miss Morales?"

"She's outside. She's afraid to come in the building."

"Why?"

"She said it's been cursed!"

# Chapter Fifty-Five

Lansing found the school teacher standing outside the double, glass doors. She stared at the entrance, clutching her arms, as if she was cold. Her eyes were wide. She was afraid of something.

"What's wrong?" he asked.

"It's your building—I'm not sure. It's just a feeling I'm getting."

Lansing looked from her, to his offices, and back. "It's just a building."

"No, it's more than that . . . as soon as I touched the door handle, I felt a chill run up my arm. I sense . . ."

"Oscar said you think it's cursed."

She gave Lansing a hard look. "Have bad things been happening around here?"

"It's a sheriff's office. Bad things happen all the time."

"I'm not talking about crimes you look into. I'm talking about the people who work here. Have bad things been happening to them?"

The sheriff was ready to deny that anything was wrong. Instead, he took a moment and reconsidered. "Maybe we need to go somewhere and talk."

"Where?"

Since his office wasn't an option, the sheriff suggested *Paco's Cantina*. Neither was hungry, but they could feed Oscar and carry on a discussion while the teenager ate.

Lansing took his Jeep. Tina followed in her car with Oscar in tow.

They found a table off to the side. All three ordered soft drinks. Oscar was thrilled at being invited to lunch. He knew what he wanted: The Enchilada Platter.

"I get the sense something did happen," Morales started. "Or else we wouldn't be here."

Lansing tried to get his thoughts organized before starting. "Saturday afternoon, one of my officers was grazed by a car. He was the one I was seeing at the clinic when I ran into you.

"Then Sunday another deputy was hit broadside. The accident totaled his unit and put him in the hospital. I don't know when he's coming back to work.

"I can expect a couple of accidents like that in a year. But in two days?" He shook his head. "I just don't know."

"What about the fire at the 9-1-1 Call Center?" she suggested.

"Yeah," Lansing agreed. "That was Friday night."

"Has anything else happened to any of your other deputies?"

Lansing recounted Jack Rivera's ordeal. That started Friday night as well—thinking he had lost his family. Fortunately, they were safe in Trinidad, Colorado. The day after he gets them home, though, they are attacked. Presumably by Poncho Chamorro.

With the distraction of Tina's fears over his offices, her ex-boyfriend had slipped his mind. "Speaking of Chamorro, we think we found his body, this morning?"

"Where?"

He told her about the barn, the burned vehicles and the body. Morales let the news sink in. She thought it was almost too good to be true. She navigated the conversation back to the original topic.

"The cat that was killed—Didn't it belong to the lady that works in your office?"

"Yes," the sheriff agreed. He thought for a moment. "Then there's Danny Cortez's son. He nearly drowned Sunday."

"How about your horses?" Oscar asked, working his way through his platter. He was half-listening to their conversation. "That's something bad that happened to you, Sheriff."

"That's true," Tina agreed.

"I talked to the vet this morning. Someone mixed mold spores into the horses feed intentionally."

"When did that happen?"

"After I opened the bag Friday."

"Has anything else happened?"

Lansing pondered. Then looked up. "Saturday, my ex-wife and son were car jacked. They managed to get away . . ."

"But still . . ." Morales concluded. "Something happened. Something bad happened." She took a sip through her straw while she stared blankly at the table. "Everything seems to have started Friday." She looked straight at Lansing. "What happened Thursday?"

The sheriff considered the question, then, "I came here to eat dinner."

"Before that. What did you do that day?"

"It was just a regular day. The only thing different was I took a short trip outside of town. I needed to contact an old woman about her son. He had died in prison."

"Who is this 'old woman?' "

"Her name is Berta Chavez."

"What do you know about her?"

"She was married to a Jicarilla Apache man. They ran her off the reservation when they thought she killed her husband. They said she was a *bruja*."

Tina's expression became grim. "What did you say to her?"

"I didn't say anything. She wasn't home."

"Why was her son in prison?"

Lansing recounted how Bernardino Chavez killed a fellow student, how he was arrested and eventually convicted.

"As far as I know, she doesn't even know he's dead, yet," he concluded.

"She knows," Morales said, decisively. "You said you came here to eat that night. Tell me everything that happened."

"Everything?"

"Yes."

Lansing admitted strange things started happening as soon as he got out of his vehicle. A bird crapped on him and his hat. No, he couldn't tell what kind of bird. He thought it was big, though. He cleaned off the mess when he got inside.

Then, while he was drinking a beer, a pretty, young lady came up and introduced herself. She sat and they talked for a long time. She claimed to be the niece of a former deputy, which later turned out to be a lie.

Anyway, when it was time to leave, he felt too drunk to drive. The two spent the night at the Las Palmas Inn. Evidently, she drove. Nothing happened when they got there. He woke early, still wearing his clothes.

He went home. Came back later. She was gone.

"I talked to the people at the motel. I talked to Paco the next morning. No one remembers seeing this woman"

"Doesn't that strike you as being strange?" Tina asked. "You were the only one who saw her?"

"But I know she was there. I know she was real," the sheriff insisted. "When I went back to the motel, I found the necklace she was wearing."

"What did it look like?"

"It was a single turquois stone, shaped like a tear. It was on a braided, silver chain."

"I've heard of those. Did she call it *Lagrima de la Madre*?"

"That's exactly what she called it."

179

"It's a *perverso amuleto* . . ." Morales said, darkly. "It's an evil charm."

Lansing looked at the teacher suspiciously. "How do you know all this stuff?"

Tina hesitated. "Since I was small, I was taught about these things—by my mother, by my grandmother. I'm a *curandera*, just like they are. Specifically, I'm a *yerbera*."

"You're a witch?" Oscar asked, wide eyed.

"Not exactly," Morales corrected. "I'm a healer. *Yerberas* are taught to use herbal remedies. However, we're also taught how to fight evil, if necessary."

"I've seen you at Saint James," Lansing observed. "Doesn't what you do fly in the face of Catholic teachings?"

"Not in the church I was raised. When the Spanish introduced Catholic doctrine to Mexico a lot of native beliefs were absorbed. As a *curandera*, my ultimate purpose is to fight evil, the same as the church. I see no conflict."

The sheriff looked at his companion doubtfully. It had been a long time since he had given "Catholic doctrine" a lot of thought. He didn't think he was in a position to argue its finer points.

"This necklace," Tina asked. "Where is it now?"

"Back in my offices. In the evidence locker."

"Sheriff, I'm going to tell you what I believe has been happening. You may believe me. You may not. But, please, don't take what I say lightly."

# Chapter Fifty-Six

*Bigo's Bar and Grill* on Pedro Cardenas Avenue was barely two blocks from the Matamoros Federal Police Headquarters. Decena was a frequent visitor. Now a retired lieutenant, Arturo Guzman Decena had once commanded the Matamoros Federal Judicial Police. His radio code had been "Z1"—"Zeta Uno." He still had very close ties to the Federal forces.

It was by accident that Osiel Cardenas Guillen and he met. They were both avid *futbol* fans. It was during an exhibition match between Guadalajara and Pachuco *Futbol* Clubs a year earlier that the two struck up an acquaintance. They had known each other for six months before they learned of each other's background. By then Decena was retired and not a threat to Guillen's business.

The former police lieutenant lamented the fact that his retirement income was lacking. He needed a way to supplement his income. Guillen had a solution. His idea, though, was much grander than Decena merely joining the cartel ranks.

Osiel Cardenas began having doubts about Humberto Garcia's ability to run the Gulf Cartel from the outset. Since his consolidation of power, though, Abrego's capacity to command had given way to blind vengeance. Guillen had taken over the day-to-day cartel operations, but everything he did needed Humberto's final approval. Abrego was nothing more than a hindrance to the Gulf Cartel business.

Too many cartel soldiers were still loyal to the Abrego name. Guillen needed a force loyal to him to attempt a coup. That's where Arturo Guzman came in. The Federal Police or army salary was nothing compared to what the cartel offered. Arturo had lured 30 members of *Grupo*

*Aeromovil de Fuerzas Especiales*, Mexican Army special forces, to join him. They would provide the muscle to oust Abrego from his position.

Decena knew the cartel had over 1,000-foot soldiers spread out over their territory. But there were only 100 in Matamoros. Those were the ones that needed to be contained. The former police lieutenant wasn't worried. One hundred street thugs were no match for 30, highly trained, special forces soldiers. Once Matamoros was in their hands, they controlled the entire cartel.

"My people will be ready by Thursday," Decena said, sitting across the table from Osiel Cardenas.

"That's good," Guillen nodded. The reason for the accelerated timeline was to prevent another massacre at a monastery, this one in the United States.

"How do you know this? I thought you said Humberto cut you out of the loop."

"My only concern is the cartel. If I have to bug *El Jeffe's* office to make sure business runs smoothly, then that's what I must do." He punctuated the statement with a shrug. "The problem I have is de los Santos and his squad are already in the States. They're retrieving their weapons from our supplier in Houston today."

"So, tell the supplier not to give them the weapons," Decena suggested.

"Humberto would know something was going on if I did that."

"Where is this monastery that de los Santos plans to visit?"

"It's in northern New Mexico. From Houston, it's nine hundred and fifty miles. I know de los Santos. He moves quickly. Today's Tuesday. His squad could be there by tomorrow night."

"You can't recall him?"

"De los Santos takes orders from no one but Abrego. Santiago and his hit squads were how Humberto retained power. In fact, de los Santos could have been sitting in my position, but he didn't want a desk job. He likes killing too much!"

"So how are you going to stop him?"

"The gringos will have to do it."

"How? They don't even know he's coming," the former police lieutenant observed.

"I guess I'll have to tell them, won't I?"

"Who are you going to talk to? The FBI? The Texas Rangers?"

"They probably switched to cars having US plates. Texas Highway Patrol wouldn't know what to look for. The FBI has too many leaks. Word would get back to Humberto."

Guillen considered his options. "I'll contact the local authorities. Make it clear that what de los Santos is doing is not cartel sanctioned. It is a rogue operation. Let them handle the situation.

"If they can stop him, great. If they can't? Not my problem!"

# Chapter Fifty-Seven

Lansing stopped Morales from continuing her explanation about what she thought was going on.

"Oscar, look at me," the sheriff ordered. The boy looked up from his nearly empty plate. "Everything that's been said at this table doesn't leave the restaurant. Do you understand?"

"But, why?" the boy was truly surprised at the command.

"What I said about things happening to my deputies—That's strictly my office's concern. No one else's. I don't want people to talk about Mrs. Chavez being a *bruja* or this supposed evil charm. And I certainly don't want people running around saying Miss Morales is a witch."

"Can I at least tell my brother?"

"No!" Lansing said in a hoarse whisper. "Not even your parents." He looked around. "Would you like to work full time at my ranch this summer?"

"Sure! That'd be great."

"One of my front acres needs to get plowed for hay. The horses need a lot more exercise than they've been getting . . . Plus, there's some painting to get done. But you're only getting the job if you keep your mouth shut. Is that clear?"

"Yes, sir."

Tina Morales understood the sheriff's concerns. If people saw Berta Chavez as a threat, her life could be threatened. After all, there was only conjecture that she was responsible for a string of unlucky situations. As for herself, just one complaint from one parent that she was a witch, even if she was a *curandera,* would end her career at Las Palmas—maybe end her career as an educator completely.

Oscar finished his lunch. The plan was for the teen to drive the sheriff's personal truck back to the ranch. Morales would follow later in her car. Lansing and the teacher stood in the parking lot behind the Law Enforcement annex and watched the boy drive off.

"I'm not saying I buy into this whole *bruja*/curse theory, yet," Lansing said. "But I thought about something driving over here. You've been hinting the people in my office have been cursed because Bernardino Chavez died in prison. Berta's holding us responsible for his death."

"Yes. That's what I think is happening," Tina nodded.

"Anna Menendez—The Las Palmas Inn?"

"The bird that messed on you was an owl. You were under Berta's influence—her spell—while you had that bird crap on you." She paused to let that sink in. "I believe Berta Chavez is more powerful than you might think. She somehow sensed what I am. She considers me a threat. The Great Horned owl is her animal spirit. That's why one attacked me Saturday."

"Well, this goes along with your theory. The judge who presided over the trial, Jason Mateo, was killed this past weekend."

"How did he die?"

"He was stung to death by a swarm of bees in his own back yard."

"Is that unusual?"

"I would call it a first for San Phillipe County."

"You're making my case for me, Sheriff."

"Okay. Let's say I do have a *perverso amuleto* in my evidence locker. What am I supposed to do? Destroy it? Take a hammer and pound it to dust."

"Just destroying it wouldn't lift the curse. Even if Berta Chavez were to die, the curse wouldn't be lifted."

"All right, teacher. What am I supposed to do?"

"First, you have to remove it from your building . . ."

"I'll go get it right now."

"If you just take it out of there, Berta will know. She'll replace it with something else. You'll have to block her ability to sense where the *amuleto* is located."

"And how do we do that?"

"Find a box. A small box, but something large enough to hold the necklace. Something lead lined would be ideal. We'll have to settle with aluminum foil. Take it to the church. Have it blessed and sprinkled with Holy Water.

"Then take the container back to your offices. Wrap the necklace in aluminum foil as well. Put it inside the box. Then you can remove it from your locker."

"What do I do with the box? Bury it?"

"Even burying it in consecrated ground like a graveyard would not end the curse. A curse is an evil thing. And Evil feeds on itself. The curse is imbedded in the *amuleto*. Only Berta Chavez can lift it . . . or, the *perverso amuleto* can be exorcized on holy ground, then destroyed."

"Fine. I'll get the box, put the necklace in it and take it back to the church. Father Roberto can do the exorcism. Then I'll pound the *amuleto* into dust."

"It can't be here. It can't be done in Las Palmas. Berta will know where the necklace is as soon as it's out of the box. You need to take it away from here."

"Where do you suggest?"

"*St. Anthony's Monastery in the Canyon.* Have you been there?"

"Of course. It's been a few years. I was down there in the early Ninety's, just after they consecrated the new church."

"I know Abbot Christian. I think if I can explain to him the problem, he would be willing to help. The stone altar in their church would be ideal for destroying the *amuleto* for good."

"Can I ask you a favor?"

"Sure."

"I have to go back and do some sheriff work. Can you handle finding a box and getting it blessed this afternoon?"

"I can do that."

# Chapter Fifty-Eight

The joy Brother Esteban experienced with his work early in the day had evaporated. He listlessly went about his chores with a weariness that bordered on despair. At Sext, just before lunch was served, Abbot Christian made the announcement. Their brothers *at Monasterio Benedicto de Santa Maria Magdelena* had all been murdered that morning. Some of the monks knew already. Most didn't. All were shocked.

Of course, Esteban was not present for the announcement. He was banned from the refectory where the monks had their meals. Part of his punishment was he ate away from the others. He was consigned to a table in the kitchen.

During the next week he would attend all the required offices of the day. But he would have to sit apart from the other men. They sat in their regular alcoves. He sat alone in the visitor's alcove.

Eucharist adoration began at 5:15, followed by Vespers at 5:50.

Esteban only half listened to the prayers and psalms. His thoughts were completely consumed by the approaching Evil. He was entirely convinced the deaths in Mexico were his fault. His dreams came to him as God's way to alert the brethren. He couldn't understand Abbot Christian's refusal to accept his view. What was worse was the Abbot's notion that no Evil would touch their monastery.

The monk sincerely regretted leaving the monastery the way he did. If he had only talked to the Abbot first. If he had only warned him of the Evil.

It was Vespers. Abbot Christian called for a prolonged prayer of intercession on behalf of their fallen brothers.

During his silent prayers, tears streamed down Esteban's face. That feeling of guilt that wrenched his guts so many years ago was back.

Unlike then, he knew what the feeling was now . . . and he understood why. He despaired.

Evil was coming.

Evil was coming soon . . . and he couldn't stop it.

# Chapter Fifty-Nine

It was nearly 7:00 by the time Lansing got to his ranch that evening. His truck and Morales' Chevy were parked in front. No one was in the ranch house, but he could smell something good cooking in the kitchen. He found a pot of beef stew simmering on the kitchen stove.

His guess was the other two were in the barn or at the corral. He found them sitting on the corral fence watching the horses. All three animals looked like they were fully recovered from the previous night.

"Oh, hi!" Tina said when she saw the sheriff walking up. "Oscar was telling me about your horses. I thought the story about how Cement Head got his name was funny. And Little Orphan Annie . . . where'd you get a name like that?"

"Her original owner liked the musical '*Annie*.' That's usually what I call her—Annie."

"Oscar said she's just a pony. Then he said you've already had her four years. How can she still be a 'pony?' "

" 'Pony' doesn't refer to age. It refers to height. The withers is part of the back above the front legs of a horse. It's where the neck starts. A horse is called a horse if it's fifty-eight inches tall or taller at the withers. If it's shorter than that a horse is called a pony."

"Annie is only thirteen hands at the withers."

"I know nothing about horses," Tina admitted. "I'm a city girl. Now, what's a hand?"

"Theoretically, if you hold your hand flat," Lansing demonstrated by holding his hand flat with his fingers together, "that's the distance from the top of your thumb to the bottom part of your hand."

Morales held up her hand and compared it to the sheriff's. "Your hand is an inch wider than mine. How do they standardize it?"

"Somewhere, someone decided a 'hand' was four inches. So, Annie is fifty-two inches high at the withers, which makes her a pony."

"You like horses, don't you." It was more of a statement than a question on Tina's part.

Lansing nodded. "With horses, you know what to expect. People, not so much."

"Oh, shoot," Morales said, jumping down from the wooden fence. "The stew! It's time to eat, gentlemen."

Lansing and Oscar washed up and joined Morales at the dining room table. Tina dished their plates. The teenager dug in immediately.

"I have to admit, it's been a long time since breakfast . . . I'm starving and this smells great."

Tina smiled. "I hope you enjoy it."

The sheriff relished his first bite. He seldom got good, homecooked meals. "By the way, how's your arm doing?"

"I'm supposed to get the stiches out tomorrow. My arm doesn't hurt. It mostly itches now."

Lansing was reluctant to discuss much in front of the Vega boy, so he tried to talk around the issue. "Were you able to find the box you needed?"

"I did," the teacher admitted. She understood what the sheriff was doing. "By the way, I stopped by St. James'. Father Roberto was in Santa Fe. The Archdiocese was having a one-day conclave of all the parish priests. They said he'd be back in the morning."

"Speaking of tomorrow morning—I'm going to Santa Fe. I have a deputy at Christus Saint Frances. He's supposed to have surgery tomorrow or Thursday. I want to check up on him. Make sure he doesn't need anything."

"Does he have any family close by?"

"His folks are in Church Rock, just east of Gallup. I'm a lot closer than they are. Besides, how can I expect respect from my men if I don't show them respect, as well."

When supper was finished, the men cleared the table and did dishes while the teacher prepared a pot of coffee. Once everything was finished the adults escaped to the front porch while Oscar looked for something good on TV.

Lansing took a sip of coffee. It was dark, already. "That bus crash outside of Raton Friday night . . . Do you think Berta Chavez could have caused that? I mean almost eighty people were killed. Is she that powerful?"

"No. I mean I hope not. I can't believe she knew that mother and daughter were on board. I think the crash was a very unfortunate coincidence."

"But Deputy Cortez's son nearly drowning and the Rivera home invasion—Did she cause those?"

"The drowning, yes. The home invasion. She orchestrated that. I'll bet you she found out about Poncho in the clinic. A lock, on a door or a pair of handcuffs, is nothing to a *bruja*. She sprung him, so he could do her bidding."

"Why would he?"

"She most likely gave him a potion. Something to control him. We know he did the home invasion."

"Yeah," Lansing agreed. "That's why I think Poncho is dead. The burned body was found in the car taken in the home invasion."

"I think Poncho was the one who killed Halley and Joe's dog. Berta did that as a warning to me," she admitted. "Keep away."

"The cat?"

"More punishment for your office."

"The judge, the two deputies hit by cars?"

"I think that was all her work."

"What about my horses? That wasn't a curse. Someone intentionally contaminated the feed."

"That was Berta, as well. Those ergot spores were incubated by someone who knew what they were doing. That's exactly the kind of evil she would concoct."

"Why didn't the boy drown?"

"Maybe her intent wasn't to kill him. She wants to drive the parent insane. They're going to wake up every day, now, wondering 'is this the day I lose my child?' "

"That would drive me nuts," Lansing agreed. Then, out of nowhere, he asks, "How does a *curandera* become a teacher?"

"I have to make a living. Besides, being a chemistry teacher goes hand-in-hand with *curandera* knowledge. Pharmacists are chemists. Compound pharmacies mix up their own medicines. A pinch of this and a sprinkling of that, combined in a *molcajete* and ground with a *maja*. That's what I do. Pharmacists use a mortar and pestle . . . same as me." She studied the lawman. "How did you become a sheriff?"

"I left Las Palmas to go to college." He found himself comfortable talking with this lady. "I had a scholarship, or else I don't think I would have gone. Anyway, my older brother was going to run the ranch. I needed a career since I wasn't going to be a rancher. Took a criminal justice course. Found it interesting. Took another, then another. Took Sociology courses on criminology.

"Before I knew it I had a criminal justice degree with a minor in crim-inology. I could have been a lawyer or a cop. I didn't want any more college. Besides I wanted to get married. So, I went to the Albuquerque Police Academy, then joined the police force.

"Boy, is there a difference between theory and application. I learned more in my first year on the streets than I did in four years of college." He finished his cup of coffee.

"Do you like being a sheriff?"

"Yes, Miss Morales," Lansing said, standing. "Yes, I do."

"Sheriff, I think it's all right if you call me 'Tina.' At least while we're alone."

"In that case, I expect you to call me 'Cliff.' "

"Deal," she replied, standing, as well. "More coffee?"

# Chapter Sixty

There was a light rap on the open, door frame. Leroy Ramirez looked up from his breakfast. "Sheriff! What are you doing here?"

"I just wanted to make sure my deputy was being taken care of," Lansing said, stepping into the room.

Ramirez looked uncomfortable. His left leg, bandaged, but not tightly, was immobilized with firm, sponge-lined supports. However, he didn't appear to be in pain.

"My dad always said he couldn't stand hospitals," Ramirez admitted. "Now I know why."

"Are they mistreating you?"

"No, it's not that. They just don't let you get any sleep," the deputy complained. "They come in at midnight to take your temperature and blood pressure. Then they come around at four and do the same thing. Then, just when you doze off, somebody wakes you so they can draw your blood."

"Are you hurting?"

"Not so much. I think they have me on morphine. It's good stuff. I see why people become addicts." He saw the look on his boss' face. "Don't worry, sheriff. It's not that good."

"Go ahead and finish eating. I'll just sit down."

"Sure, go ahead. But don't worry about my breakfast. The only thing I had left was this cold, wet goop. I think they called it cream-of-wheat, whatever the heck that is."

Lansing sat next to the bed. "So, Leroy, have they said when they might operate?"

"Probably, this afternoon. The swelling's down. They're just not sure if one operation will be enough."

"How about your folks. Have they come by?"

"I guess the office called them Sunday afternoon after the accident. They spent most of Monday with me, it being a holiday and everything. My dad had to go back to work, but they said they'd be back this weekend."

"That's great!"

Lansing's visit lasted for an hour. He informed his deputy on most of what had happened over the last few days. He intentionally omitted Tina Morales' theory about why the accident happened. Ramirez had enough on his plate without worrying about being cursed.

The sheriff reassured him there was a job waiting for him when he got back. The deputy's only concern should be to get healed up.

Back in his patrol unit, Lansing knew talking to his office over the radio was impossible. He found trying to get a phone signal in Santa Fe was just as bad. If he finally did get a signal, it would last a few blocks at best. To talk to anyone, he would have to wait until he got back into San Phillipe County.

***

"San Phillipe Sheriff's Office," Marilyn said. "Can I help you?"

"I need to speak to your sheriff." The voice at the other end had a heavy Mexican accent.

"He's not in the office, right now. Can I take a message?"

The caller hesitated, then, "My name is Osiel Cardenas Guillen. I represent a group of businessmen associated with the Gulf Cartel in Matamoros, Mexico. I am calling you to warn you there will soon be an attack on your district."

"What!?" the dispatcher exclaimed.

"This attack will be conducted by a rogue element from the cartel, but they do not represent the cartel. I want to make that clear."

"Okay. Fine. You're not responsible! What about this attack?" Marilyn didn't have to worry about writing the information down. Calls coming into her position were automatically recorded.

"There was an attack against the *Monasterio Benedicto de Santa Maria Magdelena* on Monday in San Miguel de Allende. All the *monjes* were killed."

"You mean the monks?"

"*Si*, the monks. The same men who did that raid, they are coming to your jurisdiction for the same reason."

"Who are they? Who are they going to attack?"

"The man's name is Santiago de los Santos. He will have at least four men with him. Maybe more. They are going to *Monasterio San Antonio en el Cañón*. They are looking for a man. His name is Esteban Fuentes. They will kill him and, probably, everyone else."

"When?" Marilyn was becoming desperate. "When is this supposed to happen?"

"Soon," Guillen predicted. "Very soon."

With that, the representative of a "group of businessmen" terminated the call.

Marilyn looked at Clem Montoya, the desk sergeant. He had been listening intently to her end of the conversation. "We need to get hold of the sheriff!" she reported.

"What's going on?" Montoya asked.

"It sounds like some hit men are on their way to *Saint Anthony's Monastery*. He has to stop them!"

197

# Chapter Sixty-One

It was 10:00 am when Lansing crossed the Santa Fe/San Phillipe county line. That's when he got the report about Guillen's call. His first question was, did anyone contact the monastery to check on them.

No.

Then find a number and call them. Make sure they're all right. But, don't alarm them about a possible attack    .

Just before he reached the turn off for National Forest Road 262, the dead-end track to *St. Anthony's*, Marilyn reported back. Everything was fine at the monastery. The sheriff was grateful for that. A detour to-and-from the cloister would cost him at least an hour. If the call from Mexico was real, he would need back-up.

From his first conversation with his dispatcher, Lansing employed his lights and siren. He covered the 45 miles from the county line to Las Palmas in just over 30 minutes. The first thing he requested was to listen to Marilyn's taped conversation. It troubled him immensely.

"You need to call the monastery again," the sheriff instructed. "We need to find out if there is an Esteban Fuentes there.

"Before you do that," he said, as he hurried to his back office, "get me DPS on the line. I need to talk to the State Police. Be ready to play them the recording."

His first conversation was with State Police Captain Miguel Puente, commander of District 7 out of Segovia. Puente listened to the recording. He wasn't sure what should be done. He recommended the sheriff contact Puente's superiors in Santa Fe. Probably the Bureau of Special Investigations.

The SBI had always been a thorn in Lansing's side. He had never had a pleasant experience with them, dating back to his days as a deputy. He called them up, nonetheless.

Special Agent Darwin took the call and listened to the tape.

"Sheriff, are you sure this isn't a prank call?" the Special agent asked.

"My dispatcher checked. There is a monk at *St. Anthony's* by the name of Esteban Fuentes."

"That doesn't make the call less of a hoax—Besides, what do you expect the State Police to do?"

"If there's a cartel hit squad on its way to my county, I expect the State Police to back me up."

"You don't know when or even *if* this 'hit squad' is going to show up."

"There's only one road in-and-out from the monastery. It's fifteen miles long. Give me three, four men. We can put up a blockade. Stop anyone from coming in."

"I'll tell you what, Sheriff. I'm going to pass this along to the DEA. They know all about the drug cartels. If there's a guy by the name of Guillen running the Gulf Cartel, they would know . . ."

"But . . ." Lansing protested.

"We'll give you a call back when we hear anything." With that, Special Agent Darwin terminated the call.

Lansing slammed the phone into its cradle.

Outside came the wail of a fire engine siren!

# Chapter Sixty-Two

The Las Palmas Middle/High School held graduation ceremonies in the school gym. Twenty-three seniors were graduating. There had been ample discussions about when the ceremonies should take place: morning, afternoon, evening or the weekend. It was agreed, finally, that the commencement would be 11:00 am, Wednesday morning.

Memorial Day had been an inconvenience to everyone. That was Monday. The half-day of school on Tuesday was designated as awards day. Wednesday was graduation. Everyone in the district would have been happy with graduation the previous Friday, but the state school board required X-number of school days each year. So, everyone had to come back for two more days after the long weekend.

The set-up in the gym was modest. A three-foot high platform with a podium faced the bleachers. The graduates sat in folding chairs facing the stage. Guest speaker was William Rangel, a 1980 Las Palmas High graduate who now anchored local news in El Paso. He would assist in handing out the diplomas.

Of the 23 graduates, 10 already had jobs lined up. Three were going to college. Four were going into the military. The remaining six didn't have a clue about their future. No one wore the traditional "cap-and-gown." The nearest rental outfit was in Santa Fe and that was 80 miles away. Instead, girls wore dresses. Boys wore long-sleeved shirts with ties. (Sometimes, ties had to be borrowed, but they all found ties, somewhere.)

Families, friends, teachers and visitors sat in the bleachers. Counting the graduates, guest speaker and Father Roberto, newly returned from Santa Fe, 115 people were present.

Principal de la Cruz stood at the podium and asked everyone to take their seats. Once the crowd was seated and quiet, Father Roberto walked up to the microphone to present the invocation.

Down the hallway was the library. The five, day-time 9-1-1 operators had been at their temporary location for barely 24-hours. The surroundings were unfamiliar and uncomfortable. The new occupants hoped their stay would be short.

Mary Portales answered her next call, "Nine-One-One, how can I help you?"

Instead of a voice, she got the screeching sound of a bird of prey. It was so loud she had to rip the earphones from her head. A moment later, the other four operators threw their headsets on the tables.

"What the Hell was that?" one of the other operators screamed.

Portales looked at her associates in terror, then exclaimed, "Do you smell that?"

The operator who had screamed ran to the library door and threw it open. The hallway was filling with smoke. She screamed again: "FIRE!"

There was a red fire alarm next to the exit. Portales pulled the lever, then yelled at the others, "Get out!"

Father Roberto had just finished his prayer when the fire alarm sounded. Instead of panicking, de la Cruz made the quick determination someone was pulling a prank.

"Coach," he yelled, addressing Mr. Moran, the athletics director. "Go see if you can cut that damn thing off."

The gathering waited for the interruption to end while Coach Moran headed for the exit. He came running back onto the stage and said something to de la Cruz. The principal immediately addressed the crowd.

"Everyone, please! Listen to me. This is not a drill. There is an exit to the outside to my right. Everyone, stand and leave the building in an orderly fashion. Now!"

Surprisingly, no one panicked. The exit dumped everyone out on the side of the school opposite the parking lot. They heard glass break as fire shot out a classroom window at the end of the building.

"That's my room!" Tina Morales yelled.

Since there was nothing the science teacher could do with her box or the *perverso amuleto* until the good Father returned from Santa Fe, she decided to attend the graduation ceremony. The fire alarm was jolting. The fact that the fire was in her own classroom, even more so.

The fire truck was on the scene within five minutes. A hydrant access protruded from the front of the building. The fire had been restricted to Tina's classroom and was out in fifteen minutes. By that time the graduation crowd had relocated to the parking lot.

There was immediate speculation about what caused the fire. Since it had been restricted to one location, arson was suspected. There was also speculation the chemistry teacher hadn't properly secured volatile chemicals. But there were other issues, mostly why didn't the sprinkler system work.

In a way, Principal de la Cruz and Halley Basa were grateful the sprinklers failed. Everything in the school would have been damaged, all the records destroyed, the schoolbooks and library lost.

Then there was the disruption of the 9-1-1 services—again. Someone commented, it was like they were cursed.

# Chapter Sixty-Three

Sheriff Lansing was standing in front of the school when the Fire Chief emerged. "What do we have, George?"

"Looks like arson," Chief Marron said. "Somebody got into the chemistry lab and started a fire outside the storage room. I don't know what kind of chemicals they have stored there, but it could have been a real mess if we got here too late."

"Who pulled the alarm?"

"One of the Nine-One-One operators. They were just down the hall. We kept the fire to one classroom. I don't know how much we would have lost if they hadn't been here."

"What about the graduation ceremony?"

"You'll have to ask the principal."

Looking around, Lansing spotted de la Cruz talking to a group of parents at the far end of the parking lot. As he approached, he caught the tail-end of an argument.

"Coach just checked—The gym is fine!" de la Cruz insisted.

"I don't care," one mother snapped. "I'm not going back in there and neither is my daughter."

"I'm not going back, either," another agreed.

"Can't you just hand out the diplomas out here?" a father asked. "I had to take time off work. I can't hang around here all day."

"All right, all right," de la Cruz crumbled. "Let's ask the seniors what they want. It's their graduation."

He made the announcement that all the graduates gather near him. Once they were assembled, he raised his voice. "Okay, seniors. It's almost noon. Do you want to go back and have your ceremony, or do you want me to just hand out the diplomas?"

"Can we pick them up at the office later?" one boy asked. "I have to be at work at One."

"That's an option," de la Cruz admitted. "Show of hands. Who wants the ceremony?"

A half dozen hands went up. One pulled back down when his neighbor nudged him.

"Fine. We'll cancel the ceremony. Mrs. Basa, could you please get the diplomas."

Halley Basa headed for the gym. De las Cruz asked one of the boys to help her. "Those of you who can't wait for your diploma, you can pick them up at the front office this summer. Call ahead. Make sure someone is there."

The certificates were handed out to all but two of the grads. The crowd dispersed. Most were headed to graduation lunches. Reservations had been made either at *Paco's Cantina* or *The High Desert Restaurant* in Cohino. Many just went home.

As the gathering began to clear, Lansing located Tina Morales.

"It looks to me like Berta Chavez is at it again!" the sheriff said in a low voice. "Chief Marron said the fire was intentionally set."

The teacher nodded. "Yes—and it was no coincidence the fire was in my classroom . . ." She looked around, as if to ensure no one was listening. "I also talked to the Nine-One-One supervisor. Her name is Mary Portales. She said just before they noticed the fire, all five operators got a terrible screeching sound on their headsets. She said it sounded like a wild bird."

"Yes, I know Mary . . . The *bruja* has been busy."

"Father Roberto left before I could talk to him," the teacher confessed. "When I leave here, I'll go straight to St James."

"Good. I'm expecting a call back at my office. Once you have the box taken care of, we can meet there."

Before Lansing could get to his patrol unit, he was intercepted by a very angry woman. "Sheriff, we need to talk."

"Sure, Mary. What's the problem?"

"We need protection!" the 9-1-1 Supervisor demanded. "My operators are not going back in that building unless you have someone on duty twenty-four hours a day to make sure we're not hurt."

"I can't . . ."

"I mean it, Sheriff. Two fires inside of a week? Someone's trying to kill us. We'll all quit before that happens."

The sheriff understood her fears. "Calm down, Mary. You can go back inside. I'll stay right here until I can get a deputy to relieve me. Okay?"

"Okay," she said, frowning but placated. "I'll tell the others to go back to work."

Once he got to his Jeep, Lansing contacted Marilyn. "Dispatch, Patrol One. Do we have any units near the high school?"

"Willie Estrada is heading south, out of Cohino."

"Tell her to meet me in front of the school. Our office has a new assignment. We have to start baby-sitting the Call Center, or else the operators are going to walk."

# Chapter Sixty-Four

Santiago de los Santos had been very precise about his requirements. From J.D. Morgan he wanted ten AR-15s, three loaded magazines each. He also wanted 10 Beretta 83Rs with four loaded clips. Morgan argued Uzi's were easier to get. De los Santos stuck by his order.

He could see on the map *St. Anthony's Monastery* was in an isolated canyon. He had no fear that guns shots would be reported. The intel he collected indicated there would be at least 38 monks . . . maybe a few visitors. The Beretta's were for the close-in work. If people broke and ran, his men would need more range than an Uzi would provide. Hence, the AR-15s. He also needed five walkie-talkies.

His State-side goon squad was back in Houston from Oklahoma City. Santiago recruited them for the New Mexico job, as well. Counting himself, he had ten men. The Houston office needed to provide 5 separate cars. No more than two rentals, and they had to come from different agencies. The other three cars, private, needed permanent plates—and none stolen.

Nothing would look more suspicious than 10 Mexican's piled into two SUVs following each other through the countryside. That would invite too much scrutiny. Instead, they would have two men per car. They would convoy, but spread out over a distance of two miles.

The trip was mapped out. Houston to Amarillo on Wednesday, the first day. That would be the hard push: Nine and a half hours. There would still be another 350 miles to the canyon and the monastery. With an early start, they could rendezvous at the little town of Artiga, by 3:00. De los Santos estimated they would be no more than twenty minutes away from the monastery. They could be at their destination by 3:30, when the monks were gathered for None.

The cartel hit man wasn't necessarily in a hurry. He just didn't like assignments hanging over his head. The sooner they were over and done with, the better.

Santiago de los Santos was unaware of two things: the local sheriff had been told about his mission and that sheriff would use every resource he could muster to stop them.

# Chapter Sixty-Five

Father Roberto was in his office, preparing to go to lunch, when Tina Morales arrived. She knocked at his door. "Father, do you have a minute?"

"Absolutely, Miss Morales. Please come in."

Tina entered the room carrying a cigar box. "I need to ask you a favor."

She explained about the *perverso amuleto*. He wasn't surprised Berta Chavez was involved.

The priest was very familiar with such things. He was from Las Cruces, New Mexico. He had been introduced to evil charms when he was a boy. His own uncle had gotten sick and died because he had rejected the advances of local *bruja*. After the funeral, a strange object—a broken pocket watch—was found under his mattress. The local priest said it was cursed. It caused his uncle's illness.

"I will bless your box," the priest agreed. "But, I have one stipulation. I do not want that atrocity anywhere near my church. I don't have the tools to exorcise a curse from that necklace. If I try and fail, it could bring ruin to my entire parish."

"I promise, Father. Once the *amuleto* is inside the box, I am taking it far from here."

"I don't want to hear any more details. Bring the box into the church. I will bless it on the altar. Then, please, be on your way."

\*\*\*

It was after 1:00 when Lansing got back to his office. There had been no calls from the SBI.

The sheriff sat at his desk, trying to juggle schedules in his head. He could only assign two deputies for full-time Call Center protection. They would have to be on 12-hour shifts. Clem Montoya ran the Sergeant's Desk. Leroy Ramirez was out for who knew how long. That left him six deputies to patrol over 5,800 square miles and not all the territory was paved roads.

San Phillipe county had over 36 separate communities. Some no more than a dozen people. At 5,000 each, Segovia and Las Palmas were the two largest towns. He needed to know how to protect everyone.

He could put 3 deputies on day, 3 at night, but 12-hour shifts were tough duty over the long-haul. He would be a rover, filling in as needed. The Segovia Police Department could handle their own jurisdiction. The same with the Jicarilla Apache Tribal Police. He could ask for State support. Over a 24-hour period, up to 10 State Police cars might be designated for patrol back-up. But that still was thin for over 8,000 miles of road . . . and the State Police would only be on the main highways.

His desk phone rang. "Lansing!" He was expecting his call from the State. Instead, it was Clem Montoya.

"Sheriff, there's a woman at the outside door. She said she has something for you."

Lansing found Tina Morales waiting for him.

"Come inside," the sheriff insisted. "We don't have anything to worry about now . . ."

"If I put one foot in that building, Berta will know. She'll suspect something is going on." She handed him the box, a roll of aluminum foil, and a towel. "Get your necklace. Wrap it in at least two layers of foil, then put it in the box. Wrap the box in foil. Then cover everything with the towel. Bring it to me."

Lansing did as he was instructed. He conducted the entire operation in the Evidence Locker. Then delivered the wrapped box to the teacher.

"What now?" he asked after handing over the *amuleto*.

"I'm taking it to *St. Anthony's*. I'm glad we planned ahead. Father Roberto blessed the box but didn't want anything else to do with it."

"Do you need me to come along?"

"I can handle this. I'm safe as long as the *bruja* doesn't suspect anything."

"Well," the sheriff said, doubtfully. "Call me if you need help. Just remember, once you're in that canyon, there's not going to be any radio or cell phone reception. You'll be on your own."

"I'll remember that." She turned and left.

Back inside the building, Montoya intercepted him. "Sheriff, you have a call. It's the State Bureau of Investigation."

# Chapter Sixty-Six

"Lansing, I want you to know, I took your information very seriously," Special Agent Darwin said. "When I talked to the DEA, I told them that your offices believed the call you got was credible—and that we needed a quick turn-around on their part.

"I believe they put my call on a high priority. They went to their Cartel Division . . . they even went to the FBI. Juan Garcia Abrego ran the Gulf Cartel for almost twenty years. The U.S. put him in prison a couple of years ago. The Feds firmly believe after a two-year fight, his brother, Humberto Abrego, is firmly ensconced as the *Supremo Jeffe* in the Gulf Cartel. And no one has ever heard of this Cardenas Guillen.

"They're not even sure the Monastery murders in San Miguel could have been done by the Gulf Cartel. That area isn't in Cartel territory. It would have been an overreach on their part."

"So, the Feds don't believe me?" Lansing asked, a touch of frustration in his voice.

"They don't doubt that you're concerned. But they think that call was a complete hoax."

"What about your offices?" Lansing felt the rug being pulled out from underneath him. "What do you think?"

"While I was waiting for a call-back from Washington, I talked to a few of the other agents in my office. The consensus was that we had to go along with the Feds. They have a lot more intel than we do. If they thought you were being pranked, we'd have to go along with it."

"Wait a minute," Lansing tried not to sound desperate. "The Feds don't think there's a threat, so you don't think there's a threat?"

"Sheriff, do you realize how many calls this office gets every day?" Darwin asked firmly. "Dozens. We have to put on our B.S. filters constantly to sift through what's credible and what's not. What do you want from me? I went to the Feds. They don't believe anything is going to happen. I'm not recommending State resources for some imagined menace."

"You heard the phone call!" Lansing shot back. "It's not 'imagined.'"

"All I can recommend is that you call us back if something develops."

"Listen, Darwin," the sheriff pleaded. "I'm essentially down three deputies. I need State Police back-up just to patrol my roads. If you could cut loose three Patrol Officers, we could button down that canyon, so no one could get through, no matter how many men the cartel sends."

"I'm sorry about your man-power problems." The Special Agent was losing patience. "There's nothing I can do about that. But I'm not sending anyone—Besides, most of that canyon belongs to the Forest Service. It's not even our jurisdiction."

"So, no help?" Lansing asked, disgusted.

"You're on your own."

Lansing slammed the phone down and headed to the front office.

"Marilyn, I need for you to pull Jack Rivera off patrol. I want him back at the office, immediately."

"What's going on?" Montoya asked.

"The State and the Feds don't believe that call from Mexico was legit."

"What does that mean?" Marilyn sounded concerned.

"It means that if there's an attack on that canyon, *we* have to stop it!"

Marilyn's face clouded over. "You're sending Jack?"

"Hell no . . . He's going to be acting sheriff. I'm going down there . . . and see if you can get State Patrolman Hernandez on the radio. I need to ask him a big favor."

In the small armory, next to the Evidence Locker, Lansing began assembling his arsenal: 3 Colt M4s with 2, 10-round magazines each. The

Colt M4 used .223 shells, which was becoming the industry standard. The bullets were cheaper because more departments used them. Five years earlier, his department was tasked with upgrading their weapons. He could have gone with AR-15s, but he preferred the feel and accuracy of the Colt M4.

For his daily patrol, the sheriff still preferred his Winchester 30-30. But with only a 7-shot capacity, it would be next to useless in a real fire-fight.

As he gathered his weapons, he hoped the Feds were right—there was no real threat. But in his gut, he knew they were wrong.

He put the rifles, magazines and six, flash-bang grenades in his Jeep. He added three walkie-talkies. He also made sure he had a dozen road flares. For a night attack, they could light up the access road.

He was becoming more frustrated. It took an hour for Rivera to get back to the office. Once he got there, Lansing briefed him on what was going on.

"I'm sorry you're stuck with this, Jack, but you have to figure out a schedule. Everyone is going on twelve-hour shifts. One deputy has to be assigned to the Call Center at the High School at all times. If you want to put them on six-hour rotations, that's fine with me.

"You'll have to make sure Night Dispatch knows who's on, who's not."

Rivera thought for a moment. "Those twelve-hour shifts are going to kill us, Cliff. Why don't we activate a couple of our auxiliary deputies? They're always chomping at the bit to do something.

"That way we can keep eight-hour shifts, three men per shift. We can rotate a deputy at the school every four hours."

"I knew there was a reason I named you Chief Deputy," Lansing agreed. "It's your ballgame now."

"Aren't you going to need back-up at the monastery?" Rivera asked.

"I hope not," Lansing admitted. "I haven't been there in about three years. When Road Two-six-two reaches the river, it becomes wide enough for only one car at a time. I think I can set up a choke point or two."

"Then what?"

"Then I try to get them before they get me."

"How long will you be there?"

"Matamoros is a thousand miles from here. The caller didn't say when they left or when they'd get here. I'll give them three days. If they're not here by Saturday morning, I'll have to assume they're not coming."

"That would be a good thing, wouldn't it?"

"Yes," Lansing agreed. "Yes, it would."

# Chapter Sixty-Seven

Before he left the office, Lansing had to coordinate with two other agencies.

He contacted the Carson National Forest Supervisor's office. They were in charge of maintaining all Nation Forest roads in the county. He informed them that Forest Road 262 would be shut down until noon Saturday for a Law Enforcement exercise. He apologized for the late notification. The supervisor didn't have a problem with the inconvenience. Road 262 was one of the lesser used roads in their district.

Next, he talked to the County Road Maintenance office. He needed a "Road Closed" barricade erected at the entrance to Forestry Road 262 from Highway 15. At this late notification, all they could put up was a couple of saw-horses with amber warning lights. The sheriff had to be satisfied with that.

His first stop after leaving his office was the ranch. Oscar was still there.

"I need for you to stay here, Oscar. I'm going to be gone a few days. I need for you to take care of Annie and Paladin."

"What about Cement Head?"

"I'm taking him with me. Help me hook up the horse trailer."

They attached the trailer to his Jeep. Lansing put in his saddle and blanket while Vega filled a couple of buckets with oats. While the sheriff led his horse into the transport, Oscar made an observation.

"Sheriff . . . I don't want to complain, but there isn't any food in your house."

"You can't eat oats?" the rancher joked.

"I don't know. I never tried." He wasn't sure if his boss meant it.

Lansing smiled. "I'll give your folks a call. I think they can arrange something for you."

"Thanks," the boy said, sincerely.

When they closed the trailer gate, Oscar finally asked. "Where are you going?"

"*Rio Cohino* Canyon. I have to take care of some sheriff business."

"Is Miss Morales going to be back today?"

"She should be. I haven't talked to her about it. Maybe she's ready to go back to her place." He shrugged. "She might show up. She might not. If she doesn't, don't worry about it."

Bouncing over the ruts and holes in his access road was a nuisance. It was twice as bad pulling a loaded horse trailer. Lansing promised himself he would have the road graded soon. Of course, that was the same promise he had made himself for the past two years. This time he meant it.

He checked his watch when he pulled onto Highway 15. It was already 4:00 pm. He was supposed to meet State Patrol Officer Marty Hernandez at Four.

"Dispatch, Patrol One."

"This is dispatch," Marilyn responded. "Go ahead."

"Marilyn, see if you can contact State Officer Hernandez. I'm supposed to meet him at National Forest Road Two-sixty-two, but I'm running late."

"Will do. Dispatch out."

***

Hernandez was sitting in his patrol car when Lansing finally arrived. The barricades had not been erected yet. The sheriff parked and got out.

"So, what's this big favor?" Hernandez asked.

216

Lansing tried to summarize the telephone warning, his call to the SBI and the response from the Feds. On top of everything else, he was down three deputies.

"Basically, I'm on my own."

"What about my captain? Did you talk to him?"

"Because of my manning problems, he said he was already going to shift two patrols to cover Highway Sixty-four between Las Palmas and Taos. He couldn't spare anyone else. Besides, he didn't want to buck the higher-ups. If they weren't concerned, neither was he."

Hernandez shook his head. He wanted to make a comment about his superiors but thought better of it. Instead, he asked, "So, what do you want me to do?"

"I just need the State Police to monitor traffic between Segovia and Artiga. I'm expecting at least five hit men. The caller said there could be more. I want you guys to look for anything unusual.

"If there's a car full of Mexicans—or a couple of cars that look suspicious—I want you to pass that along to my dispatch. I don't want you or your other officers to engage. The road department is putting up a 'Road Closed' sign. I know that's not going to stop anyone—but if someone goes through, you'll notice."

"If you're going to be in the canyon, how will you know what's going on?"

"The monastery has a satellite dish. That's how they get phone calls. You talk to dispatch. Dispatch will call them. They'll relay the info to me."

"Does the monastery know about all this?"

"They're getting ready to find out." Lansing turned and got back in his Jeep.

# Chapter Sixty-Eight

It was nearly 3:00 pm when Tina Morales reached the visitor's parking area. She grabbed the towel-wrapped box and hurried the 200 yards to the monastic complex. At the visitor's reception office, she found Brother John Mkubu, the Guestmaster.

"Brother John, I don't know if you remember me. My name is Tina Morales."

Mkubu stood. "I'm sorry . . . we get so many visitors."

"I understand. I have a request. Could I, please, speak to Abbot Christian? It's very important."

"I'll see if he is available. Please, know. *None* begins shortly."

"Thank you."

Mkubu left. The Abbot's private office was inside the cloister. Visitors were not allowed. It was almost 10 minutes before the two monks emerged.

"Yes, miss, what can I do for you?"

She held up the box. "I have a cursed relic. It has to be destroyed. But the curse must be broken first—the Evil has to be exorcized—in a holy place. I need your help."

The Guestmaster's face clouded with fear. Such cursed objects were not uncommon in his country. Witch doctors and shamans still held sway over much of the population. Christianity may have taken a foothold in the past 150 years, but it hadn't completely displaced thousands of years of pagan beliefs.

"I'm not sure we can help," the Abbot confessed. "There is not a lot of calls for exorcisms in monasteries."

"Please, Abbot Christian," she pleaded. "My own parish priest refused to even touch it. He wouldn't allow it in his church."

"May I see it?" Christian asked.

"I have it wrapped. I'm afraid if I take it out the *bruja*—the witch—will know where it is. She'll try to take it back."

Christian looked from Morales to Mkubu. The Kenyan nodded. He believed her.

"The hour is late, child. We have *Lectio Divina* immediately after *None*. After that Vespers and Compline. Perhaps if you came back tomorrow—that will give me time to confer with the other priests."

"Is there room at the visitor's quarters? I'd prefer to spend the night here. I . . . I'm afraid to go back."

Christian looked at Mkubu again. "Yes, miss, there is room," Brother John replied. He thought for a moment. "We will also have an evening meal after Vespers. You are more than welcome to dine with us. That will be in the refectory. About six-thirty."

"Thank you. I will."

Tina walked to the guest housing, near the visitor parking. She wanted to check her room. In the past year she had made a handful of visits to the monastery but had never spent the night. That was one of her goals for the Summer Vacation: A week retreat to the canyon.

The rooms were sparse: a table, a chair, a bed. No electricity so no lights. The room had a window that faced toward the river. A communal bathroom serviced the 13 guest rooms.

She put her burden down on the table, then sat on the bed. She thought the mattress might be a challenge for a week, but she was sure she could handle it. Wanting to explore a bit more, she reached the door, then stopped. She didn't dare leave the *perverso amuleto* alone for a second. It was too dangerous. It would not leave her side.

Past the restroom, at the end of the building, she found the common area: a room with a table and chairs, a small sofa and a kitchenette.

There was also four bookshelves with books—a few classics, mostly inspirational works, in keeping with the monastic surroundings.

She stepped back out into the warm afternoon, the cigar box tucked under her arm. The peace of the canyon was in sharp contrast to the turmoil she had experienced in the past few days. She felt sure she was in the right place.

If Abbot Christian wouldn't help her, then she would go to Santa Fe. The priest at St. Francis of Assisi Basilica could surely help. She would go all the way to the Bishop, if necessary.

She could be as relentless as Berta Chavez!

# Chapter Sixty-Nine

Lansing started up his Jeep. As he pressed on the accelerator, there was jolt as the weight of the horse trailer fought against inertia. The first mile of National Forest Road 262 snaked its way toward Rio Cohino. Then it straightened out for the next four miles. Gravel pelted the underside of his patrol unit. The tires rumbled over the wash-board surface. The strain of the trailer he was pulling kept him under 30 mph.

When he reached the river, the road took a sharp turn right, toward the north. Initially, Road 262 was wide enough for two cars to pass each other, but just barely. Now he faced a dirt and gravel track wide enough for one car. Every half mile or so the Forest Service carved out a wide spot on the river side. One car could stop, letting a vehicle from the other direction to pass.

If travelers met between turn-outs, someone had to back-up.

Road 262 now attempted to parallel Rio Cohino. In some places, construction crews had to cut into the face of the canyon walls to make room for the road. In those spots, it was a sheer drop of a hundred feet to the river below.

The road not only wound its way between the canyon cliffs and the river, it also varied in height above the river, ranging from 50 to 100 feet from the waters. On the slopes, above and below the road, vegetation flourished: Valley Cottonwoods, Colorado Pinons, Buffalo Juniper, and dozens of native grasses.

The winding, up-and-down road made for slow going, especially with a horse trailer in tow. Lansing's speed varied between 15 and 20 miles per hour. In one sense it was frustrating. He thought he would never reach the monastery. On the other hand, he was able to study for possible crunch spots—places where the enemy could be engaged with minimum chance of retaliation.

As he grew closer to his destination, a plan of action was forming in his mind. However, he needed to convince the Abbot and a few of his monks it would be in their own self-interest to help him.

A mile from the Abbey the canyon floor became broader and flatter. From the base of the cliffs to the river, the shallow slope was anywhere from 300-yards to a quarter mile wide. A wooden sign announced the monastery ahead. This was private property: no hunting, fishing, boating or camping. Visiting hours were between 8:30 am and 6:00 pm.

The road crested, then gradually descended to a low, flat plane. He could see the monastery bell tower. Two hundred yards short of the complex, he reached the visitor's parking. Even though the road continued past the monastery, a sign said, "no vehicles beyond this point."

He was able to slide the Jeep and trailer into the designated parking area. There was only one other car, Tina Morales'. Lansing wondered what kind of success she'd had.

He locked his Jeep, then walked back to check on Cement Head. The horse seemed to have survived the jolting trip. However, he protested. He was ready to get out of the cramped space. Lansing patted his neck.

"All in good time, buddy. I'll let you out soon."

The sheriff turned and started walking toward the monastery. As he passed the visitor's lodging, he heard someone call to him.

"Sheriff Lansing, what are you doing here?"

Lansing turned to his left. Tina Morales approached, the towel wrapped cigar box under her arm.

"Oh, hi, Tina . . . I see you're still lugging that lovely charm around." He kept walking toward the church.

"Yeah . . . The Abbot said they needed to confer with each other. He wasn't sure he could do an exorcism," she said, falling in step with him. "Why are you here?"

"I need to talk with the Abbot about something."

"It's five-thirty. You might be able to catch him before Vespers."

Lansing looked up the hill. The church sat on a plateau that overlooked the valley floor. To the left of the church was the walled cloister where the monks lived. To the right were the areas accessible to the public—the Guestmaster's office, which had a phone to the outside world, across the hall, a gift shop. The hallway widened into a common area where guests could gather and relax. Beyond was the refectory where both monks and visitor's dined.

"Do you know where I could find the Abbot?"

"You'll have to check with Brother John. He's the Guestmaster. He'll put you in touch with Abbot Christian—if he's available."

Morales guided Lansing to Mkubu's office. The monk was closing his office for the day, in preparation for Vespers.

"Brother John," Tina said, interrupting the monk's daily ritual. "This is Sheriff Lansing. The monastery is in his jurisdiction."

The monk extended his hand. "So good to meet you, sheriff. Can I help you?"

Lansing shook the offered hand. "I need to speak to the Abbot. It's very important."

"I wish I could help you . . . Vespers begins in ten minutes. And visiting hours are over at six. I'm afraid you're going to have to come back tomorrow. I'm sorry you came all this way for nothing."

"Brother, you don't understand," Lansing said sternly. "I am not here visiting. I am here on official business. If I don't talk to the Abbot, your monastery might not have a tomorrow."

The statement and the way it was delivered shocked Mkubu. "I . . . I'm sorry. I can't interrupt Vespers. But the Abbot will be in the refectory at six-thirty. I will make sure he knows you are here. You can speak to him then.

"You're more than welcome to join us in the church . . . or you can wait in the common area." He indicated a wide area to his right, furnished with a sofa and two, cushioned chairs.

"I'll wait out here," Lansing said flatly.

The sheriff sat in a chair. Morales sat on the sofa close to him. The church bell rang, announcing Vespers. The building grew quiet, except for the muffled sound of prayer and hymns coming from the church.

Tina studied the look of concern on Lansing's face. Finally, she said, "Something bad is getting ready to happen, isn't it?"

# Chapter Seventy

"Why didn't you tell me about all this earlier today?" Morales asked after Lansing explained the reason for his visit. She was miffed at being kept in the dark.

"First off, it didn't concern you," Lansing growled. "Second, I was sure I would get support from the State Police. We would set up a roadblock ten miles from here and stop these cartel thugs in their tracks.

"I thought the necklace business would be finished by now and you'd have left already."

"So, now what?"

"I don't know if there's anyone in that church that knows how to shoot a gun—and if there is, I don't know if they're willing to help."

"Surely, after what happened in Mexico, they'd want to protect themselves."

The sheriff shrugged. "I know exactly nothing about monks, other than they shun society. I don't know if they're a bunch of pacifists, ready to die as martyrs, or if they're willing to fight for their beliefs. I guess we'll know in a few minutes."

It wasn't long before a door behind them opened and they were allowed into the refectory. The evening meal was optional for the monks. A few would forego supper, preferring to fast until breakfast. This small sacrifice, they believed, brought them closer to understanding the suffering of others.

The dining tables were long and narrow, running the full length of the room. The Abbot sat at a head table. Monks were seated to his right. Visitors to his left. Food was served by those brothers assigned to kitchen duty that day.

Just inside the door was a pulpit that faced the Abbot. It was used to read liturgy during the meals. Other than the readings, there was no other speaking allowed.

"Please, wait here," Brother John said solemnly. A moment later Abbot Christian appeared. The Guestmaster made the introductions.

"We need to speak out here in the common area," the Abbot insisted.

Lansing, Morales and the Abbot stood alone in the visitor's area.

"Brother John says you have something very serious to talk about."

"My office received a phone call this morning. The caller said he represented the Gulf Drug Cartel in Mexico. The man said a cartel hit squad was responsible for killing a group of monks at a monastery. Did you hear about that?"

"Oh, yes," Christian admitted, stoically. "We may be removed from society, but we are not blind to the rest of the world."

"He said the reason for the murders," Lansing continued, "was they were looking for one particular monk. His name is Esteban Fuentes."

That statement visibly shook the abbot.

"He said they are on their way here!"

"Yes," Abbot Christian said vacantly, steadying himself against the wall. "Yes, I was warned this was going to happen."

"What?" Lansing exclaimed. "What do you mean?"

"You must come with me," the Abbot said, recovering somewhat. "You need to speak to someone."

The Abbot led the visitors into the refectory, through a side door, into the kitchen. A monk sat by himself at a small table, preparing to eat. He stood when the trio approached.

"Brother Esteban," Christian said. "This is Sheriff Lansing. He is in charge of San Phillipe County. The county we live in. I want him to talk to you."

Lansing had listened to the Guillen recording so many times that day, he had almost memorized it. He had also picked up additional names to augment his information. He nodded toward Esteban.

"You're Esteban Fuentes?"

"*Si*," the monk nodded.

"Have you ever heard of a man called Santiago de los Santos?"

Fuentes shook his head. "No."

"What about a Juan Garcia Abrego?"

"Yes," his forehead furrowed with concern. "He is *El Jeffe* of the Gulf Cartel." For eight years Zapata/Fuentes had been in the dark about news from the outside world. He hadn't heard about Juan Garcia's fall or Humberto Garcia's rise.

"Not anymore. He was arrested by the US government two years ago and put in prison. His brother, Humberto is in charge now. Do you have any idea why he would come after you?"

"*Si*," the monk said, sitting down. "I killed his son—eight years ago—when I worked for the cartel."

Lansing was taken aback by the confession. He had never given the monastic life much thought. He assumed monks were just monks. The idea that a man could have had a completely different life before taking vows never crossed his mind.

"Why did the cartel hit the other monastery?" the sheriff asked.

"It was the *Monasterio Benedicto de Santa Maria Magdelena*—where I took my vows." The monk admitted. "I assumed the identity of another man. A dead man. They must have thought I was there. I never thought the cartel would ever find out."

"Well, they did find out—and somebody at the monastery told this de los Santos you're here. The hit squad that struck *Montasterio Benedicto* is on its way to *St. Anthony's.*"

Esteban buried his face in his hands.

Lansing turned to the Abbot. "You said you had been warned this was about to happen. Who warned you?"

Abbot Christian nodded toward Brother Esteban. "He did."

Lansing was confused. "I don't understand."

"Dreams," Fuentes explained, looking up. "The last few weeks. I've been having dreams—about my old life—about how I killed another man—how I began my life as a monk. And at the end of the dreams, I had a feeling that something Evil was on its way."

"Nothing specific?" the sheriff asked.

The monk shook his head. "No. Just a feeling." He paused. "I thought if I left the monastery, my brethren would be safe. But God gave me a sign. I had to come back. I know why, now.

"When this hit squad arrives, I will go to them. They can take me and do what they have to do. Everyone here will be safe."

"No," Lansing said. "That's not the way things work in this country."

"What do you mean? I have free will. If I choose to sacrifice myself for the good of others, that's my decision."

"You're talking about committing suicide. That's against the law."

"No, I'm not. I'm freely handing myself over to these men. What they do after that, I have no control."

"They'll probably kill you—which means you're facilitating murder, which is also against the law. Plus, if they do kill you, I'll have to go after them." Lansing considered the situation. "Did you stop to think? After they kill you, there's nothing to say they won't come after everyone else here. They had no problem killing all your friends in Mexico."

Esteban looked from Lansing, to the Abbot, and back again. He was confused, afraid. "What am I supposed to do?"

Lansing looked at Abbot Christian. "Are you willing to defend your people, defend your monastery? Or are you going to become a bunch of sacrificial lambs?" He let the question sink in. "I came here to protect you, but I need your help. I can't do it by myself.

"If you're not going to help, I'm leaving. I could live to help others another day."

The Abbot's head was bowed in thought. Lansing gave him a moment.

When there was no response, he motioned to the teacher. "Come on, Miss Morales. I think it's time to leave."

"Wait!" Christian blurted. "Yes, our monastery is worth defending! What do you need us to do?"

# Chapter Seventy-One

"I don't know when Señor de los Santos plans to strike," Lansing admitted. "The other monastery was hit early in the day. I heard it may have been when they assembled for Mass. If that's the way they like to operate, they could be here as early as tomorrow morning."

"Do you have a plan?" Morales asked.

"If we block the road as far from here as possible and force them to walk the last seven or eight miles, we'll be able to do two things. Force them to arrive during daylight and exhaust them before they ever get here."

"How can we help?" Abbot Christian asked.

"Ask your men if any of them have ever handled a gun?"

"I have," Esteban said, standing. Then he looked at his Abbot. "Am I permitted?"

"Nearly a thousand years ago the Knights Templar were formed," the Abbot said. "They were dedicated to protecting pilgrims visiting the Holy Land. They were called Warrior Monks. Brother Esteban, if you take up arms to protect the righteous, that is not a sin."

"Father, we also need materials to build a roadblock," the sheriff said, interrupting. "Something we can transport easily."

"I'm afraid we don't have anything like that."

"That's all right," Lansing sighed. "I have something, but some of your men will have to help."

"Certainly."

"What can I do?" Tina asked.

"You can go back to Las Palmas," the sheriff snorted. "You're just going to be in the way."

"There must be something I can do to help."

"Unless you have some explosives in your car I can use to rig a couple of booby traps along the road, there's nothing you can do."

"I can make some."

"What?"

"Explosives."

"Where are we supposed to get two hundred pounds of fertilizer?" Lansing said, referring to the Oklahoma City bombing a couple of years earlier.

"I don't need all that. You forget. I'm a chemistry teacher." She explained the items she needed. She looked at the Abbot. "I'll also need a colander and a three-gallon pot from your kitchen."

The Abbot nodded.

"We can get everything I need at a grocery store and a builder's supply," Morales continued. "Probably Santa Fe." She looked at the wall clock. "It's seven already. By the time we get down there, find the stores, and get back . . . it will be after eleven. And I'd still have to put everything together."

"I know someone who can help," the Abbot said. "Brother John will have to let you into his office . . .

"I have a Chapter meeting with all the brethren in ten minutes. I will have them assemble in the refectory to explain to them the circumstances. Sheriff, if you could, please, attend. You can tell them what you need."

Lansing nodded.

Abbot Christian joined Brother John in the Guestmaster's office. Brother John dialed a number. Eileen Porter answered the phone. The Abbot explained that the monastery desperately needed their help and why. There was no hesitation on the part of either Roger or Eileen. The Porters were ready to do anything requested.

The Abbot handed the phone to the chemistry teacher.

231

"Yes, Mr. Porter. My name is Tina Morales. I want to help Abbot Christian and the other monks here. I need for you to pick up a few items."

"I've got a pen," Roger Porter said at the other end. "Go ahead."

"Five quarts of acetone. Two gallons of peroxide wood bleach. A quart of sulfuric acid . . . the kind used to clean drains. You can get all that at a builder's supply. I also need coffee filters and a candy thermometer from a grocery store."

The other end of the line was quiet. Tina didn't know if Porter was writing or hesitating.

"What are your plans for this?" the former engineer finally asked.

"Sheriff Cliff Lansing—he's in charge—he thought we might try and set up a couple of road-side bobby traps," Morales confessed, afraid she might offend Porter's sensibilities.

"I see," Porter said. He was quiet for a moment. "You'll need a few more things. I'll pick those up as well—It's a little after seven. I think we can be there by nine-thirty."

# Chapter Seventy-Two

Abbot Christian and the other monks would try to stick to their regular activities, with the exception of the Chapter Meeting. Instead of adjourning to the Chapter Room and reading a section from the Rules of St. Benedict, they assembled in the refectory.

The Abbot spoke first. He explained that the Evil that befell *Monasterio Benedicto de Santa Maria Magdelena* two days earlier was about to befall them. Since silence was a hard-fast rule of the order, there was no great cry of anguish or consternation from the brethren. But the men did look from one another with great concern. However, the Abbot declared, *St. Anthony's* would take a stand against the Devil. They were not going to roll over and become martyrs. They would meet Evil head on and they would succeed or die trying.

He then introduced Sheriff Lansing.

Lansing explained what he thought was about to happen. A group of men, 5 or more, were going to attack the Monastery. They would probably be heavily armed and attempt to kill everyone in the canyon, including himself. His plan was to block the canyon road 8 miles from the monastery. Force these men to walk.

He would plant explosive traps along the way to discourage them from coming closer. If they did get as far as the monastery, force would be met with force.

The sheriff asked if there were men there who could help with setting up the roadblock. All he needed was some muscle. Every monk volunteered.

He then asked if there was anyone there who could handle a rifle. Brother John Mkubu was the only man to raise his hand. That's all

Lansing needed. He had three AR4s. Counting himself and Esteban, they now had three defenders.

The inevitable question was finally asked. Why had *Montasterio Benedicto* been attacked? Why were these men now coming here?

Esteban Fuentes stepped from the kitchen.

"They are coming because of me," he confessed. "Many years ago, I worked for very bad men. I even killed for them. The men I killed were just as bad.

"One day, eight years ago, I was partnered with a man who told me we had to murder an entire family for no reason. I couldn't do that. Instead, I killed this man and let the family go.

"The father of the man I killed wants revenge. I think he will stop at nothing until I am dead, and he has destroyed everything sacred to me.

"I was afraid those many years ago. I ran. I took the name of another man who had died and went to your daughter monastery. There, I came to know God. I came to love God. And I learned God loved me—no matter what I had done before.

"I took my vows and became Brother Esteban. I have dedicated my life to the worship of our Lord and to better understand what he wants from me.

"I will never forgive myself for what happened in San Miguel. Every life taken will be a burden on my soul for the rest of my life.

"I can only ask your forgiveness, just as I pray to St. Anthony, St. Benedict and the Virgin Mary to intercede on my behalf—that our beloved Savior will forgive me, as well."

He was greeted with silence. The brothers slowly looked from one to another and nodded. In unison, they all stood. Single file, they approached Esteban Fuentes and embraced him, assuring him his fellowship was welcome and needed. His fate was now theirs.

# Chapter Seventy-Three

As he had predicted, it was 9:30 by the time Roger Porter arrived at the parking area for the monastery. He was delayed a little. A "Road Closed" barricade had to be moved, then replaced, on his way in. He wasn't alone, either. Eileen and Auggie were both with him.

Lansing had turned the Jeep and trailer around. It looked as though he was ready to leave. In reality, the two-horse trailer was empty. The monastery had 4 resident horses. Cement Head had been turned loose to graze with them. His oats and riding gear were stashed in an empty visitor's room.

Compline, the final office of the day, had been completed a little before 8:00. All the monks attended, including Brother Esteban. Abbot Christian's punishment had been lifted. Normally, the brethren would retire to their cells and observe the Great Silence.

Tonight was different. Abbot Christian, Brothers John Mkubu and Esteban Fuentes and ten other monks waited quietly beside Lansing's Jeep. The Porters were greeted by Sheriff Lansing and Tina Morales.

When Lansing saw the trove of materiel in Roger's trunk, he enlisted the help of 3 monks to move everything into the common room in the visitor's quarters. Everything Tina ordered was there. The acetone came in 3 half-gallon metal cans. The wood bleach in 4 half-gallon plastic buckets. The sulfuric acid was in a one-liter, plastic bottle. In a grocery store sack was a 25-pack of 12-cup coffee filters and a candy thermometer.

However, Roger Porter went far and beyond what Morales or Lansing imagined. The former Sandia Labs engineer explained the items as they were unpacked.

"I guessed from what you ordered you're making TATP. Am I right?" Porter asked the chemistry teacher.

Tina's face lit up. "Yes. That's exactly what I'm doing."

"What's that?" Lansing asked.

"Triacetone-triperoxide," the chemistry teacher explained. "It's an explosive that's been around a hundred years. However, the cooking process can be dangerous. That's why I set up that burner in the court-yard. The kitchenette isn't ventilated well enough. The fumes could explode."

"The Irish Republican Army has been using TATP against the Brits for twenty years," Porter continued. "It's ideal for use in an anti-personnel device. So, you said you were going to set up two booby-traps. I have two, one-gallon glass lemonade jars . . . the kind with the spigot on the bottom. You need something to put your devices in."

Lansing nodded. That made sense to him.

"Next," Porter pulled four smaller paper bags out of a larger one. "You need shrapnel. I have two pounds of three-inch nails and two pounds of one-inch brads for each device."

"That's going to do a lot of damage," the sheriff admitted.

"We plan to stop them, right?" Porter asked, though it was more of a statement.

"Absolutely," Tina agreed.

From a box labeled *Radio-Center* the engineer pulled out three 6-volt portable lanterns for night work. Then he retrieved three portable CB-Radios.

"What's all this for?" Lansing asked.

"We need light if we're working in the dark." He turned to Tina. "Had you given any thought to how you were going to detonate your booby traps?"

"Well, no . . ." Morales admitted. "I hadn't thought that part through. I was thinking the sheriff could shoot the device from a distance to make it explode."

"That's tricky if he misses . . . plus, the element of surprise is gone. I have a better idea." He set two of the radios aside. "Miss Morales, while you perform your alchemy, I'm going to rig detonators. One for each device. The third radio will be the trigger."

"Why CB-radios?" Lansing asked.

"That way I can set each 'bomb,' if you will, to a different frequency. We won't accidentally set them both off at the same time."

"You know how to make 'bombs?' " Lansing finally asked.

"I was a weapons engineer at Sandia Labs for over thirty years. Knowing how to design fuses and detonators was part of my job. This operation is going to be a piece of cake."

Lansing seemed impatient. "How long is all this going to take?"

"At least a couple of hours for the TATP," Tina guessed.

"About the same for the detonators," Porter admitted. "Then we have to construct the 'bombs' and figure out where to conceal them. The last thing we do is put the detonators into the devices after they're in place."

"That's going to take all night," Lansing complained. "After you leave, I have to block the road. That's going to take at least an hour. It may be daylight by then."

"Go ahead and block the road," Porter said.

"But you'll be trapped here," Lansing protested.

"That's okay with me," the engineer said, smiling.

"Well, at least, send your wife home."

Eileen had sat quietly to the side, holding Auggie. "He can't send me home," Mrs. Porter observed. "I'm his ride."

"It's not going to be safe here," the sheriff pointed out.

"We've been together nearly forty years," Eileen said peacefully. "If God decides it's time for us to join him, we'd prefer to go together."

Lansing threw his hands up in the air. "All right. Fine. I've got a road to block."

He hurried outside to round up his helpers.

# Chapter Seventy-Four

Driving in on Road 262, Lansing suspected he might have to devise his own roadblock. Seven and a half miles from the Abbey, there was a low spot on the canyon-wall side, large enough to pull his truck onto. That was where he headed. Four monks rode with him. Eight more followed in the monastery van.

When he got to the location, he pulled in and parked. The trailer still protruded onto the road. That's what the sheriff wanted.

Everyone piled out of the two vehicles. Lansing unhitched the trailer, then the dozen monks, all wearing half cassocks, work pants and shoes, began pulling and pushing the horse trailer. Lansing wanted to move it almost a half mile further down the road. With so many men, the four-wheeled, two-axil carrier was easy to handle.

When they reached the place he was looking for, he had the men maneuver the transport sideways, the hitch pointed away from the river. Then, with everyone on one side, they began lifting the trailer. The one-ton trailer tipped readily with so many hands.

The road was now blocked. The trailer was on its side, the roof portion facing oncoming traffic. The rounded top would prevent anyone from getting a good grip to turn it back over. The canyon side of the slope was too narrow for cars to drive around. The river side was a drop of 75 feet.

On its side, the trailer would only skid along, still blocking the road, even if it was pushed by another vehicle.

Anyone approaching the monastery now had to walk nearly eight miles.

Despite the fact he might be facing heartless murderers, Lansing's sense of fair play forced him to give the hit squad a chance to back off.

Before leaving the scene, he left a note taped to the trailer's roof. It was written in Spanish, addressed to de los Santos.

DO NOT GO BEYOND THIS POINT.
TO DO SO IS TRESSPASSING.
IT WILL BE CONSIDERED AN ACT
OF AGGRESSION AND WILL BE MET WITH FORCE.
YOU HAVE BEEN WARNED.
SHERIFF'S OFFICE, SAN PHILLIPE COUNTY, NM

It was 11:00 pm when the work crew returned to the monastery. Despite the desperate circumstances, Abbot Christian insisted his members adhere to the strict monastic rules. The monastery bell would still sound at 3:40. Vigils would still be held at 4:00.

Since Brother John and Brother Esteban had been recruited as "soldiers for the cause," they would be exempt from the daily rituals, but only when Lansing called them to action.

The science teacher cooked her concoction until midnight. The candy thermometer was used to ensure a constant temperature was maintained. The end result was TATP crystals had accumulated in the bottom of her 3-gallon pot. The colander was lined with the coffee filters, then the acetate-peroxide-sulfuric acid mix was poured to sift out the compound.

The final result was nearly a half-pound of TATP explosive.

The goal was not to blow up a building or even a car. The intent was to stop unprotected men from reaching the monastery. A quarter pound of TATP was enough to send 4 pounds of shrapnel—in this case, nails—a distance of a hundred feet at a velocity of over 5,000 feet per second.

The location of the two TATP bombs had to meet one criterium for Lansing. He decided he would be the one to trigger the explosions. Riding Cement Head, he would be on the cliff side of the road, looking down. The bombs had to be placed where he could see them from above. From that vantage point, he could also determine when an explosion would do the most damage.

When setting the glass jars, Lansing, Morales and Porter scooped out niches to ensure the blast would be directed outwards, towards the road. Once the engineer had set the detonator, nails were gently packed inside the jars . . . then the lids secured firmly. They wanted the blast to go out, not up.

The final "bomb" was set and the trio returned to the visitor's lodging at 3:00.

Eileen was asleep in Tina's room. Auggie was curled up on the floor next to her.

"Coffee, anyone?" Tina asked. "They have everything we need in the kitchen."

Both men agreed, caffeine was a good idea. Even though they were tired, the anticipation of what was coming kept them from relaxing.

Once they each had a cup in hand, Lansing began laying out the scenario. He would have one of his police walkie-talkies. He and his horse would take up a position on 262 where he could view the roadblock with binoculars. If men started climbing over the trailer, he would know immediately. He would radio back, so the rest could prepare. At that point, he would reposition above the road.

The State Police had been asked to monitor Highway 15 for any unusual activity. If they saw anything, they were asked to pass it along to the San Phillipe Sheriff's dispatch. Dispatch would call the monastery with the alert. Someone needed to be posted in Brother John's office. They would have one of the other walkie-talkies. Any new info would be passed to the sheriff.

"Where will they make their assault?" Porter asked.

"There's only one way in," Lansing observed. "They'll have to come up Two-sixty-two. I'll position two shooters on the visitor's quarters, here. I'll find a spot on the other side of the road."

"Do you need another man . . . or do you only have three rifles?"

"You shoot?" the sheriff asked.

"I used to do a lot of hunting. I know my way around a gun," the engineer admitted.

"Do you think you can handle an AR4 assault rifle?"

"If it's got a trigger and a barrel, I'm pretty sure I won't have a problem."

Lansing leaned back in his chair. "That's great. With my Thirty-thirty we'll have four weapons against whatever is left after our booby-traps."

"I'm going to saddle up Cement Head," he said, standing. "I need to get into position."

Lansing headed out the door. Grabbing his bridle from the temporary tack-room, he was beginning to think they may come out of this whole ordeal alive after all.

# Chapter Seventy-Five

Lansing put Cement Head into a trot as they headed down the road. If his prediction was correct, the cartel hitmen would try to reach the monastery by 6:00 am. That means they would encounter the roadblock a little after 5:30. He had two hours to get into position.

Except for the clop of Cement Head's hooves, the canyon was quiet. Even with no moon, the billion starts overhead provided a remarkable amount of light. The part-time rancher was amazed at how peaceful the surroundings were. For a few minutes he was able to forget the battle he was sure he would soon fight.

He passed the five-mile point from the monastery. That's where the second device was hidden. He stopped at the seven-mile point. He was next to the first device. He also had a clear view of the overturned trailer.

Climbing down from his mount, the sheriff tied the reigns to a scrub bush next to the road. Cement Head nosed around, looking for decent forage, eventually snorting in disappointment. It was way too early for the animal. He relaxed his muscles and locked his leg joints. Soon he was asleep, though his master couldn't tell. The stallion's eyes were still open.

Lansing pulled the radio and a pair of binoculars from a saddle bag. He clicked the transmit button twice to alert the listener at the other end. "This is Lansing. How do you read me?"

"You're loud and clear," Roger Porter responded. "Miss Morales went up to the church for Mass . . . Breakfast is at Seven-thirty. Should we bring you something?"

"Sure," Lansing agreed. "If nothing's going on, that would be great."

The sheriff found a comfortable spot to sit, then began his surveillance. In the distance he could hear the muffled sound of rushing water in the Rio Cohino. The white noise of the river, the darkness and peaceful surroundings began taking their toll. Lansing found himself constantly dozing off, then jerking awake.

Getting up and walking around helped keep him alert. Sitting immediately put him back into the dozing/jerking awake routine. He couldn't help but be a little jealous of his horse. Cement Head stood there stoically, sound asleep, oblivious to the rest of the world.

The stars began to fade, yielding to a pastel blue. A climbing sun and brightening skies were on their way. Birds announced their presence.

As the day became more awake, so did Lansing.

The hours clicked by in segments. It was 5:30, then 5:45. 6:00, then 6:20; 6:45; 7:15.

Lansing was disappointed. He was sure the cartel target-timing would be for Morning Mass. Then the doubts began creeping in. Were the Feds right? Was it a hoax? Was the SBI correct in not dedicating manpower to a fool's errand?

The sheriff shook them off. What would be the point in orchestrating such a trick? The thought of Berta Chavez and her machinations crossed his mind. He shook that off, as well. What would she know of drug cartels or Esteban Fuentes?

It was 8:30 when Tina Morales drove up. She had done her best to keep the eggs and potatoes warm. There was also a thick slice of toasted, home-made bread. Most importantly, she had a thermos of hot coffee. She also had the *perverso amuleto* with her. Lansing just shook his head.

She manned the binoculars while he ate.

"How are you going to get your trailer back up?" she asked.

"Car jacks and ropes. Fulcrum and levers. Sweat, hard work, lots of luck," he replied, not looking up.

"So, you don't have a clue?" she laughed.

"One dilemma at a time, professor," the sheriff replied, relishing a sip of coffee. "One dilemma at a time."

"Do you need to take a break?"

"I'm doing much better now," he admitted. "I've been on stake-outs before. They're tedious and boring, but I've always seemed to survive." He looked at the teacher and smiled. "The company certainly is welcome, though."

She returned the smile. "Mr. Porter is manning the phone, in case your dispatch calls. I told him I would take over when I got back. But I will bring you lunch."

Lansing nodded. "We're playing the waiting game now."

"How long do you plan on staying out here?" She gave him a look of concern.

"If I have to sit out here 'til noon Saturday, that's what I'll do. As long as Cement Head and I are fed and watered, and I can catch a few winks here and there, we'll be fine."

"What happens noon Saturday?"

"I will admit I was wrong and we all go home."

"Would you be disappointed if that happened?" the teacher asked.

Lansing thought long and hard before he answered. "Ask me again noon Saturday."

# Chapter Seventy-Six

Abbot Christian found Tina Morales in the Guestmaster's office. She welcomed his interruption.

"Miss Morales, I had a discussion with Brother Francis. He is an ordained priest and has had some experience with exorcisms. He is in our library doing research right now. He believes he can lift the curse on your charm."

"That's wonderful!" she exclaimed.

"We would like to conduct the ceremony before lunch. Would that be all right with you?"

"I am ready whenever you say." She could barely contain her excitement. She held up the towel-wrapped box. "I have it right here."

The Abbot nodded. "We will summon you to the church when it's time."

As she waited, she realized this is what brought her to Las Palmas. This was her purpose: To destroy the *Lagrima de la Madre* and stop Berta Chavez.

It was 11:00 when she was called to the sanctuary.

The candles on the altar had been lit. The Abbot, Brother Francis and another priest stood behind it, wearing their priestly vestments. A choir of a dozen monks had been assembled for prayer and chants.

Without saying a word, the priest signaled Tina to bring the charm forward. She unwrapped the towel, the foil around the box, then the foil around the necklace. Stepping up to the altar, she solemnly placed the *amuleto* in front of the Holy men.

After the teacher moved back, Brother Francis began reading text from a book held by the other priest, his hands pressed together in prayer.

The petitions and incantations were conducted in Latin. On cue, the choir began chanting the liturgy selected for the ceremony.

When they stopped, Francis again read from the Holy text. This time he sprinkled the necklace with Holy water. The choir began again.

The back and forth, readings from the text and chants from the monks, continued for half an hour.

Finally, the *perverso amuleto* was wrapped in a purple, velvet cloth. A large, heavy brass, stamp, the kind that would be used for a wax-seal, was brought out.

Brother Frances chanted a few words, then smashed the amuleto. The words were repeated, and the amuleto was smashed again. The ritual was repeated five times.

When the priest was finished, he made the sign of the cross. He folded the cloth holding the crushed, evil charm and handed it to a waiting monk. The monk disappeared behind the Tabernacle, taking what was left of the necklace with him.

The exorcism was over.

Tina Morales didn't care where they took it. She was just glad her dealings with Berta Chavez were finished.

She genuflected in front of the altar, made the sign of the cross and left the church.

\*\*\*

Thirty miles away, in her dark, dingy hovel, Berta Chavez stirred.

She was almost depleted. Every ounce of Evil she could muster had been directed against the San Phillipe Law Enforcement, the legal system, even the school that had tormented her son. She had confronted the *curandera*. Morales wasn't a threat.

She would rest for a while. Regain her strength. There was so much more to do.

In the last day, her ability to see her *perverso amuleto* had become clouded. However, she knew that was because she was tired. As long as it was sequestered in the sheriff's evidence locker, she and her curse had free reign.

Suddenly, it felt like a burning knife had been plunged into her brain. She screamed.

A vision of the *Lagrima de la Madre* flashed before her eyes. It lay on an altar. Priests chanted incantations. Standing in the sanctuary, she could see Tina Morales, the *curandera*.

A priest covered the "tear" and began to pulverize her dear charm.

Her heart was struck . . . six times. The white-hot knife that plunged into her skull now pierced her chest.

She crumbled to the floor, gasping for breath.

The curse she had so carefully crafted—and nurtured—had been broken.

Only one person was responsible: the *curandera*.

Berta Chavez was blind with hate and rage. As she tried to stand, she was consumed with only one, burning thought—destroy Tina Morales!

# Chapter Seventy-Seven

By the time the cartel convoy reached Santa Fe, Santiago de los Santos' schedule was all out of whack. His early departure from Amarillo went as planned. But he was more used to traveling Mexican roads with Mexican traffic. He expected to cover their first 240 miles on I-40 in 4 ½-hours. It only took them three. The 40 miles to Santa Fe on Highway 285 took just over thirty minutes.

Then there was the issue of time zones. Santiago never had a reason to go beyond the State of Coahuila. That was the western most reaches of the Gulf Cartel. That was also the boundary for the Eastern and Central Mexican Time Zones. He had heard of time zones, but de los Santos never had to deal with them. Crossing into New Mexico from Texas, he and his men gained an hour, going from US Central to Mountain Time Zones.

With the errors combined, instead of reaching Santa Fe in the early afternoon, it was only 9:30.

The idea of spreading out their caravan worked well as long as they were on 4-laned roads. All the roads they used in Texas were 4-lanes. Highway 285 in New Mexico was 2 lanes. It wasn't long until their five cars were bunched up, all in a row.

Out of necessity, the hit squad had to make a pit-stop in Santa Fe. They gassed up and took care of other essentials. They also purchased a current New Mexico road map. De los Santos conferred with the other drivers.

Their planned deception was out the window now. They were stuck driving in a group.

One driver suggested it might be time to pile everyone into two cars. Not yet, de los Santos insisted. They didn't want to be seen transferring weapons into two vehicles. They could wait until they reached the canyon.

It was 10:00 am. They would reach National Forest Road 262 by 11:00, the monastery by 11:20. If the monks weren't conveniently located in one place, they would ring the monastery bell to bring them together.

Santiago de los Santos didn't relish the idea of chasing monks up and down a canyon. He supposed if a few got away, it wouldn't matter. As long as he found and killed Esteban Fuentes/Pepe Zapata, he would fulfill his mission.

He and his hit squad were soon on Highway15, crossing into San Phillipe County.

*\*\**

State Police Officer Marty Hernandez was doing what Sheriff Lansing requested. He was keeping his eyes open for anything unusual between Segovia and Artiga. Deep down inside, he really didn't expect to see anything. He didn't know what he was looking for, to begin with.

He was heading south on Highway 15. Road 262, which now had a temporary "Road Closed" barrier, was five miles behind him. He had almost reached Artiga when a car passed him, going in the opposite direction.

The car had two-Hispanic males. Certainly, nothing unusual for New Mexico. But the car had Texas plates. Those were a little out of place.

What did catch the patrolman's interest was the next car he passed had Texas plates. In fact, three more cars after that had Texas plates, and each car carried two men.

He let all five cars pass. Lansing warned him not to engage—just pass on the information to San Phillipe Dispatch. Hernandez pulled off in Artiga.

He changed the frequency on his radio. "San Phillipe Dispatch, this is State Patrol Seven-thirteen. How copy?"

"State Police Seven-thirteen. We have you loud and clear," Marilyn responded. "Go ahead."

"Roger, Dispatch. Be advised, I just passed five vehicles with Texas plates coming out of Artiga—all heading toward the Rio Cohino Canyon turn-off.

"I'm making a turn, heading back north. I'll keep you notified."

"Dispatch copies."

By the time Hernandez reached Road 262, the last of the five cars was pulling through the "Road Closed" barricade. Two men had moved the yellow-and-black striped saw-horses out of the way. Once the last car had cleared the obstacle, they put the barricade back in place. So busy with their task, they never noticed the State Police unit passing by.

"San Phillipe Dispatch. State Patrol Seven-thirteen. Let Sheriff Lansing know—he has ten visitors headed his way. I presume they're armed and very dangerous."

# Chapter Seventy-Eight

Lansing backtracked 30 yards. The slope was less steep there. It was easier for Cement Head to climb. Horse and rider stopped when they reached the top of a hill, 40 feet above the road.

The sheriff had a clear view of the trailer, now a half-mile away. Looking down and to his right, he could see the niche that hid the TATP explosive device.

There was a knot of anticipation in his gut.

He had to admit to himself, he was surprised when he got the call over his walkie-talkie. It was Roger Porter. Marilyn had just called the monastery. Marty Hernandez spotted five cars with Texas plates. They moved the barricades and were now in the canyon.

He had almost convinced himself that the supposed authorities were right. No one was on their way. Nothing would happen. Even if something would happen, he guessed it probably wouldn't be until Mass the next morning.

He dismounted and positioned the horse, so it couldn't be seen. Then he fixed himself an observation post. He had his binoculars, the walkie-talkie radio, the third CB-radio and his Winchester 30-30.

He expected the call over the walkie-talkie would be from Morales. He had no idea she was attending an exorcism in the church.

He wondered why de los Santos and company were so brazen. Why would they risk an attack in broad daylight?

Then he considered the location. *St. Anthony's* was 15 miles from the nearest highway. Artiga, the closest town, was over 20 miles away. He guessed the cartel hit squad thought the conclave had no way to communicate with the outside world. Any actions on cartel's part would go unnoticed for days.

The trailer was positioned across the road, right after a sharp turn. Lansing had his binoculars trained on the road, just beyond the trailer. It was 11:15 when a car nosed around the curve. It managed to stop before hitting the trailer.

Lansing notified the Abbey the hit men had arrived. He would keep them apprised about what was happening.

A man got out of the car and walked up to the roadblock. He pulled the note from the trailer. He read it, then wadded it up and threw it away.

He signaled to the men in the car. Four men climbed out. He indicated the trailer. They all began to push, with no results.

A second car had come to a stop behind the first. More men were recruited. One man directed the action while nine men pushed. They managed to nudge the trailer an inch or two.

Frustrated, the man in charge cleared the men away. Another was instructed to operate the first car. The angle was such, the car could only push with its front, right bumper. The gravel road provided little traction. The roof began to crumple, but the bulk of the trailer didn't move.

The car backed up and tried to ram the obstacle. The curve of the road prevented the driver from getting a running start. He could only get a few feet of momentum going.

After ten minutes, it appeared the roadblock would hold, even though the roof was completely caved in.

Lansing wondered if he could get reimbursed for a new horse trailer. He doubted it. For the moment, he was satisfied his ploy was working.

A knot of men gathered around the hood of the first car. Someone produced a map. They looked from the map, down the road, then back to the map. After a few moments, the men split into two groups. They gathered around the now open car trunks. Weapons were handed out.

One by one, they climbed over the trailer-hitch end of the roadblock.

The apparent leader, Lansing presumed it was de los Santos, instructed one man to proceed ahead of the others. He was the scout. Once he was fifty yards ahead, the others began to follow.

From the trailer to the first device was a mile.

The gang of killers seemed nonchalant about their march. They were in no hurry. They were also spreading out. Two men here, two men there, engrossed in conversation, a couple of yards between each twosome.

Lansing waited. It took 20 minutes before the hit squad reached the "bomb." The scout was further down the road. Two men sauntered past the device. Two more were next to it. Five men lagged behind.

The CB-radio had 16 channels. Porter set the detonators to Channels 9 and 14. The sheriff made sure the radio was set to Channel 9. When he thought he could do the most damage, Lansing pushed the "Transmit" button.

The bomb exploded!

# Chapter Seventy-Nine

More than 100 yards from the blast, Lansing didn't feel the concussion, but the explosion was deafening. Cement Head reared up in protest. The sheriff scrambled to keep him from bolting. Once the horse was calmed, he turned back to view the carnage below. The smoke and dust began to clear.

Nine men had been knocked to the ground.

The scout came running back, yelling to his comrades. He stopped to inspect the first victim he came to.

The sheriff could only hope that their first weapon would be all the defenders needed . . . That would have been too good to be true.

Men started moving. Some got to their knees, trying to shake the ringing from their heads. A couple sat upright, dazed. In a matter of minutes, five of the men caught in the blast were stirring.

The four bodies closest to the detonation site didn't move at all.

The scout hurried over to check on them. He lifted their heads, one at a time. One of the men caught in the blast stood. He yelled at the scout. The scout stood and turned to him, shaking his head.

The first man to stand, most likely de los Santos, and the scout helped the other four survivors to their feet. The leader signaled for the men to move up the road, back the way they came. Two moved with pronounced limps.

One hundred feet from their dead companions, the remaining 6 hit men conferred. It looked to Lansing as if an argument was ensuing. De los Santo pointed in the direction of the monastery. Another man pointed in the opposite direction. Others joined in. Soon, all six were yelling at the same time. The arguing went on for a solid minute.

Fed up, de los Santo pointed his gun in the air and fired.

The men around him fell silent.

He yelled his instructions, then pointed toward the river. The men looked in the direction of the monastery, then over the side of the road. They spread out . . . looking for a way down to the canyon floor and the river. One of the men yelled. He found a spot.

With rifles in hand, the cartel foot soldiers climbed down from the road. If there were more surprises hidden along the beaten track, they would have no part of it.

This was something that never occurred to Lansing. They would avoid the road completely.

He radioed the monastery.

The roadblock worked. The hit squad was being forced to walk.

The first device was detonated. Four men were down.

There were still six other henchmen. They had abandoned the road and were making their approach along the river.

Lansing said he was returning to the monastery immediately. They would figure out their next move after he got back.

He packed his gear into the saddle bags, then mounted Cement Head. They gingerly made their way down the slope. Once they reached the road, the horse began a steady trot. Seven miles was too far to push a gallop.

*** 

Four miles from the monastery he ran into Roger Porter, coming in the opposite direction.

"You know the canyon's blocked," Lansing said when Porter stopped. "You can't get out."

"I'm just going to retrieve the other device," the engineer explained. "It's not doing us any good hidden along the road now. Maybe we can use it closer to the monastery."

"Good thinking," Lansing admitted.

"How was the explosion?" Porter asked.

"You and Miss Wizard would have been proud."

# Chapter Eighty

Lansing spurred Cement Head into a faster pace. It was 12:30 when de los Santos and company abandoned the road. The sheriff estimated it would take the group at least 2 ½ hours to reach the monastery. The best he could hope for was beating them there by an hour.

A mile from the Abbey, Roger Porter passed the rider and his horse, the TATP explosive on the seat next to him. Lansing suggested they meet-up outside the Guestmaster's office.

When the sheriff reached the visitor's quarters he dismounted. Cement Head certainly deserved coddling. If he'd had the time, Lansing would have given his steed a good brush-down. Instead, he removed the saddle bags, saddle and blanket. For the moment, the best he could do was turn the horse loose to graze with the other animals.

There was a small parking area in front of *St. Anthony's Church* set aside for handicapped patrons. Lansing broke the rules by moving his Jeep there. His plan of intercepting the attackers along the road was no longer feasible. It appeared they would make their stand closer to the monastery.

He opened the back of the Jeep. He had 3 AR4 assault rifles. In a heavy, nylon bag he had six magazines for the rifles, six flash-bang grenades and a dozen road flares. He had no idea what he could use the flares for, now. He left them in the satchel, so they wouldn't roll around the back of his unit.

Grabbing the bag, he left the rifles behind for the moment. A long, back-and-forth ramp allowed wheelchair access. Other visitors use the stairs. It took ten steps to reach the church level.

Approaching the portion of the complex housing the gift shop, Guestmaster's office and refectory, the front of the building had a portico with a low wall. The porch, like the church, overlooked a wide, treeless vista that extended from the Abbey to the river, 300-yards away.

To the right, an 8-foot wall extended 150-yards from the church to the National Forest road. Behind the wall was the cloister, the gardens, and the other restricted areas where only the monks and novitiates were allowed.

To the left was the access road and the visitor's lodging

Immediately in front of the church was the handicapped parking, then Road 262. Beyond the road was a wide pasture, the grasses kept low by the grazing horses. The pasture, a quarter mile across, extended from the cloister wall to the visitor's housing. The expanse sloped gently down to Rio Cohino, almost a hundred feet below the church.

Lansing knew the gunmen would have to make their approach across the open field. He considered putting one defender on the roof of the visitor's unit, trying to get de los Santos in a cross-fire. The problem he saw with that was his shooter would be isolated. The other defenders couldn't protect him.

While Lansing pondered his tactics, Tina Morales emerged from building.

"The *perverso amuleto* is history," she informed him.

"What?" He was so absorbed in his thoughts, he hadn't noticed her presence.

"The necklace . . . It's gone. They were able to exorcize the curse," she explained.

"Oh," Lansing said. "That's great!"

"I heard my concoction worked pretty well."

"Yes, it did," the sheriff nodded. "Too well, I'm afraid. We scared the bad guys off the road."

"How big was the explosion?"

"I don't know what to compare it to," Lansing admitted. "It was big enough to knock nine guys to the ground and kill four of them. I think another two were hurt.

"What did Mr. Porter do with the other one?"

"It's right over there." She pointed at the far corner of the small portico.

Lansing set his equipment bag next to it. "Do you know where he is?"

"Inside, having coffee with Eileen." Morales had become fast friends with the Porters in the short time they had been together.

"We don't have a lot of time. I need to give him and the two monks a quick lesson on how to handle the rifles I brought."

Lansing's small defensive unit was assembled behind his Jeep in ten minutes. He had the rifles and the 10-round magazines.

"This is how you insert and release the magazine. Always make sure the safety on the left side of the weapon is on." He demonstrated.

Each recruit took a weapon and repeated what they were shown.

"All right. Put your magazines in. To load your rifle, pull back on the charging arm, then release it." He demonstrated with Porter's gun. "That puts a round in the chamber."

The two monks repeated the demonstration.

Before firing the rifles, Lansing showed his students how to remove the magazines and clear a round from the chamber.

Finally, it was time to shoot.

The sheriff had Roger Porter step forward and chamber a round.

No specific target was chosen. Lansing only wanted them to get the feel of the weapon. Porter was told to just aim at the river.

The engineer raised the rifle to his shoulder, released the safety, and pulled the trigger.

Click.

Lansing was miffed. "Did you chamber a round?"

"Yes!" Porter snapped.

"The safety's off?"

Porter checked. "Yes."

Lansing took the weapon and cleared the chamber. The .223 shell ejected onto the ground. The sheriff picked it up and examined it. There was a dent on the primer in the middle of the rim. The dent was caused by the firing pin.

The round was a dud.

The lawman had never seen that before.

He told Porter to chamber another round and fire. Porter did—with the same results.

Now Lansing was getting worried. He asked Esteban to hand him his rifle. He chambered a round, pointed the weapon toward the river and pulled the trigger.

Click.

The same thing happened when he tried John Mkubu's rifle.

"Berta Chavez," Lansing swore, gritting his teeth. The name was spoken as if it was a profanity.

Tina Morales had been watching the operation from the portico. She came running. "What's wrong?"

"That damned witch and her curse . . . she's ruined every shell in my armory."

"That can't be true," the teacher protested. "The curse was broken."

"Breaking that curse doesn't undo what's already been done. The Call Center is still burned down. My deputy still has a broken leg. My bullets are still ruined!"

"What are you going to do?"

"I don't know, damn it!" Lansing groused. "I'll think of something!"

# Chapter Eighty-One

The field of battle was set.

Lansing moved his Jeep back to visitor's parking. No use in it getting shot up.

A monk lead Cement Head and the four Abbey horses to a safe patch of ground on the far side of the cloister.

The sheriff couldn't know for sure where the henchmen would cross the open field. He selected what would be the most logical spot. That's where he and Porter hid the second explosive device, in a clump of grass.

Now they waited.

Abbot Christian and his brethren had taken sanctuary in the church. It seemed like an appropriate time for prayer. Tina Morales and Eileen Porter joined them.

Lansing and Roger Porter had taken a position on the portico. That gave them the high ground plus the protection of the low wall, which was a foot thick.

The sheriff was armed with his Winchester 30-30 and his Remington .38 pistol containing .357 Magnum rounds. He fired one round from each, to make sure they still worked. The rifle held 7 rounds. There was also a box with 24 additional bullets. There was a total of 11 shells for the pistol.

With six attackers, he knew he had to make every shot count.

Porter manned the CB-radio. It was his job to detonate the device.

Lansing kept scanning the field with his binoculars, looking for any movement.

It was 4:00 when he finally saw a head pop up. Someone was walking up the bank from the river. Twenty yards to the man's right, another head showed. Thirty and sixty yards to his left, two more men appeared.

Lansing swept the binoculars to the right and left, looking for the last two assailants. They were nowhere to be seen. He could only conclude they were coming up the road in a flanking action.

"Let me know when they're getting close," Porter said, hidden behind the wall so he couldn't be seen.

Spread out the way they were, Lansing could only hope to take two of them out at the most . . . the two in the center. The device was planted 250 yards from the church. An explosion would do the building no harm.

"All right," Lansing said. "Now!"

Porter stood up and hit the "Transmit" button.

Nothing happened.

Porter pushed the button again.

Again, nothing.

"Is it on the right channel?" Lansing asked, a touch of desperation in his voice.

Porter checked. "Yes, it is!" He pushed the button again. He tried different channels. Still nothing.

Porter sat down heavily, his back against the wall. "It's my fault. Something on the detonator must have come loose when I moved it. I should have checked it when we set it in the field."

"Isn't there anything you can do?"

Porter shook his head. "No. Sorry."

"You'd better get inside," the sheriff said grimly. "Things are going to start lighting up here in a minute."

Porter started to move toward the door behind him, then stopped. Both men heard another door slam shut. They looked in the direction of the church.

Esteban Fuentes stood in front of the double doors.

"What are you doing?" Lansing yelled. "Get back inside!"

Fuentes ignored him. He descended the ten steps with resolve. Striding across the gravel parking lot, he stopped when he reached the road. He spread his arms and shouted:

"My name is Pepe Zapata. I am the man you seek. I killed Rodrigo Abrego. Take my life! Leave everyone else here alone. They did you no harm!"

One of the two men in the center of the field raised his rifle and fired a burst. Four bullets slammed into Zapata's chest. The monk flew backwards and lay motionless.

Esteban Fuentes/Pepe Zapata was dead.

# Chapter Eighty-Two

For a moment, time was frozen. No one moved. Lansing, Porter, the hitmen just stared at Zapata's body.

The church doors opened. Tina, Eileen and a dozen monks took tentative steps outside. Eileen, who remembered meeting Esteban only once, began to cry silently.

Lansing stepped outside the protection of the portico. "All right, de los Santos," he shouted. "You've done what you've come to do. You can leave now!"

De los Santos looked to the two men either side of him. Then looked at the sheriff.

"I have six dead compadres," he shouted back. "Somebody has to pay for that! I think maybe you! I think maybe everyone in that building behind you should pay . . . No one in this world is innocent."

He fired his weapon. The bullets fell short, popping up gravel in the parking lot.

Lansing dove behind the wall. The congregants from the church scrambled inside.

The four hitmen started their march toward the monastery.

As Lansing raised his rifle to take aim, he heard a loud squawk from somewhere above him. He looked up to see two dozen ravens, perched on the walls of the church alcoves.

More guttural harping came from the direction of the cloister walls. A hundred more ravens sat in readiness. The squawking and chattering grew in volume, drowning out every other sound in the canyon.

Finally, an unknown signal started them off. One bird launched, followed immediately by the next, then the next, then the next—soon they all had taken to wing and were heading directly for Santiago de los Santos and his three henchmen.

The birds swirled. The birds dove. The birds bit and scratched. They pecked at eyes and ears—any exposed flesh. The men swatted and bellowed.

One man fired his AR-15 in an attempt to ward off the fowl. He only managed to kill the man closest to him.

De los Santos and another would be attacker threw their weapons to the ground and ran screaming for the river.

Forty birds tormented each man. They were pecked and harassed until they fell to their knees. They rolled on the earth trying to dislodge clinging claws.

The sound of the birds had drawn the faithful from the church. Tina, Eileen and their companions stared in awe at the spectacle transpiring in front of them.

The screeching and squalling by the birds gradually began to subside.

The avian attack lasted ten minutes—then it was over.

One by one, the ravens flew off. Soon, none were left.

Where they came from, where they returned to, no one would ever know.

All that remained were four lifeless bodies in the field. They were the bodies of men no one would miss—and no one would mourn.

# Chapter Eighty-Three

Sheriff Lansing and Roger Porter inspected the bodies of de los Santos and his three companions. There was no doubt they were dead. For the time being, they left the bodies where they found them.

From the way the chief cartel hitman talked, two of the foot soldiers succumbed to wounds from the blast after they left the road. Not counting Esteban Fuentes, a total of ten bodies had to be located and removed from the canyon. Of course, no one and nothing was coming in or out of the river valley until Lansing got the roadblock out of the way.

The brethren had removed Esteban Fuentes to the cloister. They would wash his body and prepare him for burial with prayers and a vigil.

Eileen and Tina stood at the bottom steps of the church waiting for the two men. Between the four of them, there was a great sense of relief. The ordeal was over.

Husband and wife embraced.

"What now?" the teacher asked.

Lansing was walking toward the portico to retrieve his rifle and equipment bag. Morales fell in step with him. "I guess we go home and pick up where we left off," he said.

"And where did we leave off?" she asked coyly.

Before he could answer, the scene was shattered with a blood curdling screech. Something gold and brown swept past him, knocking him to the ground.

Tina began screaming.

The beast was an owl. The largest bird Lansing had ever seen in his life was now clawing and tearing at the defenseless school teacher. The piercing shrieks from the animal seemed almost human.

He jumped to his feet and grabbed the giant bird. Throwing it to the ground, he reached for Tina's arm and tried to pull her to the safety of the portico.

The bird was back on Morales in seconds, ignoring the sheriff's efforts to stop it. He reached for his rifle, then realized he couldn't swing it or fire it without hitting the victim.

He fell to his knees and tore open his equipment bag. A second later, he had a road flare in his hand. Ripping off the plastic tip, he struck the end of the flare against the rough end of the cap. Red, 3,000° flames spewed out.

He turned and rammed the burning torch into the feathers of the screeching bird. The animal emitted a scream so unearthly, Lansing nearly dropped the weapon. He held on, thrusting the flame into the back and tail, time and again.

The bird turned—It no longer cared about its victim. Its only concern now was its tormentor.

Lansing rammed the red flames into the bird's face.

It was more than the creature could take. It released whatever flesh it held in its talons. It flapped and fluttered until it was out of the sheriff's reach. Spreading its great wings, it struggled to keep from falling to the ground.

With two great flaps, it cleared the parking lot.

Flames began to engulf the bird. Its efforts to climb higher were wasted. The more it flapped the worst the flames became.

By the time it reached the river, it had the strength for one last shriek, then it disappeared below the bank.

Lansing threw what was left of the flare into the parking lot. He helped Tina to her feet. She was scratched and bleeding . . . and trembling.

He pulled her close and held her.

They both hoped and prayed for one thing: that this was the end of Berta Chavez.

# Chapter Eighty-Four

Lansing cleared what was left of his horse trailer out of the way that evening. The bodies of the four dead hitmen on the road were transported back to the Abbey visitor's quarters for temporary storage.

The sheriff, Tina Morales and the Porters were able to go to their respective homes that night to shower and sleep in their own beds.

The next day was Friday. Lansing spent part of the morning locating a horse trailer he could use to retrieve Cement Head. When he got the horse home, he would make sure the animal received special treatment.

Tina Morales made another trip to the Las Palmas Clinic. She had a dozen more bites and cuts from an owl that needed tending.

Roger and Eileen Porter opened *St. Benedict's Rialto* that morning, as usual. They never discussed the details of that previous 36 hours. They had experienced a miracle—maybe two. *St. Anthony's Monastery in the Canyon* was a special place to them—now, even more so. They knew what they knew—and they were satisfied with that.

Mid-morning, Lansing got a call from Special Agent Darwin from the SBI. The DEA had been in touch. The name Osiel Cardenas Guillen suddenly popped up. It seemed Humberto Garcia Abrego's control of the Gulf Cartel was more tenuous than they suspected. A power struggle had erupted. Guillen was a major player.

It was possible, after all, Guillen's call wasn't a hoax. Darwin asked if Lansing still wanted help.

Lansing hung up the phone without saying a word.

\*\*\*

The Santa Fe coroner's office had retrieved all of the bodies from Rio Cohino Canyon by late Saturday.

Sunday afternoon kayakers found the naked body of an old woman washed up on the bank of Rio Cohino, 10 miles downstream from *St. Anthony's Monastery*. It looked like she had been killed in a fire. She was covered with burns over 80% of her body.

Lansing had the Las Palmas EMS bring her to the funeral home. The old woman was identified as Berta Chavez. He arranged for a casket. After securing the proper permits, the sheriff made sure Berta could be buried on her own property. Save for the men who dug the grave, Cliff Lansing and Tina Morales were the only people to attend the burial.

After repeated attempts to contact the family, the State Department of Corrections relegated the body of Bernardino Chavez to the prison graveyard. He was buried next to another recently deceased inmate: Cesar Chamuscado.

\*\*\*

Other things happened that summer.

A week after the barn fire, Jack Rivera had a new car. Lansing saw the family out and about together often. They never seemed happier.

Two weeks after the fire at the high school, the 9-1-1 Call Center was back in a set of double-wide trailers behind the court house. They felt secure enough there that the sheriff was able to terminate the 24/7 protection.

It was about that time Sheriff Lansing learned Berta Chavez may not have been responsible for his armory problems. He sent a query letter to his ammunition supplier. He informed them that he had discovered several substandard rounds in his .223 stock. Had they had similar complaints from other customers?

The supplier said they would immediately replace all of the San Phillipe Sheriff's Department's cache of .223 rounds . . . —and, by the way, would the sheriff kindly not mention the situation to anyone else. Lansing saw no problem with turning the issue over to the State Department of Public Safety and the Department of Justice. Because of his supplier, he and forty other people could have been dead by now.

There was an official inquiry as to how and why ten men had died in Rio Cohino Canyon. Lansing played the Guillen tape, then explained how he alone was responsible for the "bomb." It was a desperate measure on his part. He had asked for help, but no one stepped up. As for the four men who were killed by birds, he didn't have a clue. The inquiry board found no fault on his part, particularly when the State Police admitted they dropped the ball.

Never claimed, the ten henchmen ended up in unmarked graves.

In Matamoros, Osiel Cardenas Guillen took control of the Gulf Cartel. His personal army, headed by Arturo Guzman Decena, became known as the Los Zetas, taking their name from Decena's former radio call sign. A reign of terror began that would last for decades.

A month after his death, *St. Anthony's Monastery* held a special memorial service for Esteban Fuentes. Roger and Eileen Porter, Tina Morales and Sheriff Lansing were given special invitations.

During his sermon, Abbot Christian proclaimed Brother Esteban a martyr. Esteban had been a good man, a faithful Christian, and anyone who knew him had been especially blessed. He had sacrificed his life to save his brothers—and he made this sacrifice of his own free will.

The Story of the Ravens was considered a true miracle by Abbot Christian and the other monks of *St. Anthony's*. The Miracle of the Ravens, though, became a legend never discussed beyond the cloister walls. Even the four other witnesses to the event never spoke a word to anyone outside the Abbey.

Also, never mentioned was the Great Horned Owl. Why it attacked—who it attacked—how it was destroyed—was another tale that never echoed beyond the canyon walls.

By the end of June, Albuquerque forensics had matched the teeth of the burn victim found in Jack Rivera's car with the dental records of one Poncho Chamorro.

It was only then that Tina Morales truly felt free.

# Epilogue

A pair of yellow eyes studied the man and woman below. They sat on the fence of a corral watching three horses. It was late in the day. The sun was setting.

The Great Horned Owl had made no plans for the immediate future . . . but things could change . . . true evil needed no reason to exist!

# Coming October 11, 2019

## THE WEEPING WOMAN
### A Sheriff Lansing Mystery
Book 7

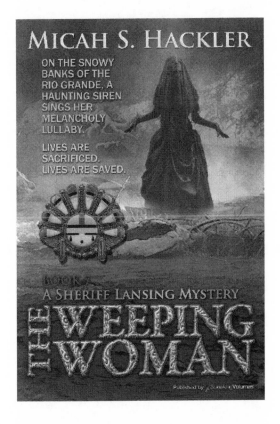

On the snowy banks of the Rio Grande, a haunting siren sings her melancholy lullaby. Lives are sacrificed. Lives are saved. All the while, The Weeping Woman beckons the living to join her beneath the waters.

**For more information**
**visit**: www.SpeakingVolumes.us

# On Sale Now!

## A SHERIFF LANSING MYSTERY
### Book 5

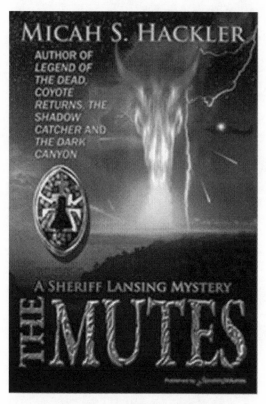

**For more information**
visit: www.SpeakingVolumes.us

# On Sale Now!

## SHERIFF LANSING MYSTERIES
### Books 1 – 4

### LEGEND OF THE DEAD
### COYOTE RETURNS
### THE SHADOW CATCHER
### THE DARK CANYON

## For more information
### visit:

# On Sale Now!

## A HOWARD MOON DEER MYSTERY
### Book 5

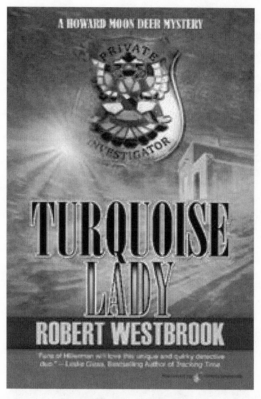

She is the Turquoise Lady, dressed in Indian jewelry and a cowboy hat, who came looking for a new life and instead found murder and betrayal. A year later, Wilder & Associate have been hired by the family to see if they can solve the mystery of her disappearance after the police have failed…

**For more information**
**visit:** www.SpeakingVolumes.us

# On Sale Now!

## HOWARD MOON DEER MYSTERIES
### Books 1 - 4

### GHOST DANCER
### WARRIOR CIRCLE
### RED MOON
### ANCIENT ENEMY

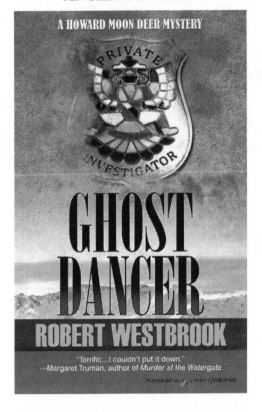

"Terrific…I couldn't put it down."
—Margaret Truman, author of *Murder at the Watergate*

**For more information**
**visit**: www.SpeakingVolumes.us

# On Sale Now!

## THE GLORY DAYS OF
## BUFFALO EGBERT

"A must read. If you haven't yet read it, get it.
It's a fine reading experience."
—Allan W. Eckert, author of *That Dark and Bloody River*

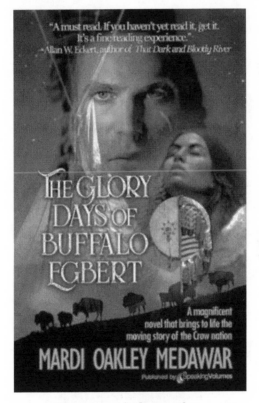

**For more information
visit:** www.SpeakingVolumes.us

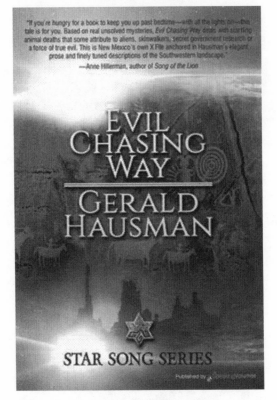

## Sign up for free and bargain books

Join the Speaking Volumes
mailing list

Text
# ILOVEBOOKS
to 22828 to get started.

Message and data rates may apply.